LUGGAGE FROM
ELSEWHERE

PARTHIAN

Aneurin Gareth Thomas was born in 1963 and brought up in Gorseinon, Swansea, and later in Brecon. He studied Philosophy in London at the Polytechnic of North London and did a Masters in Logic and Scientific Method at the London School of Economics. He is a fluent Spanish speaker and spent many years in Madrid working as an English teacher, journalist and translator. He currently lives in Brecon. *Luggage from Elsewhere* is his first novel.

LUGGAGE FROM ELSEWHERE

Aneurin Gareth Thomas

Parthian
The Old Surgery
Napier Street
Cardigan
SA43 1ED
www.parthianbooks.co.uk

ISBN 1-902638-948
      978-1-902638-94-2

The publisher acknowledges the financial support of the Welsh
Books Council.

Editor: Gwen Davies

First published in 2007
© Aneurin Gareth Thomas
All Rights Reserved

Cover design Marc Jennings
Cover image © Magnum
Printed and bound by Dinefwr Press, Llandybïe, Wales
Typeset by logodædaly

British Library Cataloguing in Publication Data
A cataloguing record for this book is available from the British
Library.

To Maureen

1. *1966*

When there were summer summers, Indian or others, the filled pit pools dug for draining water from the mine were play ponds for the children of my youth. There between where the Tawe and the Loughor flowed around that industrial orb with Swansea at its glowing centre, before it and we became underdeveloped and third-world. It was in the mid-sixties, at about a quarter to one in the afternoon, when the other children from our street had all gone home to lunch on sugary baked beans, pork fat sausages and tinned pears and milk for afters. They left behind them two little pirates from number seventeen with nothing to go home to and a tribe of head-hardened Apaches from another housing estate. They threw the elder of the two in fully clothed at the deep end after trying to scalp him with a twig and then turned on his younger piggy-faced brother who pleaded in tears. Four years old and left floating face down in the warm slag-dust swimming pool, alone with the blue-green dragonflies and soggy paper boats.

I was born in Year Seventeen of the Nuclear Age. My first memories are of a tooth-white, shining-eyed face breaking through the nothing all around. It inclined down towards me, smiled and the walls seemed to breathe in and out around us. I was crying, it was Christmas and I had dreamt of a present which wasn't and would never be there. It was before I learnt to speak that other language and my Mam murmured to reassure me in Welsh, a tongue that babies, pups, stones and other small inanimate objects seem to understand. At least they did then, when I was young. Her hair brushed whisper kisses against my brow as the curtains laced like sails over the open window moved in the air, in rhyme to her breath. Her breath moved in rhyme to the strokes of her hair against my face as she spoke.

Mam was preoccupied as she tried to console me, thinking of what exactly happened one morning when she found, looking into the mirror, that she was not as pretty as she once had thought. She'd had too many babies and too many problems, her youth wasted away, her life nothing more than living for others.

Winter and the nights each so close to the next. Chambers of air, sometimes icy, then again warm, swirled across the damp washing line hallway of our council house. I could hear voices. Waves of laughter as she took me through to the living room but stopped to adjust a hanging shirt that was dripping onto a newspaper covering the floor. I panicked and sucked on a rubber nipple as we went through the door into the light. They all stopped to look at me, ah ahing, before returning to fight as Father tried to read asleep in the only armchair. There, with my tribe before I knew who they were.

Springs onto autumns and always the house kept dark to save on the bills as we were left alone until teatime. The war started when the tribe came home from school, wishing it to be the last time, jealous of the scraggy-haired dog curled up warm in the kitchen.

Sometimes she would take me out and the street was like a ceiling pushed down onto me. Hopeless and insignificant I tried not to look up but thigh-high ahead as we went down the hill and around into High Street and the butcher's for something on offer. All the while I walked with the weight of the threatening mass of clouds layered above me.

Stretching, I could reach her hand that dragged me along, envious all the while of the warm four-wheeled prams like little tanks which passed us on the way to the shops and on to the stories of the other mothers. They told of banana boxes full of tarantulas, about the benefits of plastic versus brown-paper carrier bags, of Little Jimmy's ant-eaten tortoise in the attic and the new Co-op all-done-so-nicely funeral service. Mam was always shocked with her 'no, well I never' acknowledgements when the subject moved on to third-degree South-Walian gossip. And away we would go as she mentally added up the shopping-list deficit.

Between two rivers we were trapped in the borderline territory between English-speaking Welsh Wales and

Welsh-speaking Cymru Gymraeg. To the east there was the copper-poisoned Tawe running through Swansea, and to the west the anthracite-dusty Loughor. And all the time a constant hum of factories. The murmuring drone that accompanied those off work, the whistling kids to school and the mams chatting to the shops.

At the foot of our inclined road across the T-junction and in the alleyway between the old terraced houses was the towering mine wheel. Mam and I were out before dawn walking Father to work. She only ever went with him when she had this premonition that she'd never see him again. There were other women like her who would then hang onto the day, all the time watching the kitchen clock and half-expecting to hear the steam whistle announce disaster. We were out to show me where he went, where he had gone when I woke up, that stranger that came and went and sometimes was at home failing to control the excesses of the other children. When he left us at the gate to enter with the other men she tried to explain that he was going underground and would be back before tea, her voice betraying a fearful regret. I must have asked what it was like there below, for I remember her saying that it was like the night. I didn't quite understand and she talked of holes filled with silvery-black stars and I thought it must be comforting and warm like being in bed with the blankets over your head.

Later at school the teacher would ask us once a year what we wanted to be when we grew up. The girls were imaginative: destined not to be like their mothers; the boys, though, copied their fathers. Council roadworker, miner, railwayman, collier, butcher, tin plate worker, collier, postman, steel worker, miner, binman. One year when most of us said unemployed – pegging, my Mam called it – the teacher stopped asking us, but that was later.

One day at the end of summer I followed my brother Huw on his adventures on the slag heaps behind the mine. He would bobsleigh down them on board a plastic bag, sitting forward holding it over his feet, black coal dust and grit exhaust flowing behind. With broken front teeth, a blackened face and a handkerchief tied behind his head there was something of a pirate in him. His face was covered in little black grainy spots of coal dust. Later he would go on to add cigarette burns to them, and knife cuts, all in an effort to tattoo away his natural features. After, we went to watch him swim in the pool of water pumped out of the mine. I was afraid to enter the discoloured, stagnant pit. Other boys we knew from our street were there until dinner time, leaving us behind with a bunch of strangers that hollered like Indian braves.

We were sitting on the bank when they took us from behind, first throwing my brother into the murky pool and then me, too young to know if I could swim. There was no escape. Frantically kicking, I tried to shout until I was still and unthinking.

My family were never to treat me as if I were normal again. They looked at me in the hospital bed as if I was some strange object while inside my young body frame my thoughts were of them looking at me. Since that time I had to live with the fact that I was alone. I didn't talk again for quite a while. Later when I began, in another tongue, I could hardly stop. I sounded just like the rest of them.

In the hospital with all gathered around a question broke the silence now and then. 'Are you alright now, bach?' they would ask the little one of the family.

And I remember Father leaning over me to take a closer look before raising himself to speak.

'You'll be useless. Like me,' he said.

2. *1978*

Mam hung school photos of her kids on the living room wall. There was one of me she liked, taken in the mid-seventies. I would sometimes look at it and there I was staring out at me, long-haired, baby-faced, the features not so brutalised by puberty as in others. But that image was precisely what I didn't want to be. I was old enough to know how young I was. I was fifteen wanting eighteen.

On Friday and Saturday nights I gave up wanting to be liked for who I was. I had started trying to be mature. I was play-acting how I considered someone successful with girls would be. It didn't help. I had to wait.

I was alone in a pub waiting for the rest before going on into the centre of Swansea and unsuccessfully trying it on with Susie, the Australian barmaid. She always said no. It was Year Thirty-Two of the Nuclear Age, the night Parry

7

suggested we mug a taxi driver and Will compared morality to an empty wallet. And Susie always said no, at least then, and smiled with her blue eyes, telling me she had a boyfriend. But he was twelve thousand miles away, I protested. Anyway I was too young, she said, and it made me feel too young and all of it made me hungry for a change.

Imagining I was someone witty, I'd joke with Susie. 'I was fifteen and looking for a girl with condoms and,' I began to say.

'You're still fifteen!' she observed.

'Almost sixteen!' I corrected her and began my story again. 'Anyway, I was fifteen and looking for a girl with condoms and soft thighs. She was an eighteen-year-old-plus German-American tourist who had apparently been looking for Stratford-upon-Avon but had somehow managed to wander a hundred and fifty miles further west without noticing. When I first saw her, staring out from Swansea Bay into the blue, I told her I needed the protective arms of a mature woman. She said that the last thing she wanted was an ugly little pinky-white hairless English schoolboy's dick. I protested on the point of nationality but it made no difference, she was halfway through doing Europe in nine days.'

'What was it she said? You're pulling my leg, aren't you?' she laughed.

'No, really! She was blonde, like you. You notice these things around here.' Yes, we noticed things. We noticed Susie. Some bright-eyed marsupial we couldn't take our eyes off.

Before Susie could reply a drinker interrupted us to inform her that another piece of road had caved in over in Loughor. It happened when the abandoned mine tunnels collapsed and all moved down a little, slowly filling in space below. Life seemed to be caving in for me too in its way.

She went to serve and I noticed a solitary drinker at my side. Bony and lost under his clothes he was agelessly old with a carved-stone hardness in his face. He had drained lips and bloodshot eyes as he stared ahead. There was a constant wheeze in the miner's frightened breath. Living like a pit-pony: retired and blanketed in a woollen waistcoat and heavy jacket. Escape from all that dark and then only a sharp wind needling his face on his way home through a bitter landscape. Soon he would be gone. Would he think of the times when he had something to live for instead of slowly fading away like a distant whisper?

'Iechyd da!' I said to him.

He turned to me and nodded a same to you reply.

Almost the same as me. I was a small, flat-chested boy. A weakling. Development arrested by a dirty water-filled lung. I coughed for years, my breathing the wheeze of a distant pup's squeal, something outside of me. Later the coughs left by flu reminded me how difficult it had been. I never started smoking, just the odd puff, always fearing lack of air, needing all the breath I had. And him, almost the same as me. He had his old-age stunted by the mines, me my youth by mine water, which at least I didn't throw up any more. Just lager.

At the Swansea disco there was this girl, about my age, who must have spent hours putting on her make-up. She'd ask whoever started to chat to buy her a Dry Bluebird, a cocktail of crème de menthe and vodka, which despite the name was sick-green in colour and topped with chopped fruit and a miniature Taiwanese paper umbrella.

She had a red plastic handbag hanging down to her hip that gently bumped against her as she tried to walk on a pair of high heels two or three sizes too big for her. With her rigid smile cracking through, she was some circus clown act on stilts. The red nail varnish she wore was chipped and fading, as if she couldn't be bothered to touch up last week's paint. She was standing in a light blue dress that could have been her mother's, looking up at the glittering ball reflecting the coloured lights of the nearly deserted dance floor, when I went up to her and said hello. I was trying to be someone else again.

'Dry Bluebird,' she replied without even looking at me.

At the bar I asked how much it was and ordered a half of lager instead. The barman pointed to the dance floor and asked if it was for the high-heeled trance and prepared me her drink, charging it as a beer. I must have reminded him of a son he had somewhere, or else he just took pity on my uselessness. I gave her the drink and she went off to study one of the plastic palm trees in the entrance without even having noticed me.

There was some style in her denial of my existence. Was it because I was strange? I was dressed in black with my shirt buttons opened down almost to my waist showing off two strands of hair on my bony white chest.

From the bar I watched her climbing the stairs to the balcony over the dance floor. Waiting for the arrival of my friends I occasionally raised my head and once saw her looking down at me, quickly turning away through shyness or disgust.

In the slowly filling disco time flowed by like the beer we drank, going nowhere, getting nothing done.

Those Fridays and Saturdays were a mirror of something. Our behaviour, for example, was so predictably social it seemed genetic. There were the girls dancing around their handbags on the floor as they held lighters and packets of ten John Player's. The shouting boys watched them like predators, their hair soaked, eyes shining with a powerless desire: if only I could spike her drink.

How must we have seemed from the other side of the thirty-foot-long bar? Among a forest of heads there were those with an urge to kick someone in. They looked like five-pint psychopaths. There was always one or two and only a coma, theirs or a victim's, could calm the night. There were the young lovers with nowhere to go, embraced on the dance floor for hours in a trance that walled off the world. And there were losers like me, amateur psychologists that could only observe, too locked inside to ever take part, thinking everything's been said and done, thinking sometimes I want the ceiling to fall in, my head a five-hundred-watt amp about to explode in rhythm to the boom boom disco music.

'More Friday night sweat than Saturday night fever, hey?' my friend Will shouted into my ear.

11

I don't think I can take it anymore, I thought to say but the words just wouldn't come out and I finished in one gulp what was left of my lager.

I saw to my surprise the Dry Bluebird standing behind Will. I looked past him at her pretending to be there by chance. Will moved on when he saw I no longer had his attention. We made eye contact and I mouthed an inaudible question. She came up to me and asked me my name.

She was Karen with a K, she said. Sixteen. Wanted to run away. Hated school. Wanted nothing. Wanted all. Just had to see Berlin before she died. Hated her parents. Needed to drink. Wanted a fag. Hated the noise. Wanted to know if I'd like to go outside for some air.

At the doorway she held onto my arm and led me around the back of the discotheque to a badly-lit emergency exit. You could hear couples kissing and moaning close by among the dustbins and the empty beer caskets.

'Isn't it a nice place?' she said.

It had a damp smell of sick and cat piss. It was not her first time around the back. She asked me two things. The first answer was clearly a lie, the second also, possibly. It was just that I needed more than anything to be with her or anyone. Just for once, like everybody else. She wanted to know how old I was, I added four years and summed nineteen. And she wanted to know if I liked her.

In her drunken stupor she placed me into the darkness against the fire exit door and with her arms around my neck we kissed, our tongues mingling flavours of rancid acidy lager and crème de menthe. I put my arms around her in a rigid, protective way as if to stop her from falling over but she had the sense to take an arm from me and place my trembling hand on her braless breast. As we kissed she occasionally adjusted her handbag hanging at hip level.

I wanted to see what I was touching but all was covered in darkness and by the taste and smell of her perfume and make-up. She began to push her hip against my groin and kissed the air out of me as I tried to breathe through my nose and think of condoms.

I had carried one around in my pocket without fail for more than a year, thinking just in case, but the wrapper had become so tatty and torn in my trouser pocket and the rubber inside dried yellow and useless that eventually I threw it away. I had given up on the idea of casual wild safe sex about a month before.

One hand still cupped her breast, the other was on her buttock helping to move against her the erection trapped in my trousers. Her hands came down to pull her dress up over her waist and then to struggle to free me of my trousers. I squeezed and then stroked the warm smooth skin of her backside and she parted from my lips for the first time, quickly panting in gulps of air and with her hands made adjustments for me to enter her, or rather for her to put herself onto me. We moved in time up onto our toes and down and up, my body free and strong and I thought of precautions, of whether I should tell her that I wasn't using a condom or to ask if she took the pill. But I couldn't and didn't want to stop, or breathe or rationalise.

She pressed her kisses harder, breathing from my mouth, taking my air that was her air, our hands grabbing at each other, pulling at each other, until she became limp in my arms as I tried to hold her upright, moving in her, pushing her up and back against the door frantically and violently until her handbag finally slipped off her shoulder and I ejaculated, shuddering.

Without movement nor word we stood holding each other almost in sleep until she suddenly took herself away from me, pulled up the strap of her handbag from around her elbow over to her shoulder, took a paper tissue from it and quickly wiped between her legs, adjusted her clothes and said we should go.

She seemed suddenly sober, as if remembering who and where she was. Side by side but without contact we went around to the front entrance, beads of perspiration on our foreheads, my mouth bitter dry, my legs shaking from weakness and orgasm. She asked if I'd wait with her until her father came to pick her up at three o'clock, after he had finished work. He was a chef and she told me her parents only allowed her to stay out on Fridays.

'They say, "don't smoke, keep your legs shut, don't drink, don't do drugs," and why?' she explained. 'So that we can live a little longer, and why, to enjoy life longer? But enjoy it how? Ironic, isn't it?' She was staring at the ground, at a point of reference just ahead of her, at a shadow of herself that didn't need light. 'Sometimes I think, why bother?' she continued. 'First you live and then you die and you put up with all the crap in between and you do all this because you might have children that might be like you!'

'Do you take precautions?' I asked her after a while.

'Don't worry,' she replied without further explanation.

'Are you on the pill, then?'

'Yes.'

'You have to take it every day, don't you?' I continued, hoping she would reassure me.

'Well, I'm not taking it now!'

'Didn't you take it today?'

'Is this an interrogation, or what?'

'I don't want you to get pregnant,' I said.

'I thought you drew back in time,' she replied, suddenly sounding childish.

'But I didn't,' I exclaimed. 'I thought to ask you but...'

'Don't worry, I won't join the club.'

'You should... We should take precautions.'

'I can't imagine myself getting in the family way.'

'It's not a question of wanting or imagining. It's the easiest thing in the world to do, whether you want it or not,' I reasoned.

'Don't lecture me!' she said angrily.

It was true, I sounded as if I were blaming her.

'It's my fault,' I said sheepishly. 'I should have used a condom.'

We didn't talk more. I, because I felt both awkward waiting with her and smilingly stunned at what we had just done, while she let her gaze wander off. We waited in silence, seated on a step until her father's car stopped in front of us. When she got up she surprised me by asking if I'd be there again the following Friday, I nodded approval and she went.

I sat there some time not knowing whether to get up and go home, go back inside to tell my friends or to take off my clothes and go running in the damp early hour street, naked and crazy through joy.

I decided to wait at the entrance for them. People hung around the doorway, some discussed the possibility of sharing a taxi home. What do they want from life, I thought. I used to think that there was only one type of person, all and every single one of us wanted sex. The actions of all of us, no matter how seemingly unrelated to direct sexual intercourse, were aimed in the end at fucking someone. I then understood that I was wrong. My projections were only based on myself and other young teenage males. In fact boys were not all the same, but there were only two types. Those that wanted sex and those that didn't know what they wanted: the puberty-obsessed potential sex fiend and the blind-drunk, no-hope waster.

Soon I paid little attention to those at the doorway. I was beginning to understand the difference between the *there* around me and the *here* inside me. I was never to be fully present at anything that happened. I was never to be fully there, for I was always too aware of myself. Only afterwards could I ever feel that I liked something I saw or heard, on reflection.

Little more than half an hour earlier the Bluebird Karen with a K had been making love to me, and only the memory of it had any meaning. At the time of the act I was too inside myself, rather than inside of her, to notice the pleasure. I hadn't been there.

I can't live like this, I said to myself, all the time saying wait, I need to go away to think about this. You can't live unless it's in the immediate now.

My thoughts were interrupted by a youth who came charging out of the disco, looking for somebody. He was followed by a girl telling him to calm down. He suddenly darted among a group at the entrance and began threatening a man in his mid-twenties. I saw the man back off to avoid confrontation, which the youth took as surrender. Content with himself, he let the man go. He then glanced in my direction and came over to me, followed by the girl.

'Hiya Parry!' I said up to him from the step.

'So there you are!' he replied. I was never there, I was always here. 'See that, did you?' he asked. 'Thought he had more balls to him when he was pestering Lad but he henned out at the last minute!'

'It was all completely harmless, but King Kong here wanted to crush the Empire State Building,' the girl explained.

Steven Parry was known by all by his surname. Although he was my age, he was taller and stronger, more cocky and extrovert. I had known him all my life and there was little to know about him, he had no complicated psychology, no anxiety: his reactions were primate and all around him had to take care.

He was box-eared because his father was an amateur drunk who had hit him professionally almost every night. But he played rugby at school, and was finally able to turn the tables for the first time and knock his old man out. He then became unbearable, invincible in his own eyes until he began to go out with Lad, who seemed to restrain his excesses, except when he drank.

Lad was sensible and bright and nobody understood what she saw in Parry. Later, after they split up, she continued to hang around with us as before and Parry didn't seem to mind, surprisingly, though he became noticeably less extrovert and more aggressive with strangers. I was to be glad she'd still go out with our group, for the two of us liked to exchange invented stories, like the good young liars that we were.

Lad was short for Gladys. She had fair hair worn shoulder length and every few minutes she'd sweep a parting behind her ear. Short and slim, she preferred to dress in jeans and trainers out of school but on Friday disco nights she would wear her knee-length school skirt to get past the doorman. She had a tiny scar above her left eye since she was six, where a park swing hit her in the face when running after a ball across the play area.

Our other two friends finally came out to stand side by side, looking simultaneously around them, thinking what to do. Both small, thin and bony, both wearing glasses. But there the similarities ended. One was slightly short-sighted and wore his spectacles with an air of a young school headmaster, the other was noticeably shorter-sighted, with half-inch-thick lenses, one cracked and patched up with paper and sellotape. Dai Panda looked and was treated as a fool. The other, Will, was nobody's except his own.

Will pulled Dai Panda towards us.

'You know, resorting to violence is pointless. It's superfluous. It can rebound in your face. I mean anyone can put on being brave and loud-mouthed but what if that bloke had a bus full of mates waiting outside and all equally hard-headed?' Will declared, with Parry in mind. His words tended to mix the academic and the streetwise, as if he were both a professor of ethics and a rugby coach.

'So that's why you came out after us like a snail, is it?' Parry asked him sarcastically. 'To avoid rebounds!'

'I was looking after Panda,' Will claimed, sheepishly.

'Well, Gandhi here's got glasses anyway,' I pointed out, referring to Will.

'Is that a Welsh word? What does it mean?' Dai Panda asked me.

'Peace!' Will told him, as quick as ever.

'It's not Welsh, it's the name of an Indian...' I began to explain when Will interrupted with a hand on my shoulder.

'When you disappeared I thought you had gone home to puke,' he told me.

'He left with a piece of skirt, he did,' Parry explained to all. 'Don't deny it!' he added to me before I could say a word. 'I saw you talking to her, the mad Bluebird, wasn't it? Did you buy her one? Strange girl that.' I said nothing. 'This is even stranger,' Parry continued, showing me the small bar of cannabis wrapped in tin foil which he took out of his pocket and waved in my face. He had bought it from a friend of Lad's older brother earlier that evening. 'Come on, let's go for a walk,' Parry ordered, leading us to somewhere quieter.

Parry rolled up three small joints on a dark street corner. We surrounded him to watch, Will giving advice. I had smoked one previously with Will, but despite the great expectation of floating into surreal hallucinations, nothing happened. Parry and Lad had claimed to have got stoned a few times; Lad said she threw up the first time, which sparked an interest in the rest of us, after all if it makes you sick it couldn't be all that bad, Will argued. While for Dai Panda it was new and he was nervously looking out for signs of the police.

'Mix it up well and evenly so that we can all take a good drag,' Will insisted.

'Don't worry, we'll smoke all three at the same time,' Lad replied.

'Don't look out for the pigs,' Will told Dai Panda. 'You might make them turn up. Just act normal as usual,' he said, heavily stressing the word normal and we all laughed, including Panda.

Dai Panda, born as David Ravelli, was as slow as a panda and would often mispronounce words and occasionally stutter when nervous. Most people thought he was retarded and the glasses he wore didn't help his image. Sometimes the things he said made you wonder. Once he told me he had an alarm clock which he set to tell him when to go to bed. He was a year younger than I was and I had kind of adopted him, or rather, he saw me as his protector, he trusted me, but it hadn't always been like that. As kids I used to shout out insults at him, call him a scab and mock his stutter. I used to be one of the things that made him stutter.

There we were, Friday night and nowhere else to go for we had been everywhere there was to go.

'Except to the railway café to ask for a few drops of whisky in a cup of tea,' Will suggested. 'Before getting the bus back to Gomorrah.'

I said I was tired and wanted to get back home after the smoke. Will explained that cannabis can dry the throat and we should be prepared, laced tea being the remedy.

'But don't worry, if you can't stick it any more I'll take you back to mother,' he promised.

'I'll come too,' Dai Panda added.

'Oh, come on lads,' Parry complained. 'We haven't even lit up the shit yet and you're squealing like a bunch of schoolgirls.' At which Lad thumped him in the arm, almost knocking the joints out of his hand.

'He needs his beauty sleep to recover,' he said about me.

'Recover from what?' Dai Panda asked me seriously.

'To recover from that old mad bag Bluebird sucking him dry,' Parry answered.

'If you were smaller, he'd hit you,' Will warned him.

'You're not recommending violence now, are you?' Parry asked with a laugh.

I said nothing, took one of the joints from him and asked Lad for a match.

'So you gave her one after all, did you? Did Will help?' Parry continued.

'Help with what?' Dai Panda asked.

'Leave the man alone,' Lad demanded. 'Her name's Karen, isn't it?' she added, turning to me.

'Yes,' I replied; they were all looking at me. 'With a K,' I added timidly.

We lit the spiced cigarettes and were silently walking so as not to attract attention but passing them round after each took in a slow deep lung-burning drag. The first thing I noticed was a mild pain behind the eyes and then my heart began to pound irregularly and then seemed to stop altogether. And indeed, later, a dryness in the throat. I was at the point of telling Will about it when suddenly it occurred to me to be a foolish thing to say. Was I paranoid? I decided instead to ask about how his heart was, but I forgot what it was before I said it, then it seemed that hours must have passed without anybody saying anything and I didn't know where I was walking from or to. In all but a few minutes my body and mind had changed.

I thought about Karen. I would see her the following week and maybe we'd go around the back against the fire exit again.

A police car passed slowly by, continued down the road, stopped and turned round to come back up the road and stop opposite us. We couldn't see if it was us they took an interest in. We walked on, thinking of their eyes burning in the back of our heads and of the strange little cigarettes in our hands. I was frightened but didn't care to run. We would normally split up, each going in a different direction to diffuse any chase. But this time they let us go.

We finally reached the railway café which was usually open all night for the track workers, early morning travellers and the dropouts trying to stretch out the night. It was, unusually, all but empty but for the waiter dozing behind the counter, a kissing young couple and a postal worker eating his sandwiches as he read a newspaper before the mail train arrived. We sat around a table without ordering anything, at first in a drugged silence.

A middle-aged man entered; Lad recognised him and

pretended to read the menu. But she couldn't hide and he came over.

'How's the literature here?' the man asked her, pointing to the menu. He was dressed in a dirty cream gabardine overcoat and his tone was slightly high-pitched.

'We're not sure whether it's café poetry or modern urban fiction,' Will replied for us.

The man laughed and invited us to five cups of tea. He then shook hands with the waiter, exchanged a few words with him and left.

'He's a neighbour from Loughor. I didn't want him to see me alone with four boys!' Lad finally said.

I remembered something I had heard earlier in the evening.

'Oh, Lad, there was another landslide over in Loughor today,' I said.

'More a crack in the pavement, this time,' she replied. 'But our house has gone all wonky over the years, it's like the Leaning Tower of Pisa!'

'But without any Galileo!' Will added.

Will's confidence was all intellect. He was my best friend and we had sat together at school since Juniors' where his mother was the dinner lady. He had two things. A reputation of trying to learn more than the teachers in order to make their lives difficult in class, which he did successfully, and an older sister I had been in love with since the age of ten.

Lad noticed that the waiter was too lazy to bring us the tea and nudged Parry and he and Dai Panda went to fetch the cups. Parry asked the waiter to spice up the tea a little

23

and from under the counter he reluctantly brought out a bottle of whisky. After bringing the cups the two were soon fooling with a slot machine, leaving Will, Lad and I to talk.

'And what about that girl a few months ago you couldn't get off your mind?' Will said.

'Who?'

'You got her off your mind, then!' Lad said, laughing.

'The chemist's assistant, remember?' Will prompted.

'Oh, her!' I said. 'I remember now. Yes. From a distance she was beautiful,' I began on my fantasy.

'What, only from a distance?' Lad asked.

'Yes, only from afar,' I replied. 'Close up she looked like a mouse that had been mauled by a mangy tabby, but she had lovely flat small boy's breasts and I loved her. She was working the Christmas hols at a chemist's. I saw her being efficient through the window after I had been walking up and down the High Street all afternoon looking for loose women. It must have been about minus five and I felt like a camel lost in Siberia and had decided to go home with my frostbite and look up alienation in the dictionary. But when I saw her I went into the shop and asked for shaving cream. Normal or sensitive skin, she wanted to know and I asked if she had any abnormal. Our eyes met and we fell in love. Well, I fell in love, she just said one pound twenty please. I left with the change in my hand and thought to return the next day once my heart had slowed down but the next day was Christmas and the following Boxing Day and all was closed and I had to wait until the twenty-seventh but she had been spirited away or got bored or was busy writing thank-you letters to her many admirers, either way she wasn't there.'

'Did you see her again?' Lad laughed.

'No. I could have gone inside and asked one of her workmates but, but you know how it is,' I answered. 'Instead I went to a café and sat depressed at a table for hours, thinking of carving our names into the fake wooden formica top, but I only knew mine and didn't have a penknife on me anyway.'

'Ah, love!' Will said. 'They say it's blind, don't they? All it needs is for some charity organisation to provide guide dogs!'

It was gone half-past four when we left the café and decided to catch the night bus back home. We didn't have enough money among us to share the taxi waiting across the road from the bus shelter.

Lad and Parry were embraced and kissing, or sleeping. An old drunk who had said he wanted to get back to Port Talbot and then, as he said, on to the shithouses of Taibach on the opposite side of Swansea from us, was sitting next to Dai Panda. Both were dozing and leaning against each other. Will and I stood with our hands in our pockets thinking of the cold and our headaches and the promise of once getting home not having to get up at all, but that would be if we got home. And it was cold, a South Wales windy damp just above zero cold, and we didn't want to be there or anywhere that was not in our beds.

'Well at least it's not raining,' Will observed eventually, looking down the road for signs of a red double-decker.

'This is what sentry duty must be like in Moscow, but without the fur hats.'

And then it began to rain, an icy trickle. There we were, waiting for a bus. Soon it would be another infinite week of school until the next fleeting weekend. There we were, late February rain, Saturday five a.m. trying to survive youth.

'We could mug that taxi driver!' Parry suddenly suggested, his arms around Lad sleeping against him.

'Why? In order to get home?' Will asked annoyed.

'Yer. It's cold, we're broke and with the money we could get another cab home,' Parry explained.

'But the driver's like us. Can't you see that mun? It would be like robbing among ourselves,' Will objected. 'Mugging taxi drivers adds to everyone's poverty. The poor taxi driver freezing his balls off for a few bob a night and emptying our moral wallet in doing so. For God's sake!'

And then the bus came, red and glorious and most of all warm and moving our way.

On the way back to Gorseinon I floated on a calm haze of cannabis and Karen. The silence helped. In through the open window above the seat a cold late winter breeze swirled around my head, licking my face like a mother-hungry pup.

At the end of the ride we left Parry and Lad kissing at the bus stop. The other three of us made our way to the estate where we lived, Will soon to turn down into his street and Dai Panda and I up past the row of prefabricated council houses. With only Dai Panda to notice and a strange kind of joy in my heart I suddenly needed to run.

Dai Panda, running to keep up with me, seemed happy I was happy, without knowing why.

We waved our goodbyes and when I reached my house near the top of the hill I stopped at the gate as a light rain began to fall. I waited, breathed heavily, feeling the night before going in.

It was there – much later – standing at the closed gate that all the world would come crashing down on me, putting an end to all that could have been.

Then, that night, Karen with a K had put an end to my endless adolescent wait. With her I didn't need to hide, I didn't even need to speak much, just lie about my age. That night, still fifteen, I stood at the gate to my home and felt the oily cream of sex sticky in my underwear and the rain running from my eyebrows, down my nose, like cold tear drops. I would never be the same again.

I felt alive.

3. *1977*

'Someone once said that it's better to live miserably as a Socrates than happily as a pig,' Lad said.

'But don't both get slaughtered?' I asked.

'On hemlock,' Will pointed out.

'What? For killing pigs?' Zed asked, surprised.

'Na. Socrates,' Will said.

'He went to the chemist's and asked for hemlock, did he?' Parry asked, sniggering.

'He was feeling depressed, like an unhappy Socrates would after all that fucking thinking, why are we here, and the lot, that he decided to do himself in. Put an end to it all.' Zed began.

'So he went to the chemist's, bought hemlock and ta ra!' Parry insisted.

'No mun, he had to leave Athens or die, at a time when

28

Athens was the very centre of civilisation in Europe, so he chose the poison,' Will corrected us.

'Kind of slaughter then?' Parry asked.

'No, no! The idea is, like, that it's better to think about your situation even if it leads to unhappiness, than to live a life of wine, women and song, without contemplation,' Lad explained.

'Is it, like?' Zed asked, surprised.

'What about somebody who has sat down to think about it and has come up with the answer that yes, a life of wine, women and song, living happily as a pig, is in fact better. That's possible isn't it?' I added.

'The point is that thinking about your situation is better than ignorance, even if that ignorance is accompanied by happiness,' Lad summarised.

'I'm happy!' Dai Panda exclaimed, and we all looked at him.

'But then you're stupid,' Will said to him.

'Leave him,' I told Will, ever protective of Dai Panda.

'The point is that it's better to think about things, even if it gives you a headache, isn't it?' Lad insisted again.

'They used to lobotomise as a cure for headaches!' Will suggested.

'Like talking to a wall!' Lad said to herself, giving up on the conversation.

'Isn't that what people do after lobotomies?' I joked.

It was Year Thirty-Two of the Nuclear Age and we were outside a concert hall in Swansea where a crowd was gathering. It was way past the announced time and they still hadn't opened the doors. There were rumours that the council had banned the performance at the last moment and some people began to shout complaints.

It was a pleasant summer's evening with sunset approaching and our group were happy just to talk in a circle, with Zed occasionally responding to the slap on the back greetings of youths that recognised him as they mingled at the entrance.

There were three police vans nearby, the riot helmets inside were at the ready to defend our rights.

And we waited. We had no future, but had petty theft and bruises and scars as our tattoos. We had punk music and it was original first time around. We had nothing else. Well, at least Swansea had a beach but it was an oily seaweed-covered rubbish tip of a beach. Other places, where it was easier to live, had real beaches. Here, in the least exotic corner of the Empire, we had the sea at our door and most of the year it was locked.

The Sex Pistols had recently reached number one in the Top Ten with a song that was banned. It couldn't be heard on the radio and at Woolworth's, where they had a list of the charts, a blank spot was left at the top. Dai Panda's kid sister brought a borrowed copy of the song *God Save The Queen* to my home and the three of us listened to it in secret for the first time. It was a mysterious private experience and we felt that if it was good enough for the BBC to ban, it was good enough for us.

The discos also forbade it. We refused to dance, from boredom and in protest when we went to such places from then on. We heard punk music played at friends' houses and at parties where we would pogo away, pushing at whoever was in reach in our jumps.

Punk was different, it was ours, for a while at least when it was young and rebellious, like we were. It was something fresh, a current under commercial music, like peeling off a scab to see the wound underneath. Punk meant that one could vomit and talk of it as a virtue, as an honourable act against the system. A buffer against boredom and the rain. The music evoked Bader Meinhoff and the Berlin Wall, Belfast and Bloody Sunday, boring Monday mornings and being sick on a Saturday night.

When we talked, Lad was the philosopher, Will the encyclopaedia, Zed the brute, Parry the lover and Dai Panda the panda, I supposed.

'Here we are, thinking we're better than the rest but are we really different?' Lad suddenly asked, and then quickly finger-combed a lock of fair hair behind her ear.

'Yer, we're working class kids,' Zed suggested.

'And proud of it,' Parry added.

'Proud to be punks! That's the difference,' Zed said.

'Aren't there middle-class punks then?' Will asked.

'Yes, but it ain't real,' Zed replied.

'There are things though that don't separate us from the middle class,' Lad announced. 'Jealousy, possessions. We exploit those below us too! Take women!' she continued.

'I like to take women,' Parry said as he tried to put his arm around her to pull her towards him. She pushed him away.

I liked Lad. It was a minor miracle how she put up with us. Almost always dressed in jeans and trainers, she was like one of the boys, except she had an urgency to come to grips with the meaning of life. Her tales were becoming darker, which others found depressing. She felt there wasn't much to life. There was school, going out at the weekends, learning to defend yourself, hanging around doing nothing, and then later you got a job if there were any to be had and then later you died. But why, she would always ask, and there was never anybody who could answer her.

A youth came up to us to tell Zed that the concert had finally been cancelled. We looked around us for reactions; some people were walking away while two police officers came over to tell us to move on. It was like closing time at the pubs. But we were in the open air. We were asked to move on again and told it was a final warning. Where to, we asked rhetorically and began walking slowly nowhere.

From a distance, Zed shouted out insults at the police who were watching us and we all began to run, a pulsed animal alive and knowing it can't escape, closely chased in our imagination by unseen truncheons.

The police, immobile, watched us run for our lives.

'I'd just love to do a copper in,' Zed gasped as we slowed down to a walking pace.

We two waited for the others walk up to us, side-hugging and panting.

'Did I tell you about the last time I got arrested? Hadn't done anything,' Zed explained. 'There had been a bit of fisticuffs outside the Red Lion, I was just watching, I was, and laughing and when the police turned up they went straight for me, not for the two drunken old dickheads who were fighting. Bound over again, I were.'

For us Zed had been the first real punk we had known.

We were at school together but he was a year older and would otherwise have had nothing to do with us but for the fact that we met him at a concert. He talked of anarchy, had spiky hair dyed a yellowish orange, wore military boots and was otherwise a glue-sniffing lout who boasted of his drinking sessions and of his police record. But he stood out as different and before we got to know him well he was for us the most interesting person in the world. But then that was the summer of seventy-seven and we chose to breathe the violence of post-industrial despair.

Parry suggested that we put what little money we had together and buy some cans of beer from an off-licence. We went to one but they refused to serve us and we were ordered out. Will and Lad argued the score with the shop assistants and as we left Zed and Parry kicked at the glass door, smashing it, of course, and we had to run off again.

We met up again, again breathless. It seemed that we were getting high on exercise for a change.

'I've got to go off to see a man about a dog,' Zed eventually said, bored of doing nothing, and he went.

'A dog?' Panda asked.

'To look for drugs,' Will explained to him.

The five of us decided to make our way back home. We came across a footbridge crossing and Parry claimed he'd always wanted to see how long he could hang from it. He challenged us to a competition: only Dai Panda and I accepted. The three of us hung from our arms over the grass verge next to the passing cars, some hooting as they passed, while Lad and Will watched and timed us from above. Parry lasted out the longest, but only just and then

I teased him by saying that Dai Panda and I had let him win so that he could impress Lad.

Parry took out a comb and ran it through his hair.

'It's not a comb you need, it's a plastic surgeon,' Will told him.

Parry began chasing him down the road and there we were all running for the third time that evening.

Approaching Gorseinon, we decided to make our way to a boarded-up abandoned house on the Pontarddulais Road. We'd begun to use it as a den, but mostly as a retreat from the rain on days when we had nowhere else to go. On arriving at the house Lad began to wonder about Zed.

'Has he girlfriends?' she asked Parry.

'Yes, many, and all of them are drugs,' Parry replied.

'He talks as if he doesn't care about anything, he's a total dropout, that includes girls, sex and all. He says that's why he's a punk,' I added.

'He's still young,' Lad said.

Inside the old abandoned house, Will started kicking at some broken bottles on the floor, holding a lit match to see what he was doing.

'Tell them about your dream, Lad?' Parry asked her.

'It's not going to be a horror story is it?' Dai Panda asked. He was afraid of the abandoned house and wished we never went there.

'It's a dream, boy,' Parry reassured him.

The house was a two-up two-down toiletless semi, built in the late nineteenth century and empty of life some ten years ago. Once its occupants had died the council took the building over but just left it abandoned and boarded up. Two sisters had lived there all their lives. They died in a bedroom together, or they were both dead by the time they were found.

'I dreamt I had woken up in the morning,' Lad began as we gathered around her in the light coming through the boarded front-room window at dusk. 'There was nobody at home and an unnatural silence in the streets. I felt that I must have slept all through the previous day and now it was Sunday not Saturday morning as I somehow expected. Then I found myself in the street but there was no one around. It was as if everyone, and not just the major industries, had left town ages ago.'

'Tell them about the old woman you saw,' Parry interrupted.

'There were only rats and uncollected rubbish in the streets until I saw someone else in the distance, an old woman, hunchbacked, in a ragged overcoat and a blanket around her shoulders. She was hiding her head, dragging along a dead dog on a leash. I tried to catch up with her to ask what had happened to the town but she was always ahead of me.' Lad was staring ahead through the darkness at a plaster-chipped broken wall.

'She went out of sight, dragging the dead dog after her and when I got to the corner the old woman was gone. I felt frightened and tried to go home but I couldn't find it. I came across a broken door at the entrance to an abandoned factory and saw someone through the glass. I looked again and saw the face of the old woman I had tried to catch up with. But that woman was me. I was looking at myself, old and ugly. My face reflected in the broken glass hanging from the door. And that's all. I woke up afterwards.' A deadly silence fell, broken by Will striking another match. 'I don't want to be old and alone,' Lad added. 'Give me anything else, but not that.'

4. *1966*

Mam was thinking of Father, who was usually to be found hanging around outside the off-licence or the chemist's. She was thinking of how he would cough in the morning to see what colours he could bring up and of what she overheard his mother say of him once.

'He'd be a normal, ordinary, decent man if it wasn't for his utterly nasty habit of sleeping with women,' she said in her superior Sunday voice. Her Protestant voice that whined and scratched away at you.

I was there, I heard what she had to say when she came to visit soon after he went away for good.

He always smelt of the sodium death wish he soaked his false teeth in and of the chemically clean but hardly human aftershave he would put on before going out in the evening. He would carry the smells out and when he came

37

back with them they were joined by a sweet touch of whisky.

At the dole office, he would half-heartedly chit chat with friends until he found something to disagree with, then he would really come alive. Off they would go to drink in moderation all day long, that is, without rushing and without stopping, and watch the passing girls in their cheap dresses and perfume, coming and going without them, leaving behind them only melancholy, the source of every Welshman's irony.

'Wales doesn't exist! I should know, I was born there,' was one of his sayings on these occasions.

He would invent etymology on the spot and claim to the monoglots how *diod* and *dioddef*, the roots of drink and suffer, were the same in Welsh. And then they would get another round in and joke about the Queen and other chinless wonders of that distant haemophiliac Union Jack-waving master race.

They were the butties he sometimes brought home. They would come round all on their own after he went for good and talk nostalgically to any of us who would listen, me and the old dog mostly.

When at home he was capable of teaching me to shave, along with him in front of the kitchen mirror, me standing on a chair with my own bladeless razor and frothy soap, he with his giant hand around mine gently stroking away the foam until I got the hang of it. We'd shave as one, smiling at ourselves in the reflection, just like a Father and Son Christmas.

But we could not ever mention Christmas. Talk of

Christmas and the Queen, like going near the front door on sunny days, was banned at home.

We ended with aftershave splashed on us both. I can still smell it, and him in the morning when clean strangers pass me in the street. I can still remember him: in facial alcohol, and in booze.

He spent most of his forced early retirement at bar forums. You could tell when he had a hangover the next day. He would get up and start digging the back garden, no matter the weather, until he sweated it out, or dropped down exhausted. Or both. The rest of the time he would sunbathe shirtless on the front doorstep whenever a few rays of light escaped through the summer clouds. His head leaned back against the closed front door all afternoon as he dreamt, free from the fear of someone opening the door from the inside.

Sometimes he'd paint the walls or over wallpaper. He was slowly reducing the interior living space of our home. If he had continued we would have been reduced to a yellow floral matchbox. Then there was the bathroom he had papered pink with the *Financial Times*, rejected meat wrapping from the butcher's. But it all gave him something to do on wet afternoons until the pubs opened.

Once he brought two of his butties home to drink round the kitchen table and I was allowed to stay. Father introduced one of them as a pinter: a drinker of pints in one long, slow gulp. I remember him as Beer. He had a red round face and was bald; he seemed to whisper loudly. Fingers was older than both Father and Beer, a disabled ex-miner who noisily wheezed in breaths of air. Hearing him speak was like listening to somebody snore. He shook my hand with a crushing finger-bone grip.

Beer had brought along some homemade flagons of the stuff. When Mam invited other kids from the street home to eat and Father told us all to go play on the M4, she'd say he was turning the kitchen into a pub.

'Huw, does he want a glass?' Beer asked Father of me.

'He wouldn't say no to a sip. Would you?'

'Come over here, there's a good boy. Go on bach,' Father said and I took a sip from his friend's glass, swallowed and squirmed. They laughed at me, I was old enough to know then.

They drank for hours and eventually I took the chance to ask a question: 'Where's his hair?'

Beer leaned in his chair across to me standing at the table, answering, 'I've been moulting, I have, see. Like a dog.' He smoothed his hand back across his forehead, over his head.

'He keeps... all the hairs that've... come away in a... box under his bed. He'll... show you one... day, he will,' Fingers wheezed.

'Why don't you stick it back on?' I asked Beer and they laughed again.

They told stories, made lists, moved from one subject to another, getting nowhere like a paper bag blowing about in the wind.

They talked of useless professions.

'A Welsh-speaking bookshop assistant in Newport,' Father suggested.

'Door-to-door contraceptive salesman in Ireland,' Beer said and they all laughed.

'Inner-city... cow milker,' Fingers suggested.

'A bodyguard at Tupperware parties,' Beer said and laughed.

'Collier,' Father said, only he laughed.

'What do you... want to be when you... grow up?' Fingers asked me.

'A postman,' I replied.

'A postman! Now... there's a good... job, walking in the... fresh air... and the like,' he suggested.

'A postman with a van,' I corrected him.

They talked about the future as if there wasn't going to be one.

Fingers told me later, once when I met him in the street, that Father only ever had two interests in life. Nineteenth-century Welsh choral music. 'And... women.'

Another of their lists was hobbies.

'Collecting crab shells, Superman comics, antique hearing-aid horns,' Beer said.

'Counting the Joneses in a South Wales telephone directory,' Father said.

'Organising Harry Secombe Fan Club outings,' Beer said.

'Doing coal... stone sculptures of... mountain ponies,' Fingers said.

'Inventing,' Beer began to say.

'Inventing is a useful creation, not a hobby!' Father interrupted, a little angry.

When not drinking he would be in the kitchen inventing things, sometimes drawing out his plans or else adding improvements to already existing devices, like a nail-clipper that collected the slivers that would otherwise fly in all directions. That one was too impractical, the collecting casing restricted the cutting action. Using a newspaper spread out under the job was the easiest way in the end. He would change the winding mechanism of the plastic cuckoo clock so that a hand-drill could be used to wind it up. His fantasy was going effortlessly around the house, drill in hand, winding clocks. But we only had two. The plastic Swiss imitation birdless box over the fireplace that Eileen brought home from London as a present and the Russian alarm bell siren on his bedside table, whose ticking could be heard down the road on quiet days. Other plans too, wild ones his butties told me later. The ones he never mentioned in front of the kids. Ideas about robbing safe deposit boxes in London and escaping to Marbella.

One morning Father threw the old Russian alarm clock in rage out of his bedroom window, sick of the idea of looking for work. I was at the front gate watching Old Tommy the Commie enlightening a tracksuited Timmy Sugar Ray Jenkins, our local semi-pro boxer, as to the social function of violent spectator sports in capitalist society. Timmy Sugar Ray was just sweating and puffing indifferently as he jogged on the spot, when we saw the clock fly over our heads.

I remember Father tall and strong, but then I was still a boy the last time I saw him. He had a body built on manual work and breakfast. Raw eggs beaten into a pint glass of milk sweetened with a sprinkle of sugar and a few splashes of whisky, for the taste. And a loud smile, a wide laugh. An evergreen smile that seemed to eat you and melted women into a cream between the legs when he stared their way. He looked like a bar-room heavy, and had the weight if not the arguments: 'I'll mix him in with the floor until you can't tell which is what.'

He held something dark on the inside. He would call out in his dreams, a voice answering no, no. But he just smiled, most of the time. I began to see, as I grew, that it might have been forced, the muscles pulled into place, tight around the jaw. And the jokes, they were just the same old ones, hacked to death. He would smile at people, afraid they would otherwise see what was there, and know.

He was claustrophobic and feared the thick cockroach covering of the walls on the pit's lower levels, since as a boy he took his father's ponies underground before school during the Second World War. Colonialism, he called the work. A colony with subsidence problems. Cracks in the wall, mini-earthquakes in the street, as the ground slowly inched its way down into the hollowed-out spaces of hundreds of miles of abandoned mine tunnels below us. And above, the giant slag hills of the earth turned inside out. The mines were underground cities of dust, streeted with rainwater rivers, the drone of pumps, the curses, the screech of drills, and impending disaster.

Father was born on the other side of the river Loughor, borderline wild Welsh and American South Wales. North-east Carmarthen, borderline red Wales and green Wales, Merlin's Fort town territory. He was born to work as a bootless boy in the anthracite mine, stepping coal as brittle as glass. At home his mother dripped candle wax over his soles, to be dried and peeled off, taking the coal filings with it. When he was older he always used to look at the shoes men wore to gauge their class and income.

His mother had an old clock hanging on the wall, it chimed all the hours and halves. Behind the round pendulum weight there was a greying photograph taken in about nineteen-ten, an image of a teenage boy in a Sunday suit next to an empty chair as he posed in the photographer's studio. He was bootless in white socks, and looked just like me. Father's father, seen yes, then no behind the pendulum's swing. As a boy Father saw him die at his side underground, plastered into a shovel head by twenty tonnes of coal, the boy holding his hand until they reached the top and for a day more without ever leaving go his grip.

He had a life of candle wax, anthracite and a single mother's nagging voice, and then he met Mam and smiled at her. She had a child's smile. His smile could convince a peacock to hand over its feathers. It persuaded Mam to give him children. He also got a softer voice to listen to and an old washing machine to repair.

'Destroyed in the wash,' she would say of the great angry metal beast that roared and tore up much of what was put into it. Father tried to fix it, it was one of his useful creation hobbies, and Mam reverted to washing by hand.

She gave him five kids. The first when she was eighteen, then another when she was twenty, then twenty-two, twenty-three and twenty-six. The last one was me, unplanned.

On the dole at home he had things to say.

'Look at us! We're medieval men placed at the gates of the twenty-first century. I used to think there was progress, that we were going somewhere, but all we've done is replace the plough in our grip for a pneumatic drill. Over the centuries the control over us has changed from Catholicism to cathode rays. What's different?'

I was to go on to talk like him. Later. After.

Then, at the time, I was still learning to count. For weeks in the autumn of sixty-six I tried to understand the number one hundred and sixteen, but could only count well to ten.

He tried to explain it to me as he took a tea break from taking a bit off a scraping bedroom door by sawing away at it with the door still on. 'How much is a hundred and sixteen?' I think I asked.

'Well now, it's like you, that makes one, see, and Little Johnny, that makes two, and then a hundred and fourteen more.'

Yes, like Little Johnny, me and a hundred and fourteen more buried in their school under hundreds of tonnes of slag slurry.

5. *1970*

I awoke in the middle of the night to a slow scratching sound coming from out the back. I tried to wake my brother in the bed next to mine but he just groaned. I tried blocking the noise by pulling the blankets over my head. I got out of bed and tried going to my sister's room but I couldn't find it, I was at the top of the darkened stairs. I went down and through to the kitchen a little frightened now, the sound closer, heavier in my ears, scratch, scratch against the ground, making the sleepy house tremble. The noise was that of a huge dog slowly burying a bone in thick gravel. Shaking, I was too frightened to open the door and take a look outside.

But that was later.

There was only ever one car in our street when I was a

child, the postman's delivery van, which he brought home after work and left outside his house to rust like a solitary sunburnt old man on a deserted beach. We used to ask him for a ride, I had only ever been anywhere by bus and that to Swansea centre on the double-decker number one hundred and twelve for shopping with Mam on Saturdays or to paddle in the grey sandy mud-oiled beach of the Bay on the odd summer's day. He always said no, it's not allowed, government property see, so we asked him to rev it up, arguing that it was good for the big end, which nobody knew what exactly it was.

Transportation problems and how to be taken somewhere, elsewhere, away for a while, made me wonder when Father would get a van to take us for a ride and if not, then why not become a postman, but I never said anything. I got to travel once with the rest of the tribe, except Father, on a bus trip to Tenby organised by a dying revivalist chapel as part of some twisted plan which involved trying to civilise us. Social integration, they call it now.

On the beach at Tenby Bay trying to build sandcastles that defied the tide, one of the revivalists sat next to me on the sand, jacket, tie and all sweating under the sun like a Christian before the lions. He talked about destiny, about Heaven. I liked stories of angels and asked him if he knew one. If we are good we will go up to the sky and be saved and then live for ever he said. I asked about what we could do for ever and if 'up there' would get overcrowded.

In Heaven, the angels dressed in white with haloes and wings for hundreds of years in the infinite. Little by little

47

they began to make changes to their everyday life. Father had explained it to me. Some began working as a hobby to distract themselves, others deciding what to do with the things made by the others, until some worked for others perpetually until heaven had angels in offices dressed in ties, without the wings and haloes, he said. Eventually a board of directors' meeting decided to replace God with a plc president.

The revivalist offered to buy me an ice cream, so we got up and walked away from the beach. He led me to some public toilets and said we should go in first. Standing next to me at the china piss bowls, which were a bit like a row of ostrich-sized egg cups screwed into the wall, he asked if I'd show him my willy. I asked for some money, he said he just wanted to look. I told him I would tell Father who was a boxer and he gave me some money and I ran away to get an ice cream, leaving him to promise eternal salvation to someone else. Later the man was involved in what they called a scandal. They said he escaped to the United States and formed his own TV church.

That day in Tenby I ate soggy tomato and sandy sliced-bread sandwiches on the beach. On the way back we stopped for chips, I asked for two rissoles, only got one but shared half of Nerys's soggy sponge cod. After I went and told my Mam that I felt seasick, someone shouted out that it was a bus not a boat but she understood, holding a plastic carrier bag in front of my mouth.

Other adventures in velocity included waiting patiently for minutes that lasted hours on the pavement for a car to pass and when one did we'd run across the road in front of it.

Best of all though was when the pop lorry passed. We'd climb up onto the open back of it and ride down the hill, the petrol exhaust-fume wind blowing through our hair as we sat on the crates. Lorries were the limit of pleasure. With the other kids of my street, whom I began to call boys, we would jump onto the tail ramp of any we saw pass, holding on, spreadeagled with a devilish smile. Eventually Mam heard of an accident; feeling that I had already had my fair share of them she sent me to play with Little Johnny Evans who was quiet.

There was a water-duct tunnel behind the British Steel plant that opened out into an unnamed stream. The opening was built of brick and to enter it all you had to do was duck your head. One day Parry, Little Johnny and I went exploring with candles.

Little Johnny said it was built a long time ago by the Romans. The only Romans I knew had a chip-shop café in High Street and I somehow doubted they would drag bricks and mortar all the way around the back of the British Steel works so as to help channel floodwater. Parry agreed with me and that was that.

The entrance led into a cement tube you had to crawl along on all fours and was difficult to turn around in. Little Johnny led the way, followed by Parry and then me close on behind until Little Johnny said his knees were getting damp with water and I panicked, saying I was getting out. Parry said it was only a trickle but I crawled backwards out to the daylight all the same. I waited outside for their return. The water was only a dribble, Parry said and called me chicken and we fought.

Then, as a child, there was necessary violence, as defence. There was also unnecessary violence. Sometimes we would sit on the wall at the front of my house to watch Timmy Sugar Ray Jenkins running up and down Bryn Road at night, huffing and puffing, swinging his windmill arms, occasionally jabbing at the air of an invisible, half-defeated opponent. He practised unnecessary violence. Eighteen fights, knocked out twelve times, disqualified six times, four times for punching low and twice for head-butting.

For me fights until then were pulling and tumbling on the ground, but Parry now was swinging out at my face, punching me. I was dizzy and fell to my knees, down onto my hands, my head bobbing down, feeling a ballooning ache in my stomach: I vomited, bringing up a warm grey liquid. It was like dirty mine water. All the time I was thinking what Mam had said about it being safer playing with Little Johnny.

Johnny Evans lived alone with his mother four doors down from us. She was a big, fat-legged woman who spent all day in bed only to be out all night leaving Little Johnny alone. There was nothing in his house, except a solitary bed upstairs which he shared briefly in the mornings with his mother. Downstairs they had newspapers covered across all the floor in place of carpets and there was no lighting, just that which came in through the window. He went about his house like a blind man. He said his father had emigrated before he was born and he was waiting for him to come back home to play with him. Sometimes he would talk of him climbing in the Himalayas, braving it all without oxygen. His favourite game was to cut up worms, a piece at a time. He was amazed at how they continued to wriggle.

I went to play with Johnny Evans every day after school before the Council came for him. Father said that instead of banning poverty they prefer to ban the poor. They took and hid him away just like that Alsatian from number thirty-one that bit the milkman. They reassured me that the dog went to live with a farmer and could run free over the hills. And Johnny Evans? They never explained what happened to him, though Mam threatened me by saying that the Council would come for me if I didn't behave at home.

Home was a small three-up, two-down prefabricated house that began to get slowly filled with tiny porcelain ornaments over the years. I broke a few, playing indoors. But nobody seemed to mind that a little red gnome, a blue cottage or a white dog went suddenly missing from over the fireplace. Home was an appendix to Swansea, thrown up originally as a cross of two streets, both leading elsewhere, leaving crucified what was there. Home had three sisters. There was Eileen, or Eye as we called her, the eldest. A teenager as tall as Father eventually. She had to be in the school's netball team because of her height, but she got to travel on away games, for free in a mini-bus and I envied her.

She was beautiful. Everybody knew it and said so, but we her family who had to see her all day in all conditions never really noticed. I noticed her in her nightie with sleep in her eyes and her hair a bird's nest. I noticed her leaving the bathroom with toilet-paper towel rolled up in her hand for the kitchen fire when she was thirteen, saying that it was for the first time. She must have been down to the water duct. I noticed everything but never her beauty then when I was young.

Then there was Nerys, the silent one, Mam called her, because she didn't make silly comments and ask questions nor wonder aloud about the rest of us. Always obsessed with the physical she watched herself grow in front of the bathroom mirror, hoping to be as tall as Eileen. She ended up too short for netball travel with her pear-shaped body. Nobody said she was beautiful so she studied. As I grew I saw that her mind had grown.

At home my sisters shared a huge double bed in the main bedroom. I would sometimes go and seek the warmth and smells of my sisters in the middle of the night, being allowed to as the baby of the family, until Fan became ill.

Fan was short for Myfanwy, pronounced Van and sometimes called Lorry or Bedford as a result, this last nickname finally shortened to Bed when she was to spend most of her time there. Once when she was ten she went out on her bike and came home ill and everybody cried and I was sent to Mamgu's for a few days. When I returned Fan feared leaving the protection of indoors. At first she would hide under the kitchen table when anyone visited and then finally took refuge in her room. I loved to tease her. She was short and skinny, and she never went outside the house, not even into the back garden, and never said why, but always asked where others were going.

Finally the school inspectors came and Mam would explain things at the door, usually through the letter box.

She's bad, she would say. Later the inspectors would come looking for my brother Huw too and Mam would say that he didn't live there any more. They became people to avoid, like the rent man and she eventually gave up answering the door to people who needed to knock.

And me, a growing child, thin-boned, quick to bleed, round piggy-faced hydrophobic who thought he was all alone. It was only a child's philosophy, flat like his lung. I coughed up ideas and stale air for years and vomited dirty water when nervous or hit, or both. Nobody knew why exactly. The doctor suggested we kept a sample next time it happened but it wasn't easy to sponge the stuff up from the carpet. The local health authority's specialist in vomits said it must have been digestion acid and recommended camomile tea. The rest of us in the tribe knew exactly what it was, after all that time I was still full of pit pond water drained from the mine.

Then as a growing child I was brought up at home, first with Mam, to avoid having more than my share of accidents, and then with Father to be taught the science of forgetfulness. Lest we forget our history, our class, that we forget who we are, for a forgotten memory is like lost luggage left behind, stopping us from moving forward in life, he said. I was to remember that when, like the Council for Johnny Evans, they were to come for me too.

6. *1978*

I got up out of bed late again, black coffee and razor blades for an early afternoon breakfast and down to the library to check a fact and so prove a point to Old Tommy and in the process let myself drift to other references, learning more and forgetting more. Increasingly I found myself leaning my way through the *Encyclopaedia Britannica*. There were people already at the library, some of them students using the reference books they couldn't afford to buy. For others it was somewhere to go, to be out of the house for a bit of peace and quiet. For a third group it was a ritual, like walking the dog, for others, a municipal refuge from the rain. The inspiring concentration of the more serious students was almost palpable.

'Well jew jew, Tommy Boy, here looking for Arthur's

ghost, are we then mun?' I heard shouted out behind me as I heaved a volume off the shelf.

'How on earth did they let you in? The pubs have run dry and you've got nowhere to go, or what?' I saw Old Tommy reply.

He was seated at a table covered with the morning newspapers and spoke up to a hand on his shoulder.

'Ssshh,' came a voice from the reservations desk, worried at the prospect of a fight between pensioners.

'Look now they're going to call the fire brigade to put out your brimstone,' Tommy warned him, lowering his voice as I approached.

'Come in to rob the new revised edition of the Old Testament, illustrated and all, he has, to sell for drink,' Tommy told me. 'I came in to read the morning paper. You know the poverty of information in the *Western Mail* is staggering!' he continued.

'Well how are you, my dear man?' the stranger bellowed, wobbling slightly, his hand tightening its grip on Tommy's shoulder.

'Don't you know, bach, there's a spectre haunting its way over Europe, there is,' he said before I could reply, holding his free hand unsteadily out to shake mine.

He crushed it briefly with surprising force, his hand smooth and senseless from endless years of manual work.

Ex-pickaxe face-worker, I thought.

'Watch out, he's contagious,' Tommy warned me as I looked for signs of permanent damage.

'Ignorant pagan!' the man roared in return. An early

tang of whisky on his breath or was it impregnated in his rancid clothes?

'Now I know why he's here! It's the library's fortieth anniversary this year, he must have thought they were inviting the readers to a free booze-up,' Tommy argued, looking up to him for a response as he tried wriggling his shoulder free.

Either they were very good friends who poked at each other for a laugh or the next time they met it would be with rusty knives and clenched dentures. I saw Will's future in my old communist friend, perhaps mine too in the stranger, worn out like his clothes.

'That wouldn't be an early edition of the *Bibliography of Wesleyan Methodism in Wales*, by any chance?' the man asked, looking down at the volume under my arm.

'Hit him with it, go on, a good thumping will sober the bugger up,' Tommy recommended.

'I'm looking up the Chinese...' I began to explain.

'Now there's a country for you,' Tommy's friend interrupted just as the assistant librarian arrived to tell us to either shut up or leave.

'I only came in for a bit of peace and quiet,' the man apologised.

'I wouldn't believe anything he's got to say,' Tommy said, 'when he's as sober as Judgement Day. Don't you worry now, we're about to go out for a cup of tea and we'll leave him here to sleep it off. Look, we can lay him down nicely on the floor and cover him with these papers and he won't disturb.'

I handed the man the volume and left with Tommy.

'I'm dying for a fag anyway,' my old friend whispered to the assistant librarian as added justification for our retreat.

'But you don't smoke!' I reminded him as we went through the door.

We went to Roma's where we could talk over a single cup of tasteless tea-chest dust for a couple of hours without being thrown out and maybe not even have to pay.

'Ceylon, is it cariad?' Old Tommy asked the girl behind the counter.

'I don't know, we get it in twenty-pound sacks from a wholesaler's in Mountain Ash,' she replied dryly.

'Ah, Mountain Ash it is then!'

Bringing the cups to our table, he told me of the tea's distinctive taste.

'Due to the special climatic conditions only to be found in Mountain Ash where the morning dewdrops brush gently against the green leaves of this rather fruity northern cha variety, like, like...'

'Like caresses of a butterfly's wings,' I suggested. 'And it's dirt cheap!'

Everything in the café was false, from the imitation plastic chairs to the fly on my spoon that didn't move, but the place was all the more real for that, South-Walian real where nobody hoped to drink Champagne on a balcony in Capri overlooking the Gulf of Naples.

'You know, the Welsh are the Italians of northern Europe,' Old Tommy suggested. 'Both peoples are lost in the past and can't come to terms with the present.'

He'd talk about anything, from revolutions to tea, miners' strikes to paper recycling, history to armchairs, economics to lost peoples, philosophy to pensions, computer technology to the rain, the government to birthday cards, and all the trivial happenings and connections seen around him. I only wanted to hear about the man at the library.

'Arthur's ghost?' I said.

'Oh, Jenkins! It was something we talked about once, when we were younger and thought we were friends,' Tommy replied. 'We went through all that Celtic rubbish about the Round Table, Christian chivalry, the lady in the lake and the true Bible and all and I said that if King Arthur was to rise from the dead among us it would be to lead the workers to liberation and not to restore feudalism in Wales. Ridiculous, I know. At the time it was just a comment, but for the last two or three hundred years whenever he sees me he comes up with Arthur's ghost, the brain-dead old drunken lout. Seventy years old by now he must be mun and still believing in children's stories about the life of Jesus, it's high time he grew up. Hasn't been sober since the war, the first one. Drinks all day and then goes home to lament by reading the Book of Jeremiah out loud. Doesn't let his neighbours sleep with all that rubbish about unleavened bread and Josiah the son of Amon went forth; dogs bark at him mun and I won't go to his funeral. My only fear is that he outlives me and comes to mine. Drove his wife mad with all that Jesus voodoo, he did.'

'Did you work together?' I asked.

'No, I knew him since a boy. He was a miner,' Tommy said of him.

'Was he a scab? Did you tar and feather him?' I asked.

'No, far from it, Jenkins was a typical product of the Labour colleges, Christian utopia and all that, you know, those radical socialists who rejected Marxism because it was atheist. For them, a brother was both a fellow worker and a chapelgoer. They thought that God was on their side in nineteen twenty-six, poor devils, while the bosses were thanking their God when they forced them back to work an hour more per day for half the pay. I was sixteen, an apprentice at Richard Thomas Tinplate and became a member of the Communist Party, and still am today. It was clear that there would be no parliamentary road to socialism, only through industrial action. Jenkins and I were on an Action Council at the time, in May twenty-six, Year One of the Revolution, as we called it, he must have been about two years older than me and I must admit that for the next ten years, until Spain, we had more in common than anything else.'

'What led him to drink?' I wanted to know.

'Oh, contradiction of course, like bourgeois revolutionaries, workers who vote Tory, tee-totalling preachers who are tight all day.'

'He isn't a preacher, is he?'

'Not for wanting, he isn't. He reminds me of my father, who was a Presbyterian. My father told everybody they were going to burn in Hell, which sounded better than having to put up with him. Badly wounded in the Great War. Hated the Communists because Marx was a foreigner, unlike Christ he said. Thought that Disestablishment of the Church in Wales was the best thing since sliced bread. Mother and us children had to stand around him to

59

attention while he read the Bible at gaslight in his armchair. Always going on about the revival of nineteen o-four. He enjoyed being a bitter, nasty man, made my mother tremble constantly in fear. Now whenever I enter a dark room, hear Welsh spoken or the mention of God it makes my skin crawl, it does.'

'When I was a kid my father used to tell me anti-Christian stories, like the one about the boy-child Jesus playing hide and seek with his Jewish friends and when it was Jesus' turn he found them hiding in an oven and used his magic to roast them into dust.'

'You had a privileged upbringing, you did!'

'Perhaps your father's Puritanism has influenced you, Tommy. I mean you don't exactly spend your pension on wine, women and song, do you?'

'My pension! Don't talk to me about my pension. As for drink, I'm not against it. I'm against drunks. They waste their money, they want to drink instead of think, it's the curse of us the working class who'll never do anything for ourselves as long as we're distracted with booze, pornography and TV game shows. And that's got nothing to do with my father, may the Devil torment his soul, the miserable old bastard.'

We passed most of the afternoon, like the other ones, as a timeless parenthesis over a single cup of tea, talking because it was the only thing left for us to do. The conversation came to an end when he invited me back to his house for one of his wife's bacon sandwiches. But I had arranged to meet Siân at half past four and we parted outside the café with him patting my shoulder.

I decided to walk to Siân's bay-windowed semi-detached house in a neighbourhood with broken glass set in concrete on top of the garden walls. I wasn't late and it didn't rain so I saved on the bus fare. Her father was the head librarian in Neath and her mother, who didn't have to, worked as a receptionist for the council public health department. We had an hour and a half together every afternoon, in bed, Monday to Friday, from the time she got home from school until her parents came back from work.

I walked but my heart ran in expectation. She was a whistle that called me. It was a cold rainy Monday afternoon when I first saw her in Spar's on the High Street. She glanced at me, a brief brick in the head look, and I spent the rest of the week catatonic, walking, sleeping, eating as another person. She had short dark hair, a clean milky face and tight, faded blue jeans.

What I liked most about her from that moment on was how she looked at me, as if surprised, as though she were reading about herself in someone else's diary. And I felt naked, an open page to her eye. I was about to finish school for ever and only thought that my future held no future, until then. I hadn't even spoken to her but knew from that time what I wanted in life: to be on top of her and she below.

I watched her leave the shop and asked a colleague of my sister Nerys who she was. She said the girl almost always came at the same time every day. Judging by her uniform, she went to the other comprehensive. Nerys's colleague teased me, saying she was a polite nice girl, too decent for me. Finally she told me her name.

I never tired of repeating her name. It was a warm overcoat I wrapped around me, taking it everywhere, smiling stupidly.

I ran into her again about a month later during the school holidays, me at sixteen having just given up school for ever and having all but given up on seeing her again but still planning what I was to say to impress her in the shop. I saw her waiting for a bus and forgot all my prepared speech so I stood at her side hoping she would begin a conversation.

Nothing.

Then I realised that the bus, if it came, would take us into Swansea.

'There are only ever two possibilities with buses around here. Into Swansea or out to Llanelli, away from this no-man's land full of industrial refugees,' came out of my mouth.

'What?' she asked.

'I think I saw you once in Spar's, if I'm not mistaken? My sister used to work there.'

'Is that right?' she replied, completely disinterested, looking down the street.

'Fancy a coffee?' I said after a while, trembling.

'God,' she said to herself more than to me. 'Why don't you bog off, creep.'

'Now that's a good old Anglo-Saxon verb,' I replied cockily.

She began to walk away. I felt ridiculous, I had done everything wrong. I watched her go and then ran to her side.

'Sorry,' I said. 'I won't bother you again. You go back for your bus and I'll go home and drown myself.'

She kept on walking away, I stopped and let her go, watching in my desolation. Then she glanced back at me from a safe distance and then again and finally turned to come back. She was going to give me a real earful of insults, I thought and looked down at the ground in shame. She stopped to face me.

'What's all this about?' she asked.

I said the truth, it all came out at once.

'I saw you in Spar's, the way you looked at me, from that moment I wanted to get to know you. I went to the supermarket every day for two weeks at a quarter past four hoping to see you, the first time to say excuse me and ask where you got the baked beans from, or whatever you had in your basket, and the next day to say hello and talk of the weather and then maybe when you saw that I was normal and friendly and not a creep or a rapist or mad or anything I'd invite you for a coffee at Roma's where I'd impress you with my spontaneous wit and now what have I done, I've ruined everything by chasing you away.'

'And you thought I'd come because you wanted, just like that,' she said. 'As if I've never talked to a boy before! I've certainly known more handsome ones.'

'I've only got words on my side,' I replied, agreeing in my way.

She stared at my face, me down at my shoes.

'Pity you don't use them well!' she added.

'I used to think love was just a longing to sleep with a girl,' I finally said. 'Now, having seen you I'd be happy just to see your smile. That's what would make me happy now.'

She smiled.

'I'm going to the beach for a swim and a bit of a tan, do you want to come along, but don't you dare try anything on,' she said.

I was lucky, I had botched things up but the mess I had created had amused her. I was lucky and it had nothing to do with me, but her.

We sat together on the bus into town.

'I used to see you in the street, messing around with a bunch of punks,' she said after a while.

We began to talk, of school, what I was doing. She thought I was younger. She wanted to go to university, if she could. I was on probation, and would be always, inferior from the weakness of having told her that I wanted her. But she took no advantage because she liked me. Yes, she was beautiful and close-up my eyes felt the silky smoothness of her skin.

There was a confident, slightly lower than usual tone to her voice, there was no chirping or screech to it. Slightly smoked, a taste of bacon to it. Looking at her made me want to run fingers through the shiny strains of her short hair, to caress her delicate long neck, kiss just *there* where the hair ended, where the naked nape began.

I was in ecstasy on top of a double-decker.

We caught a second bus from the Quadrant Centre in the city out to Mumbles Head to where the sea looked cleaner, where the red-faced afternoon pier men in white vests and beer bellies avoided their children, scrounging pennies for a peek through the sixty-second coin telescopes.

I watched her swim out from the shore, the splashes her arms made shimmered silver liquid against the light of the afternoon sun and then I looked back down along the arch of the bay to Swansea Dock and its factories further ahead but did not see a thing. The city had ceased to exist, only Siân was real. Only the closed space she filled in my mind.

She came out of the water back to me, walking on the curly seaweed, twisting her hips with each step and looking at me all the while as confident as a woman who knew who she was and what she wanted to be, and barely fifteen. She sat at my side breathing rapidly to regain herself from the chilly July sea, salty drops falling around her face and she leaned closer and kissed me.

Later we walked back along the shore to the city and she told me of her secrets, of how she'd made love for the first time a few months earlier over the Easter holidays in France.

'I'm in love with a girl who's been abroad,' I exclaimed to make her smile. 'I haven't even got as far as crossing the Severn Channel to England, though my friend Will and I once thought about jumping ship to Ireland to join the IRA and destroy ourselves.'

'We are different people now,' she said and then we were silent in our other world, the one that had love in it.

We walked towards where the city had disappeared. There was only sea onto sand mingling with the first line of trees. Swansea and its wood-covered mounts, nature before mankind got to work.

'Can you see the landscape from there?' she asked on the bus back to Gorseinon.

What landscape, seascape, skyscape, roomscape? There was only her, and me thinking of her.

'I can see all the landscape I need,' I replied, looking into her eyes.

After parting we went our separate ways home. I stopped and looked back at her after only a few paces and saw her turn, stare at me and say: 'I miss you already.'

From that day on I began trying to translate my emotions into some human language. Constantly telling her how I felt, how this thing inside of me coloured the chaos of the here and now, raised me up and threw me down.

The present too, the immediacy of being with Siân also had meaning, and not just the memory of what we did. There was feeling and not just later thought. The conflict of the there around me and the here inside me seemed resolved.

The next day she said I love you in Welsh, as we made love in her bed. We didn't really make love, it was all the same, we were entangled as lovers, caressing and kissing. Her mouth, her vagina, sweetness and salt on the tongue.

I had to leave quickly before her parents came home from work.

She left me shaking, shuddering until I could be with her again. I walked differently, people noticed me, the public too have known that private feeling. The world saw through me, they knew what I knew. At home looking into the mirror I was surprised not to find an imprint of her mouth pressed onto my lips. Bruised lips and fingers, my lover's tattoo marks.

Rwy'n dy garu di.

I love you. It sang from inside me as I got into my bed alone and felt her next to me, her odour on me, the taste of her pubic hair over my face as I pushed my groin against the sheet under me and saw and loved her in my mind. As I moved the bed rocked with me until I came and fell asleep.

Knocking on the front door of Siân's place it occurred to me that it was only the second house that I had ever entered that was not owned by someone else, whether council or landlord.

She opened the door a slice, and retreated into the hallway, signalling for me to come in. She was dressed only in a white T-shirt, barely covering her hips, and in white tennis shoes. My eyes and the rest of me followed her upstairs.

While the fact that I usually left just as her parents were due to arrive back terrified me, the possibility of being discovered with a boy in her bed was for her the petty theft adrenaline of the forbidden. Her father, after all, she told me, was capable of banning me from her life or of sending her away, if ever he found out about us. She often complained of the restrictions he placed on her.

'I like the sound of my name on your tongue,' she said to me in Welsh as we entered her bedroom. She then translated it as she sat on the side of her bed taking off her tennis shoes.

I asked her to write it out for me so I could memorise it. She enjoyed teaching me Welsh, the fact that I took an interest. She picked up a pen and began to write.

'No, wait a min, I've thought of something better, by John Morris Jones,' she said on pausing and then carefully wrote out two lines of verse in Welsh with a translation below it.

Mae iaith bereiddia'r ddaear hon
Ar enau 'nghariad i.

She stared at me in silence for a few moments as I read the verse.

'Today I teased a boy who looked a bit like you on the way to school,' she suddenly said. 'I was standing against a wall and winked at him as he passed. He was too frightened to look at me or say anything,' she added with a huge smile.

'I bet he's at home regretting it now,' I said with sympathy, imagining myself in his shoes.

'He was only a kid, the wretch, if he's thinking of anything now it's of playing with his toys!'

The only time she joked, and it was only ever about sex, was when she wanted to make love. Sometimes it was to tell me of her fantasies or to comment on what she imagined as she came with me inside her. Walking back from the Mumbles along the beach, she had told me of the highlight of her trip to France, when her vagina went on holiday for the first time, since then she felt free enough with me to say what went through her head. It was a roundabout way to say she wanted me there and then, as surely as taking off her underwear and pulling me down onto her, or as surely as saying, come, make love to me, which she never said, perhaps so as not to admit any weakness in herself.

What she said didn't usually excite me in itself but I was always excited by the prospect of what was to follow her stories.

I lay by her side on the bed, placing my hand on her waist, running it down, finger toying around to squeeze her hip and up again past her waist onto her T-shirt, finger-tip feather strokes slowly around the side of her breast and along the arc of her arm as she began, eyes closed, to open and close her legs, a hushed horizontal dance; open, brushing against my thigh, closed, squeezing herself. On returning my hand, inching down to her waist, she raised an arm up over her head and arched her back and I slid the palm of my hand under her shirt up between the mounds of her breasts, up further to her throat, with spider tickles, up to her lip, to her parted mouth, at the same time

Not far away in an abandoned house a girl had become frightened by the boy that had led her there. With no way out and the only possibility of calming him having failed she shook, defenceless and small as he blamed her for being her.

'What am I to do now, hey,' he cried at her. 'Why don't you bloody care any more, it's not fucking fair!'

'I didn't mean to hurt you,' she replied, trying not to seem frightened while hoping someone would come in and save her.

He threw a punch at the side of her mouth and down she fell, shoulder slamming against the wall. He grabbed at her, pulling her head back by the hair.

'Not laughing at me now, are you?' he said, pulling

kissing her neck just below the ear as she shuddered icy yes I like, no it's almost pain against my hand, eating in gulps of air, breathing pleasure in close silence and gentle bites on my finger tips.

She took my wet hand and guided it between her legs, turning towards me, raised a leg over my waist and rocked back down onto her back, her hand in my hair, scratching and pulling at the scalp sending light-shot tickles to the brain. Pulling me over onto her, twisting her hip up against my groin I stroked her backside that moved under me. Her hands struggling with the zip of my jeans, she brought her legs up over my waist, squeezing me between her and then releasing me to slide down my trousers as I held myself up on one arm to look at her closed-eyed under me and ran a finger

her up onto her feet to face him. 'Not like when you suck their dicks for free, hey? Dirty fucking whore.'

'I'm sorry, so sorry, please let me go now, please,' she pleaded through tears as blood ran from her mouth.

He pushed her away onto the floor and kicked out a toe-capped boot, crushing it into her rib cage, then threw himself down onto his knees to look at her and squeeze her head in his hands and pull her to his groin to rub her blood covered face over his jeans. She tried to wriggle her face away from him, gasping for air between the blood and the suffocating hold on her. He suddenly pushed her away from him and she lay sobbing on the floor amid the dust and old papers, the thick-layered cobwebs, cotton bridges between the broken beer bottles, as he along the groove her knickers made against the opening of her vagina.

Now, now, she said to me with her body, pulling my penis towards her parted underwear as I led my hand from the white of her knickers to under her T-shirt to pull it up over her breasts, sucking at her nipples, hungrily from one to the other as she ran her nails down my back, over my backside and cried against my throat. With my arms extended out, gripping the headrest behind her, the weight of my body on my elbows, pushing in and out of her as her hands clenched tightly into the meat of my buttocks until she slowly released their hold on me, and again, again, to repeat it all, I thought in my fire and I fell into a timeless senseless nowhere with the last few convulsions of my orgasm.

got to his feet, standing over her and stamped his boot onto her until he could do so no more, holding an arm out to the wall, crying in his own pain and relief as the last of her life slipped from her, as he stood looking down at her motionless on the floor, crying for himself and for her and the last beat of her heart pulsed into the silence of forever.

'Will they still want you now, slag?' he sobbed at her, motionless below him all but for his kicking, jolting her lifeless body spreadeagled on the floor and then he went down on to her, opening the fly of his jeans, an arm pulling her waist up to him, her face pressed against the floor, the blood mingling in with the dust, and he pushed himself into her backside with gripped teeth, snorting heavily through his nose like an enraged bull.

7. 1979

The plan, and we usually had one, the endlessly partying misfits that we were, was to go out again at night. The idea was to meet up with Dai Panda and Will at the Mardy Hotel before moving on to join the others but Panda had already been and gone, after making a phone call, we were told. We waited for his return as long as we could and then made our way to the local disco, the Gyp, next to where the station used to be. At the turn of the century trading gypsies were welcomed there to stay and rest and what was officially called the Station Hotel became known by everyone, except the police, as the Gyp.

'There's nothing like a bit of good old-fashioned, senseless, inner-class violence on a Saturday night, now is there?' Will commented about a bit of a brawl we came across as we arrived. I immediately thought that Siân was going to be put off from coming in.

'But it's still only Friday.' I corrected him.

'And early yet,' he said. 'Now there's a sight for you! Zed and Parry aren't involved, must be scrounging a drink off Lad. Fuel for the scrums later on.'

Zed and Parry could be unpredictable, socially speaking, especially Parry, who since breaking up with Lad would look for trouble. He would lash out, without even the excuse of drink, at any and all. Although still young he had an old man's bitterness.

'I don't know why we come, really,' I moaned, beginning to regret having invited Siân.

'We come to watch and complain, as always. Anyway it was your idea. We could have gone and wrecked Panda's bedroom, again,' he replied looking around the circular dance hall. The men at the bar were staring at three groups of teenage girls slowly dancing, out of rhythm, their handbags on the floor in their centre.

'Hey look! A dead star is born!' he said, pointing to Zed who was under the DJ's platform, his head inclined sideways against a loudspeaker. 'What you having?' he added before walking towards our friend.

They soon came back together.

'Alright?' Zed greeted me. 'Heard the news, have you?'

'I heard you got done again,' I replied.

'No, that was my kid brother,' he said with a big grin across his face, showing his cracked and broken front teeth.

'Been a bit of a murder,' he went on. 'Neat. Pigs everywhere.'

'Where, here or in town?' I asked him.

73

For everyone I knew, town was the centre of Swansea, home was Gorseinon.

'Don't know. But they're looking round here. Everybody's talking about it. Heard that the Pa Pa Panda kid got nervous and got Parry to come and hold his bleeding little hand.'

'Are they here?' I asked.

'Haven't seen them,' Zed replied. 'Have you?' he asked Will who shrugged his shoulders in silence.

'Well, we haven't heard anything,' I exclaimed. 'I'm going to wait outside for Siân to come.'

'Creepy all this, isn't it?' Zed asked, nudging me with a big smile on his face. 'But it's not putting me off my drink, I can tell you.'

Will followed me to the door.

'Don't worry Romeo. If she's used to you she'll know what rough times are,' he said.

'Where's that drink you were getting?' I asked.

'All this blood and guts distracted me from persuading Zed. Give us a pound and I'll get them in.'

'Be careful!' I warned him.

I gave him the money and he went back inside. I had the idea of greeting Siân in Welsh and of warning her about the uncaged wildlife on the prowl inside. Perhaps her parents would have stopped her coming. I decided to wait and study the verse of Welsh she had given me and took from my pocket the translation scribbled on the torn envelope.

The sweetest language in this world
Is on my lover's lips.

I was articulating the words quietly to myself when I was pushed from behind. I turned, regained my balance and saw it was the bouncer helping a youth to leave. We knew each other by sight.

'Hey, can't you see I'm reading?' I told him.

'What? In this light?' he replied, looking around, ready for anything in his bow tie and mangy dinner jacket.

'It's my last will and testament,' I told him.

'It'll better be if it was you that did that girl in.'

'What? The killing? What have you heard?'

'They found a girl in an abandoned house on the Pontarddulais Road.'

The place was all too familiar to me.

'All kicked in and blood everywhere. Left in such a state, she was. Unidentifiable,' he said. He pronounced the word slowly, stressing each syllable with care, as if on reading a strange new word for the first time. 'There's going to be hell to pay, I can tell you.'

He was not a bad sort. Not nasty and arbitrary in his violence like some, despite the fact he had to handle the work alone. I had figured out his system for filtering potential troublemakers. If a couple arrived he would take special care in saying hello only to the woman, leering up and down at her as she passed through the doorway. He took no apparent notice at all of the man. The idea must have been that if the man was to react violently he could exclude him at the door. It was crude but effective. He had various nicknames, Dai Gyp the Door, Dai Bounce, Dai Bicep. Parry had told me that he had done time for head-

75

butting a policeman one New Year's Eve and came out on parole the following Christmas. But he didn't drink anymore, he only lifted weights and people he didn't like: over his shoulder and then into the road.

Will came out with the plastic glass pints but Dai Gyp warned us that there was to be no drinking outside. I turned to go in with Will when Siân came running up and touched my shoulder.

'Hiya,' she said as I turned, taking my head in her hands and slowly kissing me.

'Sorry I'm late. Did you miss me?' she purred into my ear.

'Hi there,' Dai Gyp said to her as we broke free from each other, looking down first to her bosom and then further down and around to her backside.

'Oh, cut it out, will you?' I told him and we followed Will inside.

Once inside, Zed took me aside to offer some of his pills.

'Brought over by squaddies in Germany,' he said showing me a little plastic container.

'What, bloody soldiers!' I exclaimed.

'Doing a nice trade from the Rhine, they are. Because they're our boys flown in to army bases, they are freed from most custom checks, see.'

For all the supposedly alternative, punk anarchy about him, he respected those who could make money out of the rest of us and didn't want to upset the order of things. It was a personal revolution, he would argue.

'Her Majesty's Mafia, is it then? Are they uppers or downers?' I asked him, looking at Siân and Will who had gone over to the bar.

'First they bring you right up and quick and then you float on it like and then they bring you wham smack down. Wow!'

'No thanks, not right now,' I replied. 'It's just that I'm trying out a new mixture tonight,' I added as an afterthought.

'What's that, then?'

'A heavy dose of beer and Siân.'

'That's your bird's name then, is it? Tidy. But be careful of the side effects,' he warned. 'Well, aren't you going to introduce?'

I led him over to where they were and soon he was telling her about some of the fights he had been in. I was telling Will what I had learnt from Dai Gyp the Door when I overheard her talking to Zed.

'Why not become a policeman? There are good pension prospects and you can take out all your frustrations on people while getting paid for it.'

He didn't seem to be offended, but played with the idea.

'The PC Punk Corps, now that would be a thing. Hey, boys!' he said, looking to Will and me. 'PC, Punk Corps, get it?' he burst out. 'PC means Punk Corps,' he said slowly.

We feigned ignorance to annoy him.

'Only the military have corps,' Will said finally. 'What about PC Bloggs. Plaid Cymru Bloggs!'

A fight had started close behind us and I led Siân away, leaving Will and Zed to continue in the same vein. She seemed anxious and I thought to cheer her with the phrase in Welsh. I took her in my arms and went over the words in my mind, hoping to get it right.

77

'*Mae iaith ber-eid-dia.*' I began to say, slowly concentrating, but I saw that she wasn't listening but had her attention on a point over my shoulder and I began again, this time shouting the words. '*Mae. Iaith,*' I tried as she pulled me away from the path of two falling men.

The DJ raised the volume: it was his way of calling Dai Gyp the Door and it meant look out, here he comes to everyone else.

There was a group brawling to the sound of spilt bitter and the sweet whine of senseless disco music. I could swear, looking at them as I held Siân close to me once again, her eyes closed to the violence, that their movements were in time to the beat, fist swinging, one two three, one two, lurch forward, then quickly back, one two three, one two.

When the police arrived we thought it was because of the fights. The music went off and the main lights came on and all the males were told to line up by a sergeant backed up with a dozen PCs and a loud hailer. We obeyed, most of us holding pints in our hands. No one drank and the women formed in whispering groups, some with their hands over gaping mouths.

Without the music it was if we were transported somewhere cold and sober. Even those who only a few minutes earlier were rolling around on the floor were in front of the police, shirt out of trousers and perspiring heavily, but passively giving their names and addresses. After we gave the answers to the constables they conferred with the sergeant and three were taken away for further questioning. Zed, Will and I.

I couldn't see Siân to catch her eye as we were led away and my only thought was of her getting home safely rather than what was to happen to me, until we passed Dai Gyp outside.

'Made out your last wills, then?' he asked sneeringly and I began to worry only about myself.

8. *1979*

Go back to bed. Siân was angry with the Welsh that after-noon, the day after that fateful first of March nineteen seventy-nine, for the Welsh might well have gone to bed for good.

Will thought she was on her way down the road to fascism, hating those Welsh people, the majority, who didn't think of the country as she did. Then I'd backed her up to a certain point, but understood that the people weren't to blame. I put it down to ideology, to the centralist London press, to the Welsh Labour representatives.

She was very upset, I had never seen her like that before. I too was disappointed, in the sense that a piece of the cake would have been better than none at all, but I didn't have the same sense of an illusion shattered. For Siân, Wales had just said goodbye to a millennium and a half of history. The Welsh had overwhelmingly voted for dependence.

'I can hardly bring myself to speak, I'm so confused. I can't believe the result,' she lamented like a sixteen-year-old learning she had failed an exam. 'You know,' she continued, sitting on the bed Huw would use when he was at home. 'I think I'd just prefer to run away somewhere and forget about Wales altogether. If anybody asked me where I was from, I'd say that I was English. I'll say Wales doesn't exist. It would be a relief.'

Siân didn't like my friends, didn't wish to go out with me if it meant we were to meet up with them. She got on reasonably well with Will whom she found to be bright if not very mature. I had persuaded her the day before to come and celebrate both the referendum result and my birthday with Will and me in my bedroom where we could, for once, talk of politics in peace. But the reunion had turned into a wake and my birthday was forgotten.

'What am I to say the next time I go abroad?' she asked. 'When they say, ah, yes, Galles, those that preferred being part of England than having the tiniest piece of self-government. Wales as English as Yorkshire or as Kent. I'd die, I would, I'd die. I can't bear talking about it any more. The alternative is to accept the facts for what they are and live Wales at home behind closed doors, or find a part of the country where they never speak English and draw a circle around it on the map, colour it in and call the rest of Wales England, for what it is.'

'But most of the radical Welsh nationalists also voted against,' I objected, to reassure her that it wasn't the end.

'All that was rejected was that particular botched proposal. It's not really the end of the world, it should be a new beginning. I'd have autonomy, even bad autonomy, after all a piece of the cake is...' I began to argue.

'You don't see! You don't see at all,' Siân interrupted me, waving her hands in front of me where I sat on the table under the window, her fingers pointing accusingly. 'That's not why the people voted against; they voted against because they voted against Wales,' she added. 'They said goodbye and good riddance.'

Will didn't sympathise with her. For him what had been rejected was just another expensive layer of government. For him, with council workers everywhere either on strike or working to rule and with uncollected rubbish piling up on pavements, decomposing corpses left unburied and untreated patients filling hospital corridors, devolution had become irrelevant. For him, regardless of autonomy, what was important was the struggle for socialism and a just world. On the one hand nation and class are not identical; on the other, Wales was too small to do anything on its own.

He was to change. Just a few years later even Gorseinon was big enough a place to start a revolution.

I reasoned that some voted no because they were directed by Labour leaders, threatened with arguments of Party betrayal. The most radical voted no because they wanted pure independence. Others believed a new government in Cardiff would weaken local councils, taking over local powers, and some thought the Welsh voice in the London government would be weakened through decentralised power. This jumble reflected the confused mix of the Welsh personality.

When I thought of Wales I thought of Father. A fluent Welsh-speaker who had brought up his children to be proud to be Welsh but as English-speakers, while at the same time calling the other English-speaking Welsh English. Siân's father on the other hand was an active member of Cymdeithas yr Iaith Gymraeg. He would have argued that without Welsh we would have to start to call ourselves English. The minority twenty per cent carry the rest, linguistically, on their backs in terms of nationality. The Welsh Language Society was famous for splashing paint over English road signs, but there were other protests too. At one peaceful sit-down in Swansea in seventy-one the police cracked open dozens of skulls, creating emergency ward martyrs among them, according to Siân's father.

The Welsh stubbornly accept our plight, proudly resigned to our cowardliness. A falsely smiling fightless people for whom unemployment was hard work, and almost classless because the one visible class was in the pub. A suspicious, radical, straight-jacketed, open people, hungry and lazy, old-fashioned and seduced by change. Miners and mams, shepherds and cottage tourists, road diggers and teachers, and all knowing our roles.

A contradictory people from a strange place. Some places have a different taste to them. Swansea for example is flavoured by winds of sea salt most of the year. In winter there's a touch of old books and paving-stone dust, car exhaust and beer-stained furniture and in summer of baby-milk vomit and cardboard boxes, rotten fish and tea, strawberry ice cream and gas.

Beyond physical geography South Wales was a state of mind. Sometimes as sad as a wet day, its people castaway and adrift in the melancholic downpour. Other times as alive and surprising as a rainbow, and just as fleeting.

We reflected on the rain while others had the sea or rolling hills as their point of reference, the smell of freshly cut grass or a songbird's whistle. We couldn't even name flowers and trees but we had all the time in the world to think stuck inside, in streets with the terrace houses funnelling ideas into order.

From outside it wasn't much of a land. A small unknown place lost in the wider world. What had it got? A few poems, a few poets. A rugby star. A mining disaster or two. But all forgotten, or confused with somewhere else. And the people? Annexed Englishmen, aren't we?

Then the day after my birthday in my bedroom with Will and Siân, the hangover day after the first of March, it seemed the Welsh had gone to bed for good.

9. *1966*

There was an old black-and-white Box Brownie photograph of me running up Bryn Road showing holes in my trousers and the cuffs of my woollen jersey sleeves coming undone. It was taken when I was returning from play with my dirty face marked where perspiration left white lines around the eyes and below the nose. The photograph brought back a memory of how Mam used to grab hold of me and scrub my face and neck with a damp dishcloth. For about five or six years I tried to avoid entering the kitchen when she was doing the dishes and played out in the street instead.

The first, great, never-ending temporary passion in my life was a craze that swept through our street, the name of which we didn't know at the time but which might be called perpendicular football. A dissected tennis ball, a tin can, or even a real deflated plastic football was kicked up and then came down the concrete field between our houses by two large teams for hours on end, rain or shine but mostly rain, day after day without fail during the long summer months of nineteen sixty-six, without ever a goal being scored. It must have been fever, the fever of someone else's success; no one knew what England was but we were told they had won the World Cup. Our game was medieval mock-war trans-tribal sport; we had no goal but we did have temporary goalkeepers and full-time players, the few who continued playing because they never went home for dinner or tea. Strangers, kids from other streets attracted by the commotion, sometimes never returning until the police turned up to reclaim them. Offside meant a lot to us, we would shout it when the ball went into someone's front garden, everyone after it, kicking frantically until night stopped play or a neighbour would lose his nerves over the sight of his piece of weedy grass being churned into pulp, and we'd run away to taunt him from a distance until one of his kids would own up to the fact that he was his father, and we'd send him to reclaim the ball. We also had a freeze rule, called upon when the occasional car tried to pass by, all were to stand in the place where they were until the vehicle weaved its way past or thought better and turned around.

Then in the late sixties all was play. Up to the M4 to count the HGVs pass or looking under candle-bombed Loughor bridge. Around the back of the painter's hut in the chapel cemetery, an old bearded artist with inspiration among the dead would be there, nobody knew if he was a Methodist or an Impressionist. Watching Nerys fight off the boys with words, with bog off you little sod, and she was such a nice girl with her school books. With fish and chips in her hands she threw insults. With Huw down to the local Darkness at Noon, a blackened cinema full of unemployed colliers' kids on a Saturday morning, taking sticks with us for the scurrying matinée rats. Then out into the light for war, cowboys and Germans, GIs and Indians, Romans and Vikings and the other bang-bang games from the films we had seen and all mixed in our heads.

And on rainy days I'd play with words. I wrote my first letter soon after returning from Mamgu's. Tadcu, Calon Ddu, Pontarddulais, Wales, Europe, Earth, it was addressed and sent with a toy stamp found in a kicked-over dustbin, an abandoned Christmas present post office box set for under-eights. The kid probably wanted a gun but I wanted to write to Tadcu. He didn't reply.

Later I'd rewrite English using the Welsh alphabet I'd learnt in Mr Morgan's Tech Drawing class, or with Will, learning the Morse Code together and then sending verbal messages.

Dot dot pause dash pause dot dot pause dot dot dot pause dot dot dot pause dot dash dot dot pause dash dash dash pause dot dash dash.

I T I S S L O W.

Having learnt it by heart we abandoned it for ever.

Or at home, annoying everybody with adjectives. 'A damp grey...' I began to say.

'There he goes again with his colours,' Fan interrupted. I didn't realise she was there. But she was always there. 'Damp grey! What's that?' she spurted mockingly.

For those of us that had an acute sense of greyness there were damp greys, and dry greys, dark greys, browny-green greys, rainy greys and white-sky greys to the South-Walian industrial rainbow of tones. There were late-night starry greys and overcast morning greys. The colours we see depend on the light and the eye. Will had explained it to me. At home, the sun was grey behind grey clouds and a grey central nervous system easily picked up on it, understanding intuitively.

I sometimes got bored and tried to drown people with words on wet days indoors.

Everyone blamed me for being thrown into the pit pond when little more than a baby. Mam used to warn that she'd kill me if I came back drowned. There, drowned and back from the edge to a life full of emptiness, rich in bitterness, passionately melancholic. A life nobody cared about in a place where nobody cared, like left luggage forgotten in a sleepy railway station.

10. *1968*

One summer's evening there was commotion at home. Father shouted he was going out to kill someone, anyone, and blamed Mam. She became drunk with sadness, silly, crying, laughing at nothing. They decided to send the little one on a visit to Mamgu's, grandma's house, for a few days out of the way and the following afternoon Eileen took me up on the bus.

Eileen, still at home then, said nothing on the journey. We both just stared out of the window, me thinking of our destination. Upland along the Loughor, a square, high-walled farmhouse on its own, with thick stone against the winter, white on the outside, coal-tip black within.

I was to be left alone at Calon Ddu, abandoned with Mam's mam like a dog left at the vet's. I had only ever been there on day visits and I remembered the brittle old woman speaking to me in Welsh when she forgot and me seeming to understand.

Despite statistical maps that gave a healthy forty percent minority, I had never heard Welsh spoken on the streets of Gorseinon. Only at home, and only sometimes when Mam and Father were there together, alone with their language. At Mamgu's there were two languages and two classes of smells. Indoor and outdoor smells. Stale tobacco, damp socks, mothballs, book pages and mouldy woollen overcoats. Mamgu herself smelt of cat piss, grey lifeless unwashed hair and mustard. The outdoor smells were usually of damp grass but in the summer wild mountain camomile floated in the air mixed with a stench on hotter days that came from the outside loo, a wooden shack all feared entering at night.

Calon Ddu was a turn of the century tenants' buyout from absentee landlords, part of the radical Liberal reforms. The rooms were as dark as fireplace walls, as dark as the ashes of Welsh rural life. It was rural for me but really only half so, up the road on a hillside tucked between the Black Mountains and an industrial village that lived and died on tinplate and anthracite.

I wanted to be home again, not alone with a woman who seemed crazy in a waterless, candlelit, cold house that moved in a different time, that seemed to breathe on you, that made you dream when awake or drove you mad at night.

The first night together we walked down the lane to the village for rissoles and chips to take home in layers of plastic bags to keep it all warm. The rhythm of her heels on our walk with the gnats, moths, bats and the crickets on their tiny mechanical rocking chairs joined the other distant sounds. When we passed the cemetery on the way home she stopped to look over the low wall, without moving, without a word, remembering something. At her side I called out to her but she didn't hear. At home too she would do the same. She'd get a vacant look, expressing no emotion. Then she'd take her time to notice the real world again. Perhaps you have all the time in the world in a life that you know to be ending.

Outside the graveyard in the dark I looked worriedly up at her, pulled at her hand, and was on the point of tears when she remembered she was alive again, became aware that she too would die, then looked around her and seemed surprised I was there, not knowing who I was for a few moments. She then began the walk home, mumbling to herself in Welsh, expecting me to follow, holding the dinner close to me, warming my chest.

After eating the soggy chips and savoury potato balls on our laps from the paper, as we sat in front of the empty fireplace, she got up and went to the kitchen. Soon she was back with the washing-up bowl half filled with warm water, a small towel, a tin of mustard powder and a box of matches.

Every night before bed she would soak her feet in mustard and then have me file the corns of her rubbery dry soles with a box of Swan matches. The first night I began scratching away at the tiny mounds for so long in the near darkness that I eventually fell asleep, only to be woken with a shout to continue until she herself was on the point of sleep. If I stopped she'd wake and I had to continue, and then she would sleep again. Like this it would have lasted all night but for her suddenly deciding it was time for bed. In a house without clocks she always knew the time of day.

Under the creaking, thick-mattressed double bed we shared was a large china pot that saved us from braving the outside loo in the black night. I listened to the long hiss of a snake whenever she crouched down over it in her nightie. It was a comforting sound that helped sleep fall over me.

I awoke in the morning to the fixed stare of a stuffed fox behind a glass case on a chest of drawers at the foot of the bed. Its gaze followed me as I got up and dressed among the chairs piled up with clothes, curtains and blankets as though there were no room in the rest of the house. At the top of the landing there were stacks of old books on the floor. Uncle Ieuan's old comic annuals, reference texts on European seabirds, woodwork, modern poetry and animal husbandry. I lost myself there in the hours and minutes of the morning.

I eventually went downstairs and sat around in the kitchen. Lunch was slices of cold beef, mushy peas, soaked overnight in a tablet, thick steaming gravy and for afters, tinned fruit and pieces of sliced bread floating in a bowl of milk.

After lunch I went to play in the field rising up above Calon Ddu until two older boys on the way up the hillside lane stopped and laughed at me when they saw me through the trees pretending to fist fight off the gangsters and cops of my lonely game. I returned sheepishly to the house expecting Mamgu to be there. I began to explore the place looking for her. I opened a door and entered a parlour. This was different from the rest of the house. Well-lit with modern lamps, a deep-pile, light-blue carpet, a big TV in one corner which I went straight for until a huge half-finished jigsaw puzzle laid across the table caught my attention. It was of a street market scene. I soon messed it up a little. I slowly tired of putting the pieces back, stopping and going on again, just like Mamgu getting stuck in time.

I decided to continue my search for her and left what must have been Uncle Ieuan's room before he went away to Canada for good and I re-entered the ground floor passage.

It was smaller and darker than how I remembered it. I walked towards what should have been the way back to the kitchen, and continued along a long and narrow passage. I had to touch the bare brick occasionally as I made my way down through the creepy dungeon dark, and then look behind me in fright just in case I wasn't alone after all. Eventually I came to a wooden door. I paused, turned the handle and entered.

Inside it was warm but pitch-black and had the odour of burnt wood and damp tobacco, and the strange sound of an animal sniffing and snoring somewhere in the corner. I took a few steps further inside and came to a stop at the foot of a bed. The animal was there in front of me, dreaming away in its rolling sleep. I went around the bed to see, and smelled what must have been a mangy old dog that hadn't been able to lick itself clean for months. The mound formed as my eyes adjusted to the dark and I bent down over it. An eye opened and an arm rose quickly, grabbing my hand.

'*Be' ti'n moyn?*' it growled at me.

93

In my fright I tried struggling to break free, but it was impossible to push the hand off me. It felt like touching a dead snake.

'What do you want?' it asked again in Welsh. Then I realised it must have been Tadcu. I had forgotten all about granddad. I told him who I was.

'Oh, it's you bach,' he replied letting go of his grip, disappointed at the intruder he had caught without having to get up from bed.

He told me to open the curtains and then return to his side. I was afraid to move too close to him again and stood a few feet away from the bed, just out of arm's reach. In the light of day I saw his face for the first time. The right side was all melted and stirred up like a mutilated burnt chicken. On that side the eye was permanently open and stared like a dead fish. I had never seen a man so facially deformed.

He knew I was looking at him in horror but said nothing, rather he began to roll a cigarette and coaxed me to come closer, to come sit on the bed without fear.

'Smoke this now boy,' he told me, placing the cigarette in my mouth. As he lit a match I tried sucking and chewing on the tip. 'No, idiot, you're wetting it all, mun!' he shouted out and snatched it away from me.

I got up abruptly in shock and moved away from him.

'What a waste of good bacco!' he continued angrily, rubbing the cigarette into dust. He then told me to go, and pulled the blankets over himself to sleep again in peace.

I was glad to get out of the room. Opening the door that connected onto the upstairs landing I ran down, hearing

Mamgu in the kitchen. I tried to tell her that I had seen Tadcu and went up to her side where she was washing the plates in a large plastic bowl on the table. As I approached her it felt very cold and she abruptly stopped what she was doing. She turned her head slightly and stared at the wall, icy still as though petrified.

I tried speaking but no words came out. We both stood still for minutes, her gaze fixed on the wall, me staring at her face. It was difficult to see how she had ever been young. I was distracted by a tiny black spider descending from the ceiling on the rope of its web to rest on her forehead then crawl down around the top of her grey eyebrow.

Was she dead, I thought. Why didn't she fall over? I held out a hand and touched the plate she gripped half out of the water, fearing direct contact with her.

'Mamgu!' I called out to her without opening my mouth, without making a sound and she resumed her activities. Relieved, I went out to play in what remained of the daylight to return for supper and her feet.

That second night I awoke, sensing Mamgu wasn't in bed next to me. Opening my eyes, I noticed a strange light coming in through the window and got up and pulled aside the curtain to peek out. From a distant hillside there was the flicking orange of a bonfire. Perhaps Mamgu had seen it and had gone downstairs to look.

I went to look for her, excited. At the top of the stairs I heard movements coming from behind a door on the other side of the landing. Thinking it might have been Mamgu, I opened the door and saw a candle on the bedside table, flickering orange like the bonfire I had seen from the window. In bed Mamgu and Tadcu lay face to face on their sides under the blankets, moving slowly against each other, wriggling to the rhyme of their breath. He must have coaxed her towards him, tempting her with a cigarette and then quickly grabbed hold of her and then what was the ugly monster doing to her, whispering up close to her face in Welsh?

They didn't see me so I braved moving a step closer and tried to call Mamgu to come away but nothing would come out through my lips. Then my gaze was attracted by the candle again. Soon it appeared to be the distant bonfire with tiny human figures dancing around it. Then my attention returned to my grandparents as their breathing became irregular, more intense, and they began to rise, still lying down, floating up from the bed, face to face, the blankets hanging down from their sides.

Later the next evening after a day lost in horror stories, a storm had begun to blow. Downstairs Mamgu had locked up the house and was lighting the fire at last. I sat by it and listened to her talk against the whispering wind.

'We are living in the Nuclear Age, we are. A time of those atoms they make and huge bombs. I've seen colour photographs, I have. I was born in the Steam Coal Age, right in the middle of it. Your Tadcu too! He must have been your age when he had the accident. All was black and white then, mostly black. None of them great big orange mushroom clouds. I've done my sums, I have. You were born in Year Seventeen of the Nuclear Age. Seventeen years after Hiroshima, that is, boy. Your Uncle Ieuan was born in

Year Nought. Nineteen forty-five. He's in Canada now, working so hard he hasn't time to come home.

'Your Tadcu would have liked to have travelled. Missed the Great War, but not the mines. You're thinking: why marry him with that face? We were at school together. Oh, he was so sweet to me. Through his voice I got to see something else in him. Not just his skin. Now they're thinking of putting a man on the moon. In my day we called those who thought about the man in the moon idiots. He was six, his sister ten. Like you and Myfanwy now. There was a summer harvest fire at night on the hill. We children from the village danced around it, forming a chain. She must have tripped against another child. I don't know.

'Here there were tonnes of coal and when that went my boy had to go away never to come back. The bonfire was so big they said you could see it from miles away. From Swansea. His sister fell in. He didn't think twice, your Tadcu. He ran in after her and dragged her out. The poor thing was dead. He burnt most of his little body. Spent months recovering. We were all used to that sort of thing then. They covered him in wet mud, then peeled it off and then covered him again and again. Canada's not so far away by plane, now is it? He cried so much he could hardly breathe. I feel lonely sometimes, I do. One day Ieuan will come back, I'm sure. Before it all ends with those atom things. It'll be like a huge bonfire and there'll be nobody left around to pull anyone out. It'll happen so suddenly in the middle of the night you won't have time to rub your eyes awake. You'll see.'

11. *1969*

We lived on the coast but only ever knew how to eat fish
fingers. We could warm up a few songs in Welsh but
couldn't order a cup of tea in the language. We were famed
for our close community links but were to lock ourselves
away indoors with the telly. Others had telephones, we
shouted. They had a future, we weren't even sure about the
past. But what can you expect of a land that once produced
a third of the world's coal exports but had its pensioners,
with nothing for the fire, die from hypothermia?

When I was about seven I discovered that all the cutlery
at home was marked with the engraving GCC. A few years
later I noticed for the first time that at school too the
cutlery was marked in the same way. I thought Mam must
have bought our knives and forks from the same place as
the local Juniors'. Will told me they were the initials for

Glamorgan County Council. I found out that what his lot at home ate with was also nicked from school.

At school one day the boys were made to line up in a corridor, waiting one at a time to enter a classroom set aside for the morning. We all stood there staring at the closed door ahead of us. Some of the boys left the room with blank white faces and the occasional girl protested at the discrimination. When it was my turn behind the closed door a man in white put his hand between my legs, cupped my testicles and asked me to cough. Will came up with the idea that it was for a survey, to show that ninety-five per cent of Welsh male twelve-year-olds had their sexual organs in potential working order, but then Will was like that.

The most important thing about school for me was Will. A small boy with glasses, he struck me as a miniature old man. He asked me what I wanted to do when I grew up. He said he wanted to be an inventor of words. By lunchtime, three years later, he had changed it to wanting to be an inventor of new proverbs. Parry for his part said he wanted to be someone who'd marry a woman from the catalogue's bra section. At their side I felt like an eight-year-old. Will's speciality was his tricky questions. He was a know-all but rebellious with it, sometimes he would pretend he didn't know the answer to a teacher's question. He was lousy at Maths though.

'Ah, Jones, the dinner lady's boy!' was how Taylor MA used to refer to Will whenever he came up with a point in History class. I had killed the comprehensive school head so many times in my imagination I was often surprised to see him alive, resurrected each Monday morning. He reduced our education to getting us to behave and a bit of the basics for manual workers.

There were what I thought of as class struggles at school, such as the protest over compulsory school uniform. We wore an expensive school board uniform but the poorest always stood out: we had hand-me-down tattered wear. The protest ended in Taylor MA threatening to take action against the ringleaders. But it was good to wear jeans to school for two blissful days.

At my schools, most children qualified for free school dinner. At Infants' and Juniors' we all had mid-morning milk and biscuits, it prevented those of us who hadn't had breakfast from fainting before dinner. It didn't last long. In the early seventies Mrs Thatcher as Minister of Education ensured its removal.

One summer morning at Infants' was very different from the usual. It was a special day for a handsome young man, and for us, the teacher told us. We were told the story of our Principality and then drew in coloured crayons the red, white and blues of the Union Jack. At dinner time we were led out into the playground with the rest of the classes and formed lines. The Head said that the school had managed to sell to our parents most of the commemorative mugs. Our names were called out from a list and one by one we stepped forward to receive the souvenir. We were then given the rest of the day off to celebrate with street parties.

We went running home in expectation. Some of the chapels organised their own celebrations, those from the Anglican church even went on a coach trip up to the real thing at Caernarfon Castle but best of all in our street the local council had paid for a children's party. Under the July afternoon sun and streams of little flags flying from lines stretching across the street, Bryn Road was lined with tables covered in cakes, pop, tuna fish sandwiches, paper plates, jelly and orange squash. We used the commemorative mugs to drink as much pop as we could and later as the flies and the wasps buzzed around the sticky, churned-up leftovers of the food, we played games and we ran around whooping and then we threw up.

I was carrying my Union Jack to show to Mam and Father. I was with Little Johnny Evans and Parry when we ran up to Father and his butties. I showed him the tattered flag.

'Don't they ever let you try your hand at the Red Dragon?' he asked.

'It's too complicated!' I replied.

The men talked of the Prince of Wales Investiture Street Party. They had shortened the name in one afternoon, first down to the initials of Pwisp and then even shorter.

'So the bloody council are holding a Piss, are they?' one of Father's butties said.

'Well, they can just piss off,' Father said.

'The street party was planned by bloody Alderman Roach from the Town Hall,' one said.

'Councillor Cockroach,' Father called him. 'Provokes royal tears in some and others to hand out Free Wales Army leaflets.' He took a piece of paper from his pocket, carefully unfolded it and read. 'We call upon Welshmen to organise, train and equip, to arm themselves with guns, bombs,

101

Molotov cocktails and grenades. Stock them up and bring them to Caernarfon,' he quoted.

The men talked of two students who blew themselves up early in the morning while planting their homemade bomb on a stretch of line at Abergele where the royal train was due to pass. The local stories were about the only policeman who could swim and who had spent the night before under Loughor bridge in a rowing boat looking out for bombers. The only thing he found was a fake one made of candles and an alarm clock, planted under one of the arches by a man in a canoe. Later many people claimed to have been the one who had lent the canoe.

A few weeks later Belfast exploded into flames and into the news and troops were sent to put them out, extending the fire all over Northern Ireland. It was the summer of Apollo Eleven, the man on the moon and televised riots.

'It's funny, really,' Father was to say. 'An army trained and obsessed with killing communists ending up killing the Irish. Again.'

12. *1971*

A macabre land full of industrial shadows, grey candy floss clouds above, and below, the hollow ground giving under foot. A world turned upside down: coal tips high above us, over heads bowed in reverence to the slashing rain.

'We'll have to defrost the cat, again,' Mam exclaimed, letting the scraggy creature in one frosty morning.

I was up early for my paper round; she to put on the porridge for eight, the seven of us and the leftovers for the dog, who was trying to hibernate on the armchair, pricking up an ear now and again in hope of food moving his way.

While the rest of us were still warm from bed and yawning, Mam had time to put the finishing touches to the shopping list on the back of the previous supermarket receipt.

Tinned peas, large; sliced bread, white; pork chops, if on

offer, or sausages, two pounds. The dog moved, they must have been his favourite. Baked beans, two large; cat food, small; dog food, large; biscuits, two packets; toilet paper, six rolls; washing up liquid, large; potatoes, five pounds; carrots, a pound.

'Now, that should keep you lot happy until my child benefit comes in,' she told me as I watched her through a red plastic sweet wrapper I held to my eye.

I was collecting greens, blues and yellow ones; the folds and creases in the wrappers slightly warped reality, giving me a different view on things. The best of all, then, was looking at Mam's face close up while she had her mind on something else. Any colour would do as she gently bit her lower lip, leaning over the table in concentration and then I would take the wrapper away from my eye and she would return to her white complexion.

'Oh, and *bara lawr*, a pound, for breakfast tomorrow,' she said of the laver bread: seaweed stewed into a green black mush. 'With eggs, a dozen, small, and a bit of bacon, for your father, a hundred and seventy pounds,' she added, winking at me.

I heard my sisters upstairs fighting over whose turn it was for the bathroom. Why was it that only the girls in that house locked the bathroom door to be left alone with their secrets and the spiders that came up through the plughole? Father always left the door open wide when he got up as he pissed infinitely, the beer he had fermented through the night turning into a yellowish acid, the colour of the mustard Mam's mam soaked her feet in.

I put my gloves on to go out the back for the rusty

armour-plated pram, my pride and joy since I had added a bicycle bell to warn passers by on the downhill sections when it was full of papers. All it needed was a brake. My brother had painted on the front of it a large black letter L.

Mam came out and told me to wait, adjusted my scarf and said something about me being a big boy going off to work at the crack of dawn and then warned me not to catch cold. And off I went, turning back to wave in case we didn't see each other again, which she took as a promise to be back for breakfast. And for school.

In that profession, at the lowest level but in direct contact with the clients, there were two basic openings for a young journalist. Delivering the *South Wales Evening Post* after school, or the London gutter press with the occasional *Western Mail* before it. There was also the Sunday option, the worst, with everybody wanting the *News of the World*, the same story about vicars and ladies in underwear repeated week after week with only the names changed and nobody noticing, but it set alight the fire all the same on Monday mornings.

'It shouldn't be allowed,' the curlers and fluffy slippers always greeted me.

'Child labour it is, you should be at school with the other children, not slaving away.'

'It's only a quarter to eight,' I pointed out.

She at number nine Pencwrwdrwm Lane was worse than some of those dogs I had to put up with, like that Pekinese in Llanilltyd Drive, a tiny thing with bows in his hair: he used to wait for me with saliva dribbling over the door step.

'Come in and I'll make you a nice cup of tea,' she'd say.

'But I can't missis, I've still got Chemical Way and Cigoch Lane to do,' I objected. I bet she used to get up especially early just to argue about my working conditions.

'It's a waste, it is, the best years of your life, you poor thing,' she argued desperately, holding her arms out to me as I turned to go. 'My little sparrow, you'll ruin your back,' she warned, as if I was making clay bricks in India eighteen hours a day.

'It's not that bad, really, it helps me buy sweets,' I said as I went quickly out through the gate, looking back at her through a green and yellow wrapper before turning to wait on the corner of High Street and experiment on a double-decker bus as it passed, seeing a big red through green and yellow come out dark, and then on switching to a red wrapper: red as red again, and all around as blood or black like a good day at the slaughterhouse.

At the foot of our hill on the way back home I saw Little Johnny Evans in the distance, sitting on his front wall and, by luck as I passed, Dai Panda as he came out of his house, too late for him as the door closed behind.

'Hey, Pa Pa Panda,' I called out and he started banging on the door to be let in again.

'Scab!' I shouted out as the door opened for him to disappear into safety.

We had been calling him scab even before we knew what it meant, but it applied to the worst of enemies, to the lowest form of life of all the dregs left at the bottom of the social barrel. The story went that his grandfather went to work during a strike once, years before I or anyone of us was born. No one would work with him after that, nor with Panda's father who had to travel away every morning to a private mine in the Swansea Valley. Neither Panda nor his father had any friends and the woman of the house never left it, because of the shame that the grandfather she inherited on marrying had caused before she was born.

Little Johnny Evans came down to see the commotion.

'Your mam back yet?' I asked him.

He nodded timidly and asked if he could come with me on the paper round the following day.

'If you like, but you'll have to get up early.'

'My mum can wake me,' he promised.

He followed me home to wait outside, on the wall. When I parked the pram Mam came to the door to greet me.

'Is that the Evans boy out there, I bet he's had no breakfast!' she said. 'Johnny Evans come in here!' she shouted out to him before I could answer and we entered together to see my lot finish theirs.

She sat him down next to me to share what was left of the porridge while the dog waited under the table, moaning.

I thought she wanted to adopt him. Father thought she was turning the place into a soup kitchen, at his expense. She said it would be at his expense when he got a job, and she had her way again.

On Sundays when she made a roast she would send one of us out with a plate to a widow who lived across the back. Whenever I went she gave me a sweet in return, a boiled tasteless fruity crystal ball wrapped in paper. Useless blind greasy paper, you couldn't see a damn thing through it. I hated them but always said thank you Mrs Green and ran back home to eat my favourite, roast potatoes, saving the sweet for Little Johnny, before the council came for him. And Mam thought the sun shone out of me for doing so.

That day Mam walked with me to school and Little Johnny came along too. She asked him about his mam and he said that she was ill in bed and wasn't going to get up. He never liked to admit that she went out at night and rested during the day, only that she was tired, or ill.

Putain, Mam would call Little Johnny's mother. I didn't know that Welsh word at the time.

Mam left us on the corner of High Street to do the shopping and when she was out of sight, Little Johnny went running off back home to stand in the dark until I came back from school later that afternoon to play with him.

From my desk in Miss Williams' class I could look out at the pit shaft wheel slowly spinning behind the row of terraced houses across the road. It was the last of them around, the one at the bottom of our road had already closed. Miss Williams told us a story about a wooden rocking horse that won a race, a doll its jockey. She then set out to get us to stand up one at a time to tell the rest of the class our surnames and if we knew their origin. We all thought they were Welsh. Well, they all were by then, she said and went on to say that since the end of the previous century a lot of different people came to Wales to work in the mines and there were, in our class, not only Welsh surnames but also English, Italian, Irish, Spanish, Polish and Russian ones. Then she showed us a wallmap of the world where Swansea didn't appear and had the word England spread across Britain and Ireland. After school I told Mam about the map and at teatime she told Father, who was very sensitive about geography and got very angry, shouting about Harold Wilson and his Labour Government.

Later that evening Eileen took me out with her to sell photos of babies' faces to the neighbours to raise money for Oxfam, for poor children starving in Biafra. We knocked on dozens of doors and if a woman answered she would carefully look through the booklet and choose the face she liked best, adopt it by tearing the photo out and give a small donation. If a man answered he would tell us to bugger off.

We were out until midnight, until I was chilled to the marrow, we hadn't even got round to spending the money we had collected.

The next morning I woke up with the flu and a week off school.

Mam did my paper round the first day. I warned her about the dog in Llanilltyd Drive. When she got back she started cleaning the house because she didn't like the look of my temperature, she said. She had called the doctor, who must have wanted the house disinfected, and when he came with his cold hands and sterilised thermometer he confirmed that yes, in fact, I was bad after all. The fact that one could call for a doctor and then one would come for free amazed Mam. Despite Father's curses it was enough for her to vote Labour all her life.

In my dazed half-sleep I felt that my hands and feet were balloons and lying down in bed I was ten feet tall in the enclosing shrinking unlit room. When Father came home from the pub he too placed his giant hand on my brow and also confirmed that yes, in fact, I was bad after all. He stayed with his head-cooling hand until he thought I had nodded back off to sleep.

'You'll be of no use,' he whispered to me.

Again.

They gave me tinned soup four days running. Scotch broth, mixed vegetables and chicken cream, alternatively, twice a day.

Cats seem to know when we become ill, they have a premonition for death and lie on the bed of the sick, perhaps in hope or in mourning. Mam suggested that Twpsyn, our kitten, had come to keep me company, there next to my legs, using a knee as a pillow. Guiltless pleasure is allowed when you're ill, and I stretched out a lazy fevered hand to stroke its back and we wheezed and purred our way into sleep.

When I was finally up but still weak we played in the back garden: lion-tamer games of cheat and cheater until Twpsyn jumped over the fence to other adventures next door. I would call her and she would come to see if she could be tempted to danger. I held cupped hands to my mouth, made squeaky bird sounds and threw out emptiness into the air towards her.

Twpsyn came home limping and bleeding a few weeks after my flu. Maybe she had picked a fight with a dog or, more likely, with the neighbour two doors down who used to complain about her scratching up his vegetable patch only to haunch onto her hind legs and plant little presents.

I picked her up in the garden, hanging useless from my arms, hoping she would lick herself well again but she was giving in. When she was still I whispered her name into her ear. I put her on the ground, standing over her with my arms at my side, fists clenched, squeezing my thumbs, and I cried with utter desolation.

The following day I took out my revenge on the neighbour when I knew he was out, smashing up his little plastic greenhouse with an old tennis bat. And I felt good with each blow, liberated, swinging my axe until all but a piece of wooden handle was left in my grip.

Father surprised me after my attack had ended, at first I thought that the neighbour had come back to creep up on me. He had heard the noise and saw me come home clambering over our garden fence. He lifted me over with one hand and carried me quickly into the house out of sight behind a slammed shut door.

I felt like a small plastic doll in his arm.

'The boy's going mad, mun,' he shouted at Mam as I stood at his side in the kitchen.

'Poor dab! He needs some air,' Mam replied, unsure.

Father then sat in his chair staring at me. I was mad and Twpsyn was dead. After a long silence he finally said he would take me fishing the following day.

'It'll do his flat lung some good.'

When the neighbour got home he marched up and down our street shouting about his greenhouse and threatened to tell the police and get the unknown culprit arrested, but he never did. No one ever got the police in to deal with their problems then.

The following day Father took me fishing up the Amman Valley. It was the first and only time I had ever been alone with Father. He lay on the ground in the midday end of winter sun, shirtless and enormous, talking of life as he played absent-mindedly with some blades of grass in his hand and I listened, mostly not understanding.

I'd had to learn to be really sad in order to know what it was to be really happy, I thought as I looked at him through a red sweet wrapper.

'Nice here, isn't it, bach? You'll see, we'll catch something, we will. Got to forget about the cat, like. I could do with a drink, maybe on the way home? A bit of patience, that's all. But, you know, it's sometimes too easy to get angry. Too easy. Got offered a job, but seven days a week, mun. Is bad enough Monday to Friday. Ideally, for me, Tuesday to Thursday with Wednesdays off, for fishing up here and the like. That's the life for me. But what can you do? Wouldn't you like to live somewhere else? A better future for all of us. Maybe there'll be some trout. God knows there's little enough around here. Even if you study. I've tried that, you know. But in this life it's not what you know, it's whose wife you know. Luckily, sometimes. I can't see why we bother. But for women. There's nothing in this world like a woman's voice, all sing-song. And the curves and the rest. They want to keep their legs closed. It's easy to get angry. Teased like. But I'm still young. I've got it in me for a while yet, you know. Just the other week, there at the local. Chattered away with me until we fell over. But I still got it up. Filled her with it, like. You'll know what I mean. It's what keeps us going. Putting up with all this shit

112

they pile on by the bucketload and then expect a thank-you. But we get our chances with the girlies, and for free sometimes. Got to use the right bait, that's all. When I was younger it was all I thought about, screwing and drinking. I'm older now. But I'm still the same. Just have to smile at them sometimes. In a better world we'd do it all the time, I bet. Screwing and drinking. They can get jealous sometimes, then you got to watch out, there's nothing like that, when they get annoyed you can forget about groping out the back.

'Nothing like a good pint. Quenching your thirst on a hot day. When it's sticky. But then you just have to wipe it all clean again. But it's easy to get angry. Fisticuffs and all. They fight like monkeys sometimes. But my father taught me. The uppercut, keep to the centre, jabbing. I'll show you how one day and then you'll be alright. Got to be careful not to catch something nasty. Fucking crabs, the worst. Can't tell these days who's clean and who's not. Always wash, if you can, beforehand. Remember that. An office job would be best. But it turns them into nancy boys, big girl's blouses. But it's an easier life, doesn't break the back nor make you cough to death, like the mines. I bet you want another cat?

'I like the sun, I do. When I was your age, with my father. How old are you now? Anyway, try to be a scholar if nothing else. But don't you go poofy on me now, will you? Hate them bloody snobs, lording it over. I'd fuck their missis when they're out bossing and telling the rest what's best. They could do with it, all alone. And I bet she'd open up to me. Lap it up and I'll fill her. Four times stiff rigid, until it bleeds. We could buy a car. You'd like that, wouldn't you? Yes, mun, a small car. I could take lessons and we'd live somewhere else. Wish I could fly away sometimes, you know, bach. But I've got to take care. Jabbing. And watch out for the crabs. Alcohol doesn't kill them off. I've tried but nobody will give me a job these days. Fucking crachach. You know who they are, don't you? Make the money and we fucking work the shit out of ourselves.

'It's good here. Should come more often. Pity about the bloody weather most of the year. Can't stand the cold. Hope there's still trout in this effing river. I'll get you another little pussy. I like them in dresses, I do. In the summer down the Gower. Invite them dancing on a Saturday afternoon when the old man is at the rugby and then somewhere quiet when the light goes. And give them one. Every inch of it, and she'll know a real man. You'll know, bach, it's like having wings, it is. If I had money I'd take you with me. A better school and all. Talk posh to fool the crachach and screw their little darlings behind their backs. You'll like that one day. Got to punch hard. Never run. But never work too much, I've seen them drop like flies. Never knew your grandfather, did you? Crushed under tonnes of coal before you were born and for what? Couldn't catch a thing, except muddy weed. Didn't even have a pension. But that was before your time. God it makes me sick it does. Used to hit me at school, but I spat at them later when I put on a little muscle. Look. Still firm, despite the drink. Better with a car. Could taxi you, wherever you want. Touch a girl up in the back. But take

114

care. Crabs, you see. Keep it clean, wash it every day and polish it at the weekends and then the paint won't rust. Better Tuesday to Thursday. Ideal, mun. Caught anything with that bloody rod yet bach?'

13. *1973*

He was always snivelling and snot-nosed, worse, he wore horrible NHS glasses badly patched-up with sellotape. He had eventually got into the habit of taking them off before being beaten, and he was beaten a lot, even by kids a lot younger than himself. He was someone who was picked on and as a result had the look of one, which attracted more of the same. I myself didn't really hate him: he was ugly and shabby beyond our shabbiness, but I didn't hate him. I hit him because it was the thing you did and it didn't mean anything, it wasn't something you thought about. Nobody had ever defended him.

It was during a summer rainstorm and I saw him alone half-way up the coal tip. I could have gone up to thump him, looked for stones to throw, gone home or ignored him. Instead I decided to shout insults from a distance.

'Pa Pa Pa Panda, you sc sc sc scab. Go on, tell me to fu fu fuck o o o off,' I shouted at him and laughed.

Surprisingly he came down towards me and I thought he wanted me to hit him. The sky was becoming dark and the rain was pelting pebble drops. I sheltered my eyes with my hands as he came nearer.

'L L Look,' he said and offered to share the plastic sack he had been sliding on to protect us from the rain. I accepted and we stood at the base of the coal tip holding the bag raised over our heads, watching the rain form black streams. We talked, he slowly, me occasionally turning to look around in case anyone saw us together.

I asked him if he always played alone. I knew the answer just as someone opening the wrappings of his own gift. He was always alone, or at home with his kid sister avoiding the street.

I asked him about his stutter.

'W W When ne ne ne nervous,' he explained.

'And when is that?' I asked him.

'Oh, al al almost ah ah ah all of th th the time,' he replied and then spent a minute trying to tell me that he went to a therapist, like important people did.

When the streams grew to ankle height around us we ran back to our street. When I got home Father who had been reading the paper talked of how petrol rationing coupons were being stockpiled. Mam looked me up and down and warned me not to play around the tip when it rained and I wondered how she knew I had been there.

'Oil crisis, wage freezes, public spending cuts. Heath

117

will have to sell his effing yacht and the royals emigrate to bloody Saudi Arabia!' Father joked.

I wished I could have emigrated when I saw Dai Panda following me on the first day at High School. He was a year younger and had to wait to go. I tried to ignore him from shame as he walked behind, in case others would associate me as his friend, but I didn't hit him anymore. At the end of the day, laden down with new secondhand textbooks that were handed out to us I saw him waiting for me as I walked to the gate with Parry and Will. I chickened out and said to them that I had left my new fountain pen in French class and told them I would catch up later. Some ten or fifteen minutes later Dai Panda was still outside waiting proudly but a little worried, like a young mother for her little Dafydd on his first day at Infants' as the school yard emptied. I felt I had no choice but to let him walk home with me, almost at my side but not too close.

A group of young kids, half our size but devilish, saw Dai Panda and taunted him. They came closer and tried hitting him, each running forward in turn. They were like a pack of hyenas, hungry for a fight but unconfident. At first I did nothing and then looked about me to check no one else was around before chasing them away.

'You're my friend,' he said without stuttering.

'No, you're a scab!' I reminded him.

'I'm only ten,' he said, surprised.

Closer to home two boys about my age saw us. One went for Dai Panda, while the other gave instructions and encouragement as Dai Panda cowered, crouching down,

118

still on his feet but curled in a foetal position, taking off his glasses and covering his head with his arms. I stopped the hitting and we fought, the other boy still giving out orders.

Back home my brother Huw told Panda something unusually profound.

'They beat you because you don't fight back,' he explained, as if he were a boxing champ. 'Once you begins to stand up to them, even if they bugger you they'll begin to think twice next time to avoid the hassle, so you has to fight back,' he went on, jabbing at the words bravely.

I didn't think anyone else took much notice but I was impressed. When I told Will and Parry they mocked, saying I always made friends with the weak ones like Little Johnny Evans. He had gone by then and there was another family living in his house after his mother did herself in. One morning soon after Little Johnny disappeared she swallowed fifty-nine sleeping pills and didn't wake up for the following night.

'Silly *putain* cow!' Mam called her.

Will and Parry were only jealous that I had befriended Dai Panda, saying I needed another fool hanging around waiting for me after Little Johnny Evans went for good. True, Dai Panda was loyal as a friend and always did what I told him to do, though I never pushed it too far, except to rob for me. It was like having an obedient dog at your side. He would come back with a present and a smile.

He was good at petty theft. Tiny furry dolls that gripped onto pencils and swayed sweeping around in time to spellings; synthetic wire clothes brushes that wiped all hair and dust away for good; cover versions of the Mamas and Papas' songs on tape; toddlers' boots, men's hats and women's oversized underwear.

In a Swansea department store we were almost caught and he began to stutter, shouting warnings. His stunted repetitive outburst confused a sales assistant lost in his baggy suit. I whooped and wailed with Dai Panda, exaggerating his hesitated syllables into a spasmodic shout. Out the door and past a pensioner looking for a refund on shear thin knee-length black cotton socks, that present from a distant grandson and last year's receipt gripped in both hands, and then we were mingling with the crowds in the safety of the Saturday street.

And we weren't caught. We were never caught shoplifting. Even our incident at the newsagent's was met with local indulgence. It was during the miners' strike in seventy-three and a state of emergency had been declared. Troops were already on the streets of Glasgow, there were power cuts, sugar rationing and a three-day week.

The day after Boxing Day Panda and I as brothers in arms were on our way to different shops looking for something to put in the tea when we passed a newsagent's. Will had said the tabloids were heavily criticising the miners and we stopped to literally piss on a pile of them stacked and tied in cord on the pavement. The newsagent chased us off and we ran whooping to watch the mess from across the road. A passing pensioner suggested he put on rubber gloves, put them into a black plastic bag and send them back to Rupert Bloody Murdoch in London.

Pushing open the front door later that day I heard

Eileen's laugh upstairs. She was home. I ran up the stairs in hope of a glimpse of her smile.

'Eye! Eye!' I heard myself shout out to the top of the flickering landing closing in on me. A candle on the sink threw a dark orange light through the open bathroom door.

The house was a child's castle, cast in darkness. I was going up to the tower, my sister's voice a sweeping wind. I wanted her to hug the air out of me, but all she did was to gently tousle my hair with her fingertips as if mixing make-up powders. But I didn't care, she was home.

'Merry Christmas,' she said.

'Home to stay?' I asked, hoping.

She laughed.

'I'll get the train tomorrow, I've got to get back to the...' she began to answer.

'Take me with you!' I demanded.

'When you're older,' she promised me.

'But I'm older now,' I insisted.

'Yes, you're growing. What did you get for Christmas?' she added, changing the subject.

'I don't know, what are you going to give me?'

'You must have got something!'

'No,' I pretended, staring at the dim floorboards.

'No,' she replied, copying the slow tone.

'Yes, he did. And he's broken it already!' Fan told her. I didn't notice her there behind Eileen.

'Do you remember when he used to go through the cutlery drawer and wrap stuff up in newspaper and give them as presents, in February, he did,' Fan explained. 'Now he goes out robbing, like the rest.'

121

'No I don't! What rest?' I added, to see which friends she would accuse.

'Still got your paper round?' Eileen asked me before Fan could reply.

I nodded.

'And your presents?'

'I got a chemistry set, but everything fizzed away and the test-tubes burst!' I lamented.

'So you did get something then,' she reminded me.

'He burnt the table!' Fan informed.

'But I've still got the burner. Next I'm going to see how LPs melt,' I said, turning to where Fan must have been in the dark.

'No you won't! Touch my Elvis and I'll skin you alive with a blunt penknife!' she threatened.

'I got a jigsaw puzzle, from Nerys. D-Day Landing in a thousand pieces. I tried starting it but we had to eat and clear the table,' I began to explain.

Eileen laughed. I was glad she was happy at seeing me again. Laughing at me or with me, it was all the same when you are still a kid, when you live for laughter.

'And where's Nerys?' Eileen asked.

'She's at Elen's,' Fan replied.

'No, she's at Will's,' I corrected her, for Nerys was with her friend Elen at her brother's, Will's house.

Equally it was true to say that my friend Will lived at Elen's, as Mam would also have it. I didn't mind whose house they said it was for I secretly loved Elen and all her six beautiful years older than me.

Fan never stepped outside but was forever curious about

where others went. A compensation I supposed, like reading. Like people who fear planes but flip through tropical holiday brochures. She just asked where people were, and why, and all without moving except from bedroom to bathroom to kitchen to bedroom, for breakfast, dinner and tea, and always back to her room and her records and her pointless, necessary questions.

There was a knock at the door below.

'That must be her now,' Eileen exclaimed.

But it was never locked, I thought.

I followed my eldest sister down.

'Who was it?' Mam called out from the kitchen, before time.

I stood peeking, behind Eileen's waist as she opened the door.

They asked if Father was at home.

'Mam!' Eileen called out after a contemplative pause. She was always able to do the right thing.

'I didn't do nothing!' I whispered up to her as we backed inside.

'That means you at least did something,' Eileen whispered into my ear, sounding just like Will being dry and calm on a crazy wet day.

How did they know where I lived?

Mam came, serious as always when a visitor had to knock, like the doctor. Or the police.

One of the officers explained the story. Mam turned to find me and grabbed at my arm, pulling me in front of her. I looked up at the two professional monsters, big and proud in the serious black of the street.

'Just you wait! I'll give him a good hiding, I will,' she said to me and them. 'I'll demolish you, I will!' she added.

I tried backing away inside the darkness but her grip became tighter.

'It's just a warning, madam,' one of the officers reassured.

'Is that it then?' she asked.

That was it.

'All the fuss over a few soggy papers, I thought they'd bring out them torch things and start nosing in the corners,' she said as she led me by the scruff of the neck into the kitchen.

Father sat trying to read the paper by firelight without much success and ended up using it as fire.

'Been up to mischief?' he asked me nonchalantly when she let go, glad the call was not for him.

I was relieved they were not angry with me, Mam who would usually and quickly punish in her way, slap, slipper or tea towel, whatever was at hand, and Father who just needed to look at you as if on the point of shouting, so I smiled a reply as I pulled my jersey collar down into place.

'The shame of it,' Mam exclaimed to herself. 'A shame it is, two grown men they needed to come here and tell off a little boy! And Christmas and all. Almost had to sing *God Save the Queen* to get rid of them.'

She had mentioned Christmas, again, and set Father alight after he cindered the paper.

Oh, Christmas was one of her exasperated expressions all year round. Adding JC or Iesu Grist to a phrase gave it a flare of blasphemy, almost taboo still for her even after all those years of Father's influence.

'In the future parents will frighten their kids into silence with the words Welsh Chapel! That black Hell full of hypocrites and visionary charlatans peddling guilt. Yes, our Welsh Inquisition...' Nobody took any notice of Father except me and the dog. All because she had mentioned Christmas again. Well, it was the twenty-seventh of December.

There were a few prominent atheist fundamentalists in my life. For Father, atheism was a profession, the rest were part-timers, except Old Tommy the Commie. It's a wonder I didn't rebel against them in my youth and end up becoming a practising Methodist.

Because I'd caused trouble I decided to help Mam with the tea while Eileen went back upstairs to avoid it all, and worse, have to answer Fan's questions.

Father jokingly toasted the monarchy with his empty cup of tea and then asked if food was ready.

'It's Chris... dinner for Eileen,' Mam corrected him, as I cut a finger opening a tin of beans in the dark, pulling back the lid recklessly with an index.

'Mam, look,' I exclaimed proudly.

I couldn't actually see the blood but I felt it wet and hot and it wasn't sweet tomato sauce. A few drops must have landed in the dog's face for he began following me around the kitchen.

'Now what?' she asked as I waved the gash in her face.

'It's bleeding!' I replied as she tried to see.

Wanting to clean the wound she grabbed hold of me for the second time in ten minutes.

'Let me see. Ych a fi! Oh Duw,' she said, leading me to the sink cupboard. 'I'd better put some ointment on it,' she continued, squeezing out some cream onto her finger and turning on me.

I struggled and awchted in pain as she tried to cure me.

'It'll go all sceptic,' she argued, holding me still.

'Tell him to think of England!' Father said. 'That should make him feel bloody worse!' he laughed.

After she put on a sticking plaster I went to show Father, the dog still following me, the old tired wolf in him awoken.

'Wow! Sabled were you? Mind it doesn't turn into Foot and Mouth!' he joked, tousling my hair like he did with the dog.

Over Chris dinner, delayed by Eileen, we were almost a complete family. Only Huw was missing but then he was always missing. There was Mam, Father, Eileen, Nerys, me, and Fan. It was easy to forget that Fan was there since she wouldn't open her mouth. She was so skinny she couldn't be seen in a bad light. I was surprised Mam put a plate out for her, but then Mam was Mam in those days, not like later.

'A candlelit dinner! We live like the crachach!' Mam said as we ate the pork chops, mash potatoes and baked beans flavoured with tomato sauce and blood.

'It's lovely, thank you Mother,' Eileen complimented her.

Father must have been enjoying the tea for he began to joke, something he did a lot lately, since he didn't have to work.

'The paper says that without the telly they expect the birth rate to go up,' he began.

'During the war at Calon Ddu we spent nights awake watching the city below in flames,' Mam contradicted.

'Ah, but that was different,' he replied. We all looked at him waiting for the difference. 'It must have been one long big firework display for the kids from the hills,' he said after thinking. 'February, forty-one.'

Four years before the Nuclear Age. Prehistoric.

'But the other nights? An early bed for all. During the war Mam gave birth three times,' he said.

'Three?' Nerys asked. 'But you've only got one younger sister, not three!' she added.

'In those days Mrs Philips the midwife would count their tiny little fingers and toes and if anything was missing the little one went missing, if you know what I mean. One I heard! It began to cry on coming into the world and as we were wondering boy or girl there came a chilly silence. We all knew. There was no room for weaklings then. Duw it was hard enough with seven mouths,' he explained, trailing off.

'What did she do to them?' Fan asked through the silence. 'What did she do?' she repeated raising her voice and turning to Mam demandingly.

Mam held a hand tight over her mouth and nose as an answer.

'Oh, Mam, really?' Nerys said almost in tears. 'Dad, it's not true, is it? The poor things. Just think, just.'

Father didn't reply and began to eat a fried sausage. He always left them until last, like giant fingers alone on the plate, healthy ones there were room for in the world.

After eating we all waited at the table. Some for the

presents from Eileen, others for when Father couldn't wait any longer and said he was going to the pub for a quick drink in the dark, never put off even when the barrel pumps were. He always did like to live as an amateur and drink like a professional.

'Who runs Britain, the government or the miners?' Prime Minister Heath asked during the seventy-four electoral campaign. The electorate voted the government out of office as an answer.

Following a thirty-five per cent pay increase the miners' strike was over. Dai Panda and I were especially pleased. Will had convinced us that we had helped them win, for word must have got round about us wetting the press. For years after Dai Panda would say 'Remember how we won the strike.'

'We've finally won, when we've already lost. All too bloody late for it to mean anything,' Father said.

He had recently been expected to get up early for a boring job in a plastic toy assembly plant.

'Work, they call it! God help,' he said holding the letter from the dole in his hand.

Soon he was to disappear, as though he had gone out for a quick drink for good.

14. *1974*

The tumbling waves, frothing over the lip of the pebbled beach, spat sea spray at the sunbathers at the water's edge. Close by, the youngest children screamed as they fished in the crab pools, using their fingers as bait. The sun shone all summer long onto the Gower, the pig's chin peninsular of the open mouthed, floppy eared, pork-head profile that is the aerial view of Wales.

Close by and just ahead of us, two girls were chatting at the water's edge.

'Let's go over and talk to them,' Parry suggested. 'You too, Willy, come and say something intelligent for a change.'

'They're too old for us,' he rebuffed timidly.

'All the better. They'll know about precautions and all that,' he replied to Will, and winked at me.

'I'm going over to the shade by the rocks,' Will said as he got up from his towel.

He adjusted his too-small T-shirt over his too-large shorts and wiped the perspiration from the bridge of his glasses with a little white handkerchief.

'You'll lose the chance of showing off your willy,' Parry shouted after him and the girls looked towards us for the first time. Will increased his pace, almost tripping in the sand.

'Well come on then, you,' Parry said to me.

'You go first,' I replied, afraid their screams would be all the precautions they needed.

Parry went alone with his bare, almost teenage chest and thick legs and came back grinning. He was more advanced than either Will or I and saw the sexual implication in everything. Are you coming? He's a growing boy. It's a hard life.

The two girls tracked Parry until he swung round to face them, walking the last few paces backwards to his towel. They simultaneously turned their heads away, talking to each other in a hush. I, for my part, didn't exist for them, as though Parry were talking to an unseen ghost.

'A good sign,' he said nudging me as he sat down.

'So what did you say to them?' I asked.

'Good day for it, isn't it?'

'Was that all?' I said, surprised at how easy it was to talk to strange girls.

'Yes. It gives them something to think about. And that's what they're doing now,' he said lying down onto his back, crossed hands pillowing his head, closing his eyes and smiling.

'They must be at least fourteen! Real women!' he said. 'We'll give them a few minutes, and this time you're coming with me, you just have to chat to them that's all, and we'll ask them to go for a walk along the beach. What do you say?'

One had a salty look to her, wide-eyed, skinny and squinting against the sunlight as she placed her reading glasses in a cloth bag at her side and got up to march valiantly in a black one-piece swimsuit and bandy legs into the chilly sea, only to be bowled over back again to the sanctuary of the shore. Her fair-haired friend had salt cobwebbing her dried stretched skin; she watched her friend with concern, rising to adjust her bikini top, a flowery pattern over budding breasts. Both girls back at the towel, us boys surveyed their provisions for half an afternoon on the beach. Suntan lotion, fashion magazines, bottled water, eyeliner, sun glasses, lipstick, beach mats, cigarettes, tomato sandwiches, homework, raincoats and, Parry hoped, condoms.

Parry was convinced they liked us. My forehead began to feel very hot. Perhaps we would kiss them, I thought. They were older and might have let us touch them, see them naked.

'I've got Eileen to think about!' I said, not wanting to make a fool of myself. 'I've got to tell her.'

'We're not going to elope with them!' he said. 'We'll tell her we're going for a walk and be back in time for the lift home.'

'She'll tease me for a year or two if she sees me with a girl.'

'We can say they're from school,' Parry countered. 'Don't hen out on me now mun. There's two of them and I need you to come along and look after the specs. Where's Will anyway?'

'Looking for traces of tyrannosauruses in the rocks.'

Those days everything was confused: a sexual awakening connecting body and brain but repressed by the excruciating shyness of early puberty.

I must have been about ten when I first noticed Will's sister Elen. Sitting next to her I was captivated by her perfumes, powdered face and that other, secret, arousing aroma. She had come to visit, with Nerys after school to listen to T-Rex and Bowie records. I'd play the harmless clown to get noticed. It all ended once both found their first boyfriends, and Elen never came to our house again, but waited on the doorstep for Nerys to change before going out. They substituted listening to records with me for youths with big hands and tight flared trousers who kissed them brightly in bus shelters on damp cold-moon nights.

It was soon after we had broken up for the summer holidays after our first year at High School and Eileen had taken the three of us to Oxwich with a bank clerk called Dave who had a car. She was back from London for a week and, although twenty years old, felt she still needed an excuse to go off for the day with a man. The excuse was him offering to treat the poor kids to a day out in his white Mini Cooper. On the drive down she talked of London and he talked of Swansea and international money orders.

Cramped on the back seat, Parry stared out of the side window at the girls we passed, Will read from a library book on dinosaurs and I tried to decipher the coded messages passed between my sister and our chauffeur.

We crossed the windswept green of the Gower peninsula to face car-park charges.

'How much? It's only a Mini!' Dave gasped.

'We just want to park, not buy the place,' he added as he calculated how much cheaper it would have been to have taken us to Barry Island on the bus.

'We'll get out here and you take the car back up until you find somewhere else to park,' Eileen suggested.

'Oh, thanks. It's miles back up that road, it'll take me hours.'

'Well pay the man then!' my sister demanded and she opened her door for us three to clamber past the seat.

He was still talking to the car park attendant when we descended to the beach.

'Don't wander, mess or fight,' Eileen warned us, walking away in her bell-bottom jeans toward the sea. 'Come and find me when you're fed up and want to go home,' she shouted back.

'Thank God for that, I thought she was going to tie us to her ankle,' I said once she was out of ear shot.

'A good sort, your sis,' Will said to me.

'A sexy piece,' Parry added.

'What, sexy? My sister?' I gasped at him. 'You must be loose!'

'Let's throw him in the sea to cool him down,' Will suggested.

'Just you try,' Parry warned and he suddenly pushed us both and ran off onto the sand.

We didn't follow but stood there watching him run and taunt us from a distance.

'I shouldn't have come,' Will sighed, eventually.

I started thinking about school, a few months before I had wandered over to where Parry was surrounded at the far end of the yard by a group of boys. He was reading aloud, purposely slow, to listeners either possessed by the giggles or open-mouthed concentration. Over a shoulder I saw text at the side of a large double-page spread photograph of two women and a man, naked and in an impossible twisted chaos of arms and legs next to a bench in a gym changing room.

'Don't come yet comma I pleaded as another climax almost shattered me full stop,' Parry read slowly.

'I just couldn't get enough of his cock semi-colon the length really did make all the difference full stop I swear I could feel every inch of Damian's throbbing love stick as he thumped it in hard to the hilt yet again full stop paragraph I was completely saddle sore comma my hips aching from riding him up and down comma when I felt Damian finally spurt his load up inside me full stop that hot wad hit the sides of my cunt hole hard comma and after he'd come I felt him pull out his thick shaft and roll it around on my love lips and clit until I came for the fourth time full stop paragraph.'

'Four times!' someone gasped, 'It must be that one there with her legs round his face,' he said referring to the photograph and the rest of us laughed.

134

'I'm going to copy it as my English lit composition, for Mrs Meredith,' someone exclaimed.

I didn't say anything but thought to ask Will what clit and love lips meant.

Our group had attracted the curiosity of a teacher on patrol. We separated and walked away as he approached. Some boys watched from a close safe distance while Parry carried the magazine under his blazer and walked into the main school building.

It was lunchtime when Parry and I found out we had been squealed on by some anonymous boy. We were hauled before the Head, Taylor MA, with our form teacher carrying the printed evidence. Parry bravely accepted sole responsibility as owner of the photographic material and I was told to leave the office. He was caned. Six times. It was a rare thing to see Parry with tears in his eyes, even after a beating at home.

He threatened revenge on Taylor MA every day for weeks, forever adding to a list of tortures he had invented for him. He was patient and didn't show the least animosity towards him until he felt the moment had come. Two years later the Head was found unconscious in the teachers' car park, attacked from behind by an unknown assailant armed with a blunt instrument. Such was Parry's patience and respect for what Will sarcastically called the justice of revenge.

And here we were on the beach, close to girls with their soft thighs, love lips and juices. They could have been in search of real men and multiple climaxes but avoided the distant leers of middle-aged married men taking the afternoon off in their depression.

'Let's go for it then,' Parry decided.

I followed on behind as the girls watched him move towards them.

'Got a fag for my friend?' he asked.

'What? For him?' the flowery bikini said. 'He's too young to smoke. It'll stunt his growth, the poor thing!'

'He's older than you!' Parry defended me. 'And anyway he's already got smoker's cough.'

'Pull the other one!'

'Go on, cough for them,' Parry turned to invite me to his side.

'He can bring up black phlegm in the mornings, he can. Show them, mun.'

I didn't move. I hadn't thought that they would talk back to us. I wanted to run away and hide or find Will or die.

They watched and waited, all three expectant. I felt ridiculous.

I had seen Nerys in the cemetery up the top of our road the previous summer, among the headstones. A youth was on top of her. Dai Panda and I were playing Frankenstein and Dracula at sunset while they played husbands and wives and I secretly watched as he pinned her down to the ground between the tombs, not knowing if I was jealous or worried in case he'd hurt her. They didn't move or say anything; her legs were open, he between them, supporting the weight of the upper part of his body on outstretched arms, looking down at her. When Dai Panda came running and whooping to surprise me, he was in his horror story and I was in mine.

136

'Go on, give them a demo,' Parry ordered. 'He can walk on his hands too,' he added to save me. 'But not on the sand. What can you two do on the sand, hey?' he asked them and turned with a smile for me.

'Cheeky monkey,' the flowery bikini exclaimed.

Her friend remained silent, without for a minute taking her eyes off Parry.

'So you can do the cheeky monkey, can you?' he quickly replied. 'You know how that goes, don't you?' he asked me.

I shook my head.

'And you two?' he asked them. 'Come on, I'll show you. Let's go along the beach away from the prying eyes.'

'There's chopsy for you,' the flowery one said and looked to her friend for approval before they rose together from the towels.

'Don't worry about all that, we won't be long,' Parry reassured them as they looked down at their stuff.

'I'll stay and look after your things if you like,' I offered, feeling two feet tall and sinking lower in the sand.

'No, mun,' Parry replied angrily. 'Nobody steals around here anyway.'

Parry walked off, merrily chatting between the two girls, I following behind like his forgotten dog. I turned to look for Will and saw him watching from a distance. I waved for him to come and join us but he just turned away. I continued to follow them along the length of the beach towards where the sun would set, deliberately slowing my pace so that they were well ahead when I finally stopped, turned round and went back to find Will.

Sometimes there is art in nature. A hand seemed to have

scratched a single central cloud into patterned lines across the light blue sky. Below an oil tanker stationed in the distance looked like a castle on a flat blue horizon. Seaweed washed up and dried under the sun as snakeskins. Foam met the grey-green of the sea. I walked along the shore among the sea's bones, passing boys my age playing at being younger with a plastic beach ball carried by the wind over the heads of a young family. A woman alone hoping for a lifeguard to stroke oil over her back, whisk her dark glasses and scarf away and take her back to when she was twenty. Men playing cards and holding in their stomachs, thinking if only the scarf would ask. Cans of Pepsi and Heineken were tangled up in the seaweed and shredded plastic bags and murky excrement inched up and down with the tide.

Will, a pathetic figure, traced my progress.

'Eileen's been looking for you,' he said, raising his glasses with one finger to wipe specks of sand off the bridge of his nose with another. 'They've had a row and she wants to go home. I'm supposed to be looking for you,' he explained.

'Where's Parry off to? We'd better go and find her. I sent her off to look in the opposite direction. I didn't want you lovebirds to be disturbed, now did I.'

'Oh, it was only Parry fooling around,' I said.

'Why didn't you go with them?'

'They're not my type,' I answered offhandedly.

'There too old anyway,' he repeated.

Both of us hid our shyness behind clichéd adult excuses. But we couldn't look each other in the eye.

'Listen, I'll go and get Parry and you your sis, alright,' Will said. 'And we'll meet back here.'

On the drive home neither Eileen nor Dave talked at all. To cheer them up Will calculated how many pints of sea there were in the world, while Parry whispered complaints into my ear. He said that next time the men would go out and come back, alone. He also moaned about there being no topless beaches in the Gower.

I asked him how he got on with the bikini and friend.

'Nothing,' he whispered. 'Must be frigid. You were better off not coming along. I'm just glad that Willy boy came to save me, but the bugger said, "Your mummy is looking for you, Teddy!" He called me Teddy and the bitches laughed, but I don't mind. I'll let him off this time.'

With eyes closed I thought of the girls on the beach, of Will's sister, of the porn mag at school. And of Dai Panda's younger sister.

'Let's see now. If there are a hundred and forty-one million square miles of sea surface area and about twenty-eight million square feet to a square mile.'

'Next time the boys go alone.'

'Because there are six hundred and forty acres to a square mile and four thousand eight hundred and forty square yards to an acre.'

'Just you and me. So we can do what we want. Without interruption.'

'And nine square feet to a square yard. That makes almost four thousand billion square feet, but we want cubic feet! How many pints are there to a cubic foot?'

'And you, why don't you take up swimming? That's good

139

for building a chest. Next time a few hours in the sea, right! Must remember to buy some condoms for next time.'

Once I went to Dai Panda's house and found he wasn't there. His sister who was playing with her friends told me that he was shopping with their parents and that I could wait if I liked. I could play with them if I liked. Ten years old, hiding and seeking in the darkened house. When it was my turn I pretended at first not to be able to catch anyone until I saw her alone in the front room, while her friends were more adventurously hiding under a bed or in the airing cupboard. As part of the game I lay on top of her as if to stop her from running away. She struggled playfully, and I, in order to feel my body against hers, pushed my groin against hers. I don't know if she felt anything, she didn't protest or stop me, but then she was too young to know.

What if later, as a woman, she were to find a memory return, as from a battered old suitcase from the past, a different time, another place. The thought of me on top of her. How would she feel on discovering later that an older boy had been sexually assaulting her? A friend returned to switch on the lights and there we were on the floor, reacting rapidly to separate ourselves.

Dai Panda's sister had asked me if I'd come to play with them again. Maybe, when they were older, I had thought. 'We'll see,' I'd said.

Reaching home my face was hot. Salty-lipped and wide-eyed I went upstairs to the bathroom and lay on the bleached floor, face down. Through the sound of my wheezing lung came Parry's voice reading from the magazine. I saw the twisted legs of the photographs and the faces of the girls on the beach. Eyes closed eyes tight, I pulled my trousers down over my knees and pressed and rubbed my groin against the lino and thought of the cemetery boy on top of Nerys, and smelled Will's sister; her secret odours became my salt. I rubbed against the floor that was Dai Panda's sister and holding the base of the lavatory bowl I clutched at Elen's breast. With heart thumping I trembled and kicked out at the door and was released for the first time. I slept unknowingly fulfilled on the bathroom floor as the remains of the bleach disinfected the creamy juices covering my stomach.

15. *1979*

He took off his T-shirt and slapped at the dust and cob-webs, creating clouds of tiny particles in the light entering through the cracks in the boarding across the window frame.

'It'll be better once my mam has a good go at it,' he promised.

'Do you live here now then?' I asked.

'Well, I live and I am here!' he replied staring at me strangely. 'Nobody charges rent or comes and asks how I am while wishing the death of me.'

'But I've come!' I reminded him.

'Yes,' he said, suspicious of me. 'Only you, and I wonder why? I suppose someone's got to keep them informed and you're good as a spy, aren't you? They told me. But I'm not leaving here to go back you know, not ever,' he insisted, raising his voice.

'I haven't come to take you away, you know that. Much less spy or anything,' I tried to reassure him.

In fact I had no idea why I had gone back there, it must have been to ask him something but I had completely forgotten what it was. Parry always did like the old house, where we would go to talk and sniff glue when we had no alcohol. Now nobody ever came and he was free to do as he liked, even spending the night there alone. Despite his efforts to tidy up, he treated my visit as an invasion.

'Then you've come to rub it in, or what, hey?' he asked.

'No, come off it! You know that's not like me...' I tried to explain.

'I know now why you've come,' he interrupted. 'You want me to do in Taylor MA for you, don't you?'

'Ah yes, it must be that,' I agreed, unsure of myself. True, we all hated the school Head and I had a vague feeling we'd all decided on it earlier.

'Well I'm not going to do it, 'cause I'm not leaving here, so drop it, will you!' he shouted.

'Alright, alright! Calm down! It was just an idea, that's all, what with the exams beginning and all,' I said. 'What if I get him to come, then you won't have to leave,' I added.

'But nobody must know I'm here. Can't you get that into your thick head?'

'I'll trick him into it somehow,' I insisted.

I noticed that he was holding something behind his back. He was careful not to reveal it to me as he moved and gestured expressively with his free hand as he talked. Despite the bad light, I also saw his look: unblinking.

'He'll only bring the rest with him and they'll force me to leave,' he said.

'But anyway it's not so bad on the outside these days.'

'Dead dogs everywhere!' he objected. 'I look at the people and only see their raw flesh, skinless and horrible. Everyone is, you too now. All they do is fuck, dirty whore pimps all of them, all the time, sweaty bodies. And the girls, not like us men, can't talk to them, not like a real mate, know bugger all about rugby. Have you seen how they drink? Timid sips! People are like pigs, they bleed and squeal, they're fit only for bacon and black pudding. So I'm not bloody leaving. My mam can come to clean and bring me a portable TV and some beer. You didn't bring any, did you? But then you're like that, aren't you?'

'Like what, Parry?' I asked surprised.

'Like a parasite. Leeching on all. Only think of yourself. You stopped taking notice of me a long time ago,' he complained and I felt inexplicably guilty.

'Did you bring the gun?' he added.

'What?' I asked completely dumbfounded.

'You promised, you did,' he moaned.

I was glad he was no longer angry with me and began to wish I had brought him a gun. I slapped at my trouser pockets to convince. But then I felt a long object and pulling it out saw that it was a piece of twig naturally curved at a right angle.

'Look, here it is,' I exclaimed, giving it to him.

'I knew you wouldn't let me down,' he said, wedging the twig into the front of his jeans behind the zip.

'But you didn't want to hand it over, did you?' he said,

his tone changing. 'They told you, didn't they? Be chatty and trick him to come out, hey?'

'No, no. I must have forgotten, that's all. I know now! So as not to attract attention on the way, I convinced myself I had nothing to hide and...'

'You sleep with everybody, I just know it,' he interrupted. 'Lower your knickers for all at a blink, even the fucking tramps and pensioners, but not me. No, not me. Don't bloody care how I feel, do you?' he shouted menacingly.

'I'm sorry. I didn't mean to hurt you. It's all been my fault, I know. You're right to blame me but you've got to understand,' I tried to apologise, frightened of his reaction and prepared to say anything to calm him.

'Understand? I just can't understand. Why me? What have I done?' he began to sob.

'It's just that I, that I,' I tried thinking as I spoke. 'I love you, you know that, but... we can still be friends, can't we?'

'You've no bloody right. Why can't we be the same as before? You can't leave me all alone. What am I to do? Tell me?' he asked, wiping the tears dry with both hands, holding in one a short-handled hammer he had been hiding behind his back.

'I know, let's make a fresh start as if nothing had happened,' he suggested with an air of dead-end optimism. 'If we do I'll forgive you,' he added. 'Forget all about it, yes, as if nothing had happened. I didn't mean to kick you so hard, you know. But you deserved it and now I'm going to give you a second chance. But you'll have to help me clean up all this blood.'

I noticed his hands were stained with blood and he had smudged it around his eyes when he'd wiped his tears. Looking around the room I saw there were splashes running down the walls and dripping from the ceiling.

'Please, let's get back together again,' he insisted and went down on his knees and held out an arm to me.

I had let him talk. He had tried to convince me but when he began to beg I felt angry with him.

'Don't lay your paws on me! Look at you? You're pathetic,' I snarled as I stepped away from him.

'I shouldn't have gone out with you in the first place,' I complained. 'You're ridiculous. A creep. Always groping at me like a drunken gorilla lost in the dark. You've no idea. You never turned me on, you impotent dick, but I bet you went boasting to all your mates. What? Four or five times, one after another, was it? I used to pretend, just had to moan a little and you thought you were Superman. Pathetic!'

Everything seemed strange to me, even my own words. I was speaking someone else's script. Although I felt I had him under control I was working out how I could leave, there seemed no door to the room, and escape through the window was impossible.

'Don't say that,' he cried. 'Don't provoke! You don't want me to hit you again, do you?' he said, drops of blood tapping onto his forehead like water off the leaves of a tree.

As long as he was on the floor and whimpering I had nothing to fear from him and even thought of giving him a thumping.

'You don't want me to kill you again?' he said, his tears gone. 'You know, like before?'

I had some such vague memory of being close to death there in that room.

'You didn't like it first time around and if you're not a good girl you'll get what you deserve. Again!' he warned in a calm voice as he stood up, freshly determined and strong again.

He stepped towards me and raised the hammer above his head.

'You're ugly like all the bloody rest. You used to be different, pretty but now you've changed. Your face is as horrible as a skinned goat's head,' he shouted.

I tried to scream but my throat was blocked and he brought the tool down hard towards my head and as I moved out of the way it brushed against my shoulder knocking me off balance. I fell against a mouldy rolled-up carpet. It opened, revealing a dead body as I slumped down beside it.

'It's my father!' Parry said laughing, lowering the hammer down to his side.

Seeing the face of the corpse, I got up and stood back in horror.

'No, my father!' I screamed.

He continued laughing next to the body and I pushed out of the room against a door that opened into a small parlour without a wall on the far end. Passing between a low coffee table and a leather settee I ran through the room and out into the bright orange red daylight. I began to walk then, shading my eyes with cupped hands. I heard a voice call out but I couldn't quite see who it was and anyway it sounded as if it was addressed to a girl, not me. My eyes

147

adjusted to the light and I saw the sun set, massive on the horizon, trapped like a hot air balloon at the bottom of the street between the rows of houses. In the doorways old men leered at me, one came out into the road and asked if I was working and how much it cost for an hour. I noticed for the first time that I was wearing a woman's flowery summer dress. I walked quickly away and the men began to whistle behind me and I felt a hand pull up the hem of my dress. I turned and slapped out at one of them and began running. I ran hard but moved slowly. I blamed the high heels. I turned a corner into a boarded-up dead-end terrace street as night came down. I thought to climb over the wall at the end but it was topped with barbed wire and I would have had to take off the dress. I didn't want to provoke the men, should they have followed me. I saw some steel drums in a corner and hid behind them but I didn't feel safe there. As I waited, I heard a roar of engines and I saw two huge bulldozers coming for me armed with flame throwers. They had me cornered. I tried escaping but the fire burnt my dress, my hair, my skin. I went to run but couldn't move as I became a ball of flame and black smoke. I wanted to scream but no sound came as I choked silently.

It was in the earliest hour of the morning and the street was abuzz with doorstep gossip as the police arrived, sirens fanfaring their welcome, and warrants to search our homes. Mam didn't want to let them in until she had a chance to quickly go over the place with a duster. Even Fan came out of her room, knowing something was wrong.

When they finished with our house Mam put on her

overcoat and still in her slippers marched down the hill towards the houses of Dai Panda and Parry, where the police were taking greater interest in their search for clues. She wanted to talk to someone in charge and to know when her bach, poor dab, would come back home. Others followed, partly out of solidarity and partly out of morbid interest. Someone suggested they march on the police station either to get better news or their sons let free. And that is what they did because everyone remembered seventy-four and some remembered twenty-six.

Although we were all under age, with the exception of Zed who had just gone eighteen, the police released our names to the press.

Old Tommy was told by a neighbour who had watched the news and was making his way to our house when he came across the commotion outside the police station.

I heard the noise from the inside and shuddered at the thought that they had come to lynch us until I heard what sounded like a soprano choir of angry mothers.

Old Tommy, thinking of the Bastille or the Winter Palace, urged them on with his shouts against the police state, the social services, labour relations and unemployment.

Police reinforcements arrived in black Marias from Swansea and in rudimentary protective riot gear they linked arms and began to push the women away down the street. A piece of road chipping was thrown against a window of the station. Popular imagination converted it into a heavy, red oven-baked brick, and then began what was to be the first and only ever riot in the history of Gorseinon.

Later the local press put it all down to late-night drinking and called for a religious revival.

The mothers retreated first into High Street, body-blocking it and the connection between Swansea and Llanelli. The nightshift lorry drivers moving steel strips from Port Talbot to Trostre works stopped at the scene, went on strike and joined the women. So too did the postal workers and firemen when word got around that it was another Grunwick's and some were expecting Shirley Williams to turn up followed by London camera crews. Some old boys from the sixties wrote Free Wales Army on the walls and others broke into the TV rental shop and an off-licence, but then again that wasn't unusual on a Friday night. Someone else tried to take a photograph but the flash wouldn't go off and the history of major social conflicts lost out. The oral version of events however benefited from unrestrained exaggeration.

Do you remember seventy-nine? Do you remember when we brought down Callaghan's Labour government? Do you remember that night we never slept and the mothers of South Wales had bricks in their hands?

There were, inevitably, differing versions of events. The first version I learnt on being released was my Mam's, across the kitchen table at half-past nine in the morning.

'On the way, there must have been no more than a dozen of us. By two in the morning we had turned into quite a crowd.'

Many had turned up out of curiosity, some for political reasons, hoping for the final crisis of capitalism.

'Then a young police constable popped his head out of a

150

window and shouted,' Mam continued. 'Saying we were interfering with police business. He had no right; Mrs Cook warned him with going in to change his nappies, what a laugh, I almost had kittens. But they wanted to bring out the Ravelli boy.'

'Dai Panda!' I said. 'I didn't even know he'd been arrested.'

'Ay. To take him to the scene of the crime. Your friend Old Tommy had turned up by then with other men, hearing there'd been four arrests. Some of the more sober men tried to calm us but then an ambulance arrived to take Zed to hospital and all hell broke lose. We knew it was Zed because his mother said she would know him under a blanket any day.

'His mother stepped in front of the ambulance and others came to surround it while we banged on the door of the station and more police arrived from behind and formed a line to push us all away. I'm glad to see you're alright, it nearly broke my heart when the police came. If Zed was slapped it was because he must have done something to deserve it, now mustn't he?'

'Oh, yer? Come on Mam!' I complained. 'It could have been me in that ambulance.'

'No, don't say that, I won't sleep,' she pleaded. 'Oh, you should have seen us, what a state? We tried staying put but they pushed and shoved and we ended in High Street, they said it was for throwing, but I didn't see. Then at about five they brought Steven Parry in, found wandering in the centre of Swansea with blood on his clothes. Oh, I don't know, I thought it was all a mistake. Poor Edith Parry, we were on first-name terms and then she fell down all faint. It broke her, it did. Soon after a police inspector approached with a loud-hailer thing and announced that Will and you would be released if we dispersed. But we would have none of it, we wanted the Ravelli and Parry boys too.'

'Good on you,' I agreed.

'Well, it was Will who was let out first. The boy stepped free and joined the crowd and was almost arrested again, what a sight it was!'

'I was taken home in a police car and Fan let me in, but you didn't know much, did you?' I said to her.

'I stayed until they drove the Parry boy away,' Mam explained. 'They had let your Dai Panda go by then. They had decided that it was Parry they wanted, and oh, what is Edith thinking now? And that poor girl! So what did they want from you then?' she suddenly asked staring at me.

'We were at a dance with Siân at the Gyp and they came and rounded up Lad's friends, that's all. Well just the boys. But not much happened, like. Questions.'

She told me to go up and rest and whether I wanted cocoa, at ten o'clock in the morning.

It was Mam who finally went to bed that morning after and I, finding sleep impossible, went to see Dai Panda. His mother told me he didn't want to be disturbed and then I tried Will's house, and he told me what he had learnt.

'Were they arrested together?' I asked.

'I don't know. But apparently they identified the body by about the time we got to the Gyp so then they began rounding up her friends.'

'They found Parry wandering around town, still in the same clothes, my Mam said.'

'And Zed. Did you hear about Zed? Had an accident with a copper's knee, repeated several times. Didn't touch me.'

'What, nothing?' I asked surprised.

'They were accusing but I refused to say anything, just I don't know, no comment, I want a lawyer, and things like that or ignoring the questions all together, it seemed to work,' he said causually.

'I was only slapped on the back of the head. But I was frightened,' I explained. In fact I puked during the interrogation.

'The bastards! Depended on who you got, I suppose,' Will replied. 'I got interrogated by a big detective constable with a northern accent. Tried everything to annoy me, calling me a murdering Taffy git and all.'

'My two wanted to know if I slept with Lad, if I fancied her, if I tried it on. They accused me of first trying to seduce her and when things went wrong I raped and killed her! They kept on and on. When I said no they slapped me. I couldn't see when they were going to do it next. Eventually I was flinching. God, it was only what, four hours ago!'

'Bastards! One of these days that police station will get burnt down!'

'What do you think Parry's going through now?' Will asked.

'Ay. I can't believe what he did,' I wondered aloud.

'Oh, I can. Let's face it mun, he was out of his head. You know what he's been like recently. Remember New Year's Eve?'

It was just over two months earlier and Parry, Dai Panda, Will and I were drunk at the Workingmen's Institute dance.

'One minute Parry was chatting nice and all to a bloke who knew a cousin of his and suddenly one of them must have said something and their moods changed,' I said.

'Ah, and we put it down to being that guy's fault at the time. I don't mind arguing the toss but I just hate fights. I'd never seen him so aggressive before.'

'It all happened so quickly. They would have given us a good hammering if it wasn't for Parry,' I suggested.

'If it wasn't for Parry we wouldn't have needed to scrap in the first place! He was behaving as if he wanted to kill someone, perhaps not just anyone, we know now.'

We talked, unable to sleep, the adrenaline still high. We talked, relieved we had survived, relieved Parry carried all the blame.

When I could finally sleep that afternoon I had a dream, repeated many times before and since. I awoke in the middle of the night to what seemed to be a dog scratching at the back door. A slow scraping sound that never paused. I tried to wake my brother Huw but he just turned on his side and began snoring. I found myself walking down the stairs to the kitchen. At the door the scratching sound was closer, coming from the small garden outside. I gripped the door handle, feeling it sticky from the sweat of my hand. Trembling, I opened the door and looked out into the night. A dark silhouette hunched over a spade stopped digging, slowly stood up erect, turned to me and growled.

'*Cer yn ôl i'r gwely!*'

154

Go back to bed, the voice commanded.

Two days later, on the Monday, we went to see Zed in hospital, surprisingly cheerful with his dislocated ankle and three fractured ribs. They had wanted him to sign a confession and of course nothing ever happened to the two policemen that beat him. In fact Zed was lucky that the police didn't charge him with assault, with the bruised knuckles and knees he left them.

Sat on the bed with the ward full of old men coughing, he said that although he was due to be released the following day he couldn't stand it any more. He'd much rather a drink and would have left if he could walk properly.

We joked about him needing a wheelchair. I went to fetch one. We pushed him around the second floor until a porter told us to leave since it was the end of visiting time, so we left, borrowing the chair and taking Zed with us. We wheeled him round the streets of Swansea in the rain, crossing busy roads, Zed shouting where he wanted to go. It was all good rehabilitation therapy for us all, but Zed was never to walk properly again.

We had failed to see Dai Panda who stayed in his room for weeks. His mother said he was alright, but what did she know? She was just glad he was not involved in the scandal. Dai Panda was not to leave home for a while and when he did he was silent and angry. They broke his glasses. He never talked about it but the police had scared him and he began stuttering again with strangers.

I saw him one day staring out of the boxroom window and tried to call him down, but he just stared out as though staring inwards.

16. *1979*

'Zed's not properly wrapped mun. You know, badly packed,' Will said as we made our way through the streets of Gorseinon with Dai Panda tagging along behind us.

'Oh, he's alright. At worst he's just a sheep, badly wrapped, in wolf's clothing,' I replied.

'And what the hell are we doing going back to that house?' he asked.

'Well, when there's nothing else to do on a cold and boring night,' I said, shrugging my shoulders. 'And it is Halloween after all.'

It was Celtic New Year and as we walked we passed through the fumes swirling over the top of the terrace houses. It carried with it the taste of burning damp twigs. We saw a small group of kids in fancy dress on the prowl, their screeching cries like the brakes of an old bus.

'Who owns the place now anyway?' Panda asked me as we stopped at a gate, staring at the small front lawn overgrown with nettles and a rusting washing machine. Beyond lay the lifeless building, where Parry had killed Lad five months earlier.

'It's not much better on the inside,' Will warned.

We walked round to the back through an alley that sided the wall of a neighbouring house, passing under an asbestos drainpipe that creaked as it swayed over our heads. I had brought some candles with me and asked Will for a light.

'Wait until we're on the inside,' he whispered, swiping his hand across his face against imagined fears.

I began pulling violently at some planks of wood that blocked the doorway.

'Shh,' Will and Dai Panda warned me in unison.

'Try sliding them apart, there must be some technique to it,' Will suggested.

'You try sliding them,' I told him.

'Who's there?' a voice asked from the inside.

'It's the wolf, you lame dickhead,' Will answered.

'The door's no good. Try the window, Einstein,' the voice instructed.

The voice was right, there was nothing blocking the way in through the kitchen window, except a fear of what we would land on inside.

'Ah, here they are. The Three Wise Men,' Zed exclaimed, seeing us enter against the light of a candle he held out to us.

We followed him as he limped into the front room and joined another youth sketching on the wall in felt pen.

'This is Merlin,' he said.

'Hiya,' Will and I replied.

Dai Panda said nothing. Letting us do the talking for him, happy to be switched off. He occasionally pulled at a thread of stitching undone on the hem of his waxy unwashed jersey.

'Alright,' the youth replied without turning away from his work.

'He's known as Merlin 'cause what he can get hold of makes magic, like,' Zed said of him.

We watched them at work. Zed was colouring in a series of Satanical symbols which consisted of an inverted cross and a pair of six-pointed stars, all in black, while his friend concentrated on a large portrait of a devil's head. Merlin constantly snivelled and occasionally twitched his head to the right at which he moaned Oh fuck each time. The rapid movement of his jerks flicked specks of liquid wax from his candle onto the dusty floor, while the felt-tip he held in his other hand wobbled off course.

'I got a bit of a cold I haven't been able to shake off,' he said, turning to face us for the first time, wiping his nose on the sleeve of his denim jacket. He had long lifeless hair which lay flat over the side of his head and fringed into his eyes.

We stood staring at their backs in silence. A circle in the centre of the room was formed by seven burning candles, which shot the boys eyebrows up to the ceiling. Occasionally Will and I turned to face each other knowingly, thinking what a pair of basket cases we had on our hands.

158

'Hasn't anybody brought something to drink?' Will asked desperately after a while.

'What? You didn't bring anything with you? What a party!' Zed replied and pulled out an almost full half-bottle of vodka from his jacket.

'Here,' he said, handing it to Will before returning, with a hop, to painting a few quarter moons. 'And don't drink it all at once. I don't want to be carrying you home to mammy later.'

'Ych a fi!' I exclaimed in disgust, having a sip that left a nail-varnish taste.

'Good stuff, hey?' Will said before his turn.

'Kills more Russians than the snow,' I told him.

Dai Panda drank in nervous silence.

'Alright?' I asked him. He made no comment but remained fixed at the two would-be artists.

'This is as good a place as any to get blown out of your head, like,' Merlin commented.

'Or for killing someone,' Zed said with a grin.

There was a chill in the room's lifeless air.

'L L Let's go, mu mun?' Panda whispered to me.

'Have another drink,' I said to him. He hadn't stuttered for a long time.

Having finished their drawings they joined us next to the circle, Zed supporting himself on Merlin's shoulder.

'Goes with the place, don't it?' Zed said, admiring his art and taking the vodka from Dai Panda.

'It's going to become a temple,' Merlin exclaimed.

'And a slaughterhouse for pigs, yer!' Zed added. 'I can't wait. One day let's go and do one in?'

159

'You couldn't do in a tortoise,' Will objected. 'Let alone go for one! How? Hopping?' and we all laughed.

'A temple and altar for the sacrifice of white virgins,' Merlin suggested.

'I don't think she was a virgin, somehow,' Will replied as he sat down against a wall to roll a joint.

'Yer, Zed's been telling me about it,' Merlin added.

'Telling you what?' Will asked him.

'You know, the vibrations of the place, you can really feel it,' Merlin said, looking at each of us in turn for approval as Dai Panda and I sat by Will. Merlin and Zed sat in the flickering light of the candles.

'Parry certainly felt it,' Zed said with a laugh. I didn't know whether he was mocking or being cruel.

'It was Lad who felt it,' Will added, slapping a fist into the palm of his hand. His words were just a spontaneous play on words, but I threw him a vicious look.

'What lad was that then?' Merlin asked.

'The girl the other lad did in,' Will replied.

'Her name like,' Zed told Merlin. 'Short for something or other?'

'Gladys,' I said to help.

'Yer, Lad from Gladys, like,' Zed agreed.

'Something happened to him when he was here, I know it,' Merlin continued, staring down at the glow. 'The place. Feel it! Was there some force that brought him here against his will or did he follow a plan, a pact with the very devil?'

'Yer, tempted by Satan himself,' Zed added encouragingly.

'Parry had psychopathic tendencies, they say,' Will said. 'And,' he started.

'The chief of the fallen angels. The vibrations of the place!' Merlin cried out and then gave a jerk of his head.

It was like talking to someone undergoing ECT. Dai Panda couldn't take his eyes off him.

Will lit up a joint and passed it on to me, while Merlin took a few small paper packets out of his denim jacket.

'Alright now?' I asked Panda in a whisper and he nodded a timid reply. He had always been happy to do anything as long as it was with me but there in the abandoned house he was paralysed, perhaps partly by memories of his arrest.

'Was he drugged?' Merlin asked.

'Parry? Yes, with hate,' I replied.

'He wasn't stoned or drunk or anything,' Will suggested. 'Though he seemed to have acted as if nothing had happened afterwards. After killing her, I mean.'

'What do you mean? Afterwards?' I asked him. We really hadn't talked much about it.

'You know, don't you Panda?' Will said, leaning forward to look at him past me.

'Oh, n no, d d don't,' Dai Panda begged him. He had never talked to us about that day. I knew that he, like the rest of us, was badly shaken by that night. The police had broken his glasses and he'd thought they were going to send him down.

'When the trial comes up you'll have to give evidence, as a witness for the prosecution, you know that don't you?' Will warned Dai Panda who held his face in his hands and stared down at the floor between his knees.

'Will we have to go to court?' I asked.

'Only Panda here,' Will assured me.

'Well isn't someone going to tell us?' Zed insisted.

'Well, Parry had a phone at home, you see,' Will explained for Merlin's benefit. 'His father's a miner who's actually got a job. When the family finally got a phone Parry wrote out the number on dozens of pieces of paper so that everyone he knew could call him. But no one ever did, did they Panda?'

'Oh, d d don't go on ab ab about it!' Panda pleaded.

Dai Panda's stuttering merged in with Merlin's sniffing, forming a concerto of hapless musicians.

'No, n n no one ever d d d did,' Will continued, mocking Dai Panda. 'Did they? Not until he started going out with Lad and at last he had someone to phone him, reversed charges from a box in the street.

'Well on the famous day in question he went and called on Lad's house, late afternoon it must have been, insisting they went for a walk to talk things over once and for all. He wanted them to get back together. Anyway she agreed and when they passed by here with the street outside pretty quiet at that time of day he must have decided to drag her in here, or else planned to murder her all along.'

'Yer, yer, we know all that. Reach the point will you?' Zed insisted.

'Anyway later that evening Panda here was waiting for us at the Mardy when he overheard that there was a murderer on the prowl. He still had Parry's phone number after all this time, and because we hadn't turned up he got worried. Didn't you?'

162

'No, d d don't,' Panda begged and then stood up as if to leave but he remained standing.

'God bless his little heart. So he left to find a phone box and called Parry to come and take him home. Can you imagine it? Parry, still covered in blood and wild eyed and all, went back out to go and hold Panda's hand.'

'Yer? Really,' Merlin asked.

'But he acted as if nothing had happened, didn't he?' he said turning to Dai Panda. 'Or Panda didn't notice.'

'I no no no ticed the st st stains,' Panda stuttered out and then burst into tears.

Zed laughed at the scene and then tried to hobble over to Dai Panda to offer him vodka. I rose to my feet instead and took the bottle from Zed, handing it to him. I was angry with Will for making Dai Panda feel stupid. Was it the place that made us hate each other? I told Dai Panda to sit down with us again and then began my story.

'After splitting with Lad he decided in order to attract girls he had to put on a bit of arm muscle. You know what he was like, trying it on with everyone between fourteen and forty.'

'Yer,' Panda laughed timidly, wiping his nose and tears on the sleeve of his jersey.

'He spent every morning lifting buckets of water in the bathroom, cheaper than buying real weights I guess, but he ended up with thicker biceps than thighs. You know, he fought really hard to be someone.'

'Yer,' Panda said again, cheering up.

'But at the same time he'd pick a fight with anyone, after the split. He must have gone crazy and it got worse. Must have thought of killing her as his only relief. And do you know why Lad split with him in the first place?' I asked. Dai Panda shook his head and I then turned to Will.

'Apart from the obvious reasons,' I continued. 'She was a bright girl after all. Well, she became fond of someone else. Know who made her heart flutter anew? Willy boy here,' I said to everyone's surprise.

His face went white.

'I never realised,' he mumbled.

'So Parry killed her because she left him for Will!' Zed exclaimed. 'Wow!'

'Wait a minute,' Will objected feebly.

'She told me! But don't worry, you won't have to take the oath,' I laughed at him and Dai Panda joined me. ''Cause I didn't say anything to the police!'

'You didn't give her one, then?' Merlin asked Will. He was preparing a huge marijuana joint.

'She was waiting for him to make the first move. Anyway Parry would have killed him, literally we all know now,' I explained.

'Bastard,' Will exclaimed under his breath as I sat down at his side again.

'W W Want to ph ph phone?' Dai Panda asked him, faking his own stutter and he and I laughed again.

'Cut it out, won't you?' he said and then he was quiet.

'All heavy stuff this,' Zed said, turning to Merlin.

'Listen! It's the vibes!' Merlin replied, looking up. 'I know it, I just know it,' he added, lighting the joint with one of the candles and taking cigar puffs at it.

'How about something stronger?' Zed asked him and I waved the bottle of vodka at him.

Merlin responded by waving the joint at us.

'Jamaican-style spliff, just weed, no bacco,' he said as Dai Panda went to exchange it for the bottle.

'Look, perhaps he went berserk, spontaneous like, when she was telling him about Will,' Zed reasoned, taking a swig.

'Hang on now,' Will protested.

'Perhaps,' I agreed. 'We'll never know.'

'You were lucky, like,' Zed said to Will. 'Not being around here at the same time!'

'Luckily it wasn't Dai Panda she had in mind when she split with him, what with the phone call later and all,' Will said desperately trying to move the focus of our conversation back.

'Now that would be a thing!' I exclaimed and laughed, Panda joining me.

I pulled a puff on the joint and offered it back to Merlin.

'No ta, for you,' he replied. He was concentrating on preparing the contents of the packets he had brought along, and slowly our attention was taken by his ritual.

After tapping some powder into the palm of his hand, he unrolled a tablespoon out of a paper bag, took a little plastic bottle from his jacket breast pocket then tried to comb with a free thumb his fringe out of his eyes. He mixed the powder in the spoon with a few drops of liquid and heated it with a candle flame held underneath until it began to bubble. Finally he put the liquid into a syringe.

'It's a good night to try it,' Zed said.

'Your jacket. And your belt,' Merlin told him and without standing up Zed took off his self-slashed nylon bomber jacket, tugged the sleeve of his T-shirt up onto his shoulder and pulled his belt out of his jeans.

'Ready,' he said in excited anticipation.

After tightening the belt around Zed's bicep Merlin paused to jerk his head and then inserted the needle into Zed's forearm. He retrieved a little blood to mix with the drug and then reinjected it all back into his arm.

'Wow,' Zed exclaimed as Merlin helped him to release the belt.

'It's like, like everything you ever wanted and all at the same time, isn't it?' Merlin said to him.

Zed placed his arms at his side, pushing against the floor as if to support himself as the world spun until the moment had passed and he nodded off, mumbling to himself.

'Ta ra,' Merlin said to him, smiling.

The floorboards above us creaked and tiny grains of plaster dust floated down, spitting on contact with the candle flame. We all looked up. It was impossible to go upstairs because the place was crumbling away with woodworm and vandalism.

'Have we called up the spirits or what?' I asked.

'Yer, the vodka!' Will said.

'I like it here mun,' Merlin said and waved his packets at us.

'What's that, then?' Dai Panda asked him sleepily, still standing, he alone smoking the marijuana without realising it, his stutter gone.

'Good stuff, like. I can get hold of anything. Just ask.'

'Like what?' Dai Panda asked.

'Well there's narcotics; the sleepy stuff like the light

166

rubbish you're smoking, marijuana or hashish, and the serious business like opium, codeine,' Merlin listed.

'She never said anything to me,' Will said, leaning towards me, oblivious to Merlin's words.

'Then there's morphine and good old heroin. Then we got analgesics and the rest of the painkiller beasts. Then there's the hippie hallucinogenics thing,' Merlin went on.

'Did she really?' Will whispered into my ear.

'Mescaline, psilocin and psilocybin and LSD, you've heard of that one, haven't you? Stimulants like amphetamines and coke, that really make you go, uppers like, and depressants...'

'He might have killed her when she told him about it!'

'...downers like barbiturates...'

'Just thinking about it makes my skin crawl, it does.'

'...and housewife's sedatives to keep the hysteria at bay.'

Zed, deep in sleep had nodded his head chin down onto his chest and was still.

'Is he alright?' I asked Merlin.

'Dozing. Floating on his dreams, really relaxed like,' he said, then jerked his head violently to the right and added an Oh fuck.

'It's a pity he's missing the party,' Dai Panda observed and Merlin laughed at him.

'How old are you anyway?' he asked Panda and after looking at Will and I for approval, stopped laughing.

'Sixteen, why?'

'Just wondering, that's all,' he said offhandedly. 'What was she like? The girl?' he asked, before jerking his head again.

167

'Nice, like,' Dai Panda replied.

'Alright in the dark,' I joked.

'Yer, I know. With the lights off, hey?' he laughed. 'Was she a real goer? A bit of a slag?'

'I bet you're a hard-core druggie who exploits kids, yeah?' Will challenged.

'Hey, friends, like? All I said was that I can get hold of what people want,' Merlin defended himself.

'Are you working now?' Will asked him. 'I bet you've calculated how much you can squeeze out of us!'

'Hey! Are we cool, or what?' Merlin protested. 'Or I'll go,' he warned.

Dai Panda now stoned, went over to the painting and began to draw slash marks around it with the red felt-tip Merlin had left on the floor.

'Splashes of blood,' he said, laughing to himself.

We all looked at Dai Panda.

'He's off too,' Merlin said to us. 'Look, just to show we're friends I'll mix up a little more for you to try, on me it is. What do you say? No hard feelings, hey?'

'I'll try!' Dai Panda said.

'That's more like it. You know if you're careful, taking only a little and only occasionally it's impossible to get hooked,' he reassured us.

'Anymore of that joint left?' Will asked Dai Panda.

'Marijuana,' Dai Panda replied, holding it out to him, almost stumbling over.

'How about you two?' Merlin asked, holding up the syringe delicately between two fingers.

'Well if Zed is OK it might be interesting to try, just once,' I said.

'No, never,' Will exclaimed, puffing on the last of the joint.

I laughed at Will, Dai Panda joining me.

'Oh, come on Will, don't be medieval. Let's see what it's like.'

'No,' Will insisted. 'I'll stick to booze and the odd joint. Heroin kills!'

'No fear! I know what I'm doing. In control, like,' Merlin promised us as he sniffed again. 'OK, just for you two then.'

Dai Panda, smiling stupidly, went over and sat next to Merlin as he prepared the same used syringe for the two of us. Zed remained in deep sleep on Merlin's other side.

Will didn't look pleased. He said he was going out for fresh air but I asked him to stay around to check we were alright. He got up to take the bottle of vodka from next to Zed's feet, paced the room a few times and then went back to nudge Zed.

'He's sleeping,' Merlin said.

There was no response from Zed.

'Does it leave a bad hangover?' I asked Merlin.

'You'll feel great after, really relaxed like nothing in this world,' he replied.

'Hey, I can't wake Zed,' Will exclaimed.

'Let him dream,' Merlin said.

'We won't be knocked out all night, will we?' I asked.

'Relax!'

Will held a candle close to Zed's face.

'He's really in Noddyland,' Will said, turning back to me. 'Hey,' he looked at Zed again. 'He's not breathing!'

'Let me look,' Merlin got up, the prepared syringe still in his hand. He slapped Zed's face but there was no response. 'Oh, shit,' he moaned.

'He's gone cold,' Will cried out. 'I think he's dead!'

'Always looking for trouble, can't do anything with you around,' Merlin said panicking, cursing Zed to wake, to get up, kicking his leg, pausing to jerk himself and then kicking out again, missing Zed and hitting the wall.

'Bad vibes, I knew it. Fucking dump,' he screamed.

Will was holding the vodka and staring at me to do something while Dai Panda just watched Zed motionless.

'Let's go and phone an ambulance,' I said to them. 'He might be in a coma, or something.'

'No. Slow down. Let's think about it first,' Will suggested, trying to be calm.

'But somewhere else, hey,' Merlin said as he collected up his packets, throwing the syringe at Zed.

Suddenly Dai Panda began to sob again, and laugh at the same time, Zed's belt tight round his readied arm.

'Let's just think about it,' Will said again, not moving.

'Not with me here, it's worse than bloody Port Talbot!' Merlin said, cursing Zed to himself as he left, his head twitching violently to the right. We never saw him again.

Meanwhile I had got up to shake Dai Panda by the shoulders, and to my surprise he grew calm.

'Let's take him out and then phone,' I told Will.

Dai Panda began laughing again as we pushed him through the kitchen towards the window ledge.

170

'Shh, the neighbours,' Will warned him.

'Shh you,' Dai Panda laughed at him.

We managed to get him out and round to the front of the house, marching him between us as we went along the street.

We were silent at first as we walked, thinking only of Zed, one minute partying the next minute dead. Then Will told me of his plan. First he suggested that we should phone anonymously, to say that there was someone unconscious in the house. He didn't want problems with the police again, and this outweighed his desire to blame Merlin, who we didn't know anyway. He told Dai Panda and I that we should never tell anyone, stressing to me that that included Siân too. Then he suddenly changed his mind.

'Hell! We'll have to return to clean the place up first!' he exclaimed. 'We've left fingerprints!'

'Panda home first though,' I said and we began walking again.

'Alright?' I asked Panda. 'Sure? You were right, we shouldn't have ever gone back there. I'm sorry. I'll come and see you tomorrow, in the afternoon,' I added.

We helped Dai Panda take out his door key and put it in the lock for him, hushing each other as he made his way in.

'And if anyone asks, we were at my place, OK?' Will said to him and he was gone.

We rushed back to the abandoned house. 'He got really stoned,' I said to Will.

'Sometimes I think he plays the fool just to avoid all responsibility,' Will said to me.

171

When we reached the house we stopped for breath and Will pointed to the gate. Since Lad's death the old place had been re-boarded and a sign put up.

WARNING
ENTER AT OWN RISK

Warning: nobody dies of old age around here, I thought.

We made our way in through the back as before. The candles were still lit and without speaking or looking at Zed's body we collected up the butts and kicked roughly to wipe possible footprints out.

'Should we leave the needle?' I asked Will when I thought we had finished with the cleaning.

'Yes, of course. No! Oh, I don't know. Let's see. If we do, with Merlin's prints on it he might get caught and then he might name us,' he argued.

'But if we don't leave the needle the police will be suspicious, looking for those that took it,' I replied.

'What if we burn the place down?' he wondered aloud. 'They'll blame the candles.'

'Oh, hell. I don't know. How?'

'No, you're right. Don't touch the needle nor put out the candles,' he said picking up the almost empty bottle of vodka and the unused candles we had brought along with us.

'I've got a feeling. We aren't going to get out of this one. I know it!' I exclaimed. 'We should tell the police exactly what happened, we didn't do anything after all,' I argued, changing my mind at the last minute.

'Panda's prints on Zed's belt!' he exclaimed, not listening to me and began wiping the belt clean with the tail of his shirt.

He then turned to me as I stood motionless. 'But they'll accuse us of heroin pushing,' he tried persuading me.

'Let's think about it for a min,' I said.

'No. Fuck, let's go,' he shouted and I agreed without further argument.

Having to decide on your feet, when events get complicated is the hardest thing. It's nothing you can learn to do. You can never tell at the time what's best and even trying to rationalise about it later I was left feeling that our reactions were the survival impulses of an animal on the run. We couldn't do other than leave a body to grow cold.

Will had persuaded me into betraying Zed. Later he would betray me too.

As we approached home after telephoning for a ambulance, sharing the last of the vodka in the worried silence, there was a flash of lightning in the distance, followed by the alternated roar of a motorbike.

'What were you saying earlier about vodka and the Russians?' Will asked me, regaining his composure, taking a timid sip of alcohol.

'Just that it's killed more Russians than Hitler.'

'And that other thing you mentioned. Ah, yes, did she really break up with Parry because of me?' he feigned.

I said I had made up the story because I was angry with him for having a go at Dai Panda. Will shed all responsibility, as if it was more important to him not having a part to play in the chain of events that led to Lad's

173

death than the fact that we had just left our friend's corpse to rot. He threw the empty bottle at the ground ahead of us to celebrate his relief.

Nothing happened afterwards. The police didn't even bother to ask Zed's known friends and the local press said of him that he was a heroin addict who got what he deserved and blamed the teachers who were always willing to go on strike.

I tried to act as surprised as anyone at the official news but with Siân I felt guilty about it all, in case she found out the truth.

A few weeks later the council came and knocked the old house down in an attempt at laying ghosts to rest under a rubble of broken bricks and rotten wooden beams.

17. *1980*

Life was on the whole pretty meaningless, yet full of significant events. We were making our way from pub to pub along the Bay in the humidity towards the Mumbles. We were sitting on bar stools, and I leaned forward to tell Siân: 'A poem would be to glimpse down your cleavage to the little bow tie in the middle that holds the cups of your white bra as you lean drunkenly forward towards me on your stool, inclining over my Guinness.'

She acted out a free translation of my verse and fell off the stool, spilling the beers. In the commotion we talked to a man and told him we were searching for a flat and he gave us an address in Sketty. Two weeks later Siân and I moved into a ground-floor bedsit in the centre of Swansea.

'If it wasn't for me falling off,' she said, looking for direction in a passionate but drifting relationship. 'Anyway,

it's small but a beginning. And so close to the university!'
she continued.

'Better sharing a single bed than alone in a double,' I
agreed.

'It could do with a mirror, a big one,' she said offhandedly. 'And more chairs. And...'

'There's no room!' I protested. 'Anyway, what's that old
saying in Welsh about the best piece of furniture being a
good wife!' and she suddenly, but not unexpectedly moved
towards me to thump my arm, failed and then pushed me
down onto the settee from where I watched her unpack. All
I owned were two plastic carrier bags of dirty washing, an
old portable red plastic record player and a box of LPs.

'You've brought too many clothes. Can't you see that
you're making the room claustrophobic?' I teased her.

'I've left most of them at home,' she replied in all
seriousness, a dozen pairs of tights in her hand.

'Bring your teeth over here!' I said, motioning to the
settee. She paused. 'Your teeth and the rest of you.'

She came smiling and cwtched up to me. As I placed an
arm around her she surveyed the room triumphantly.

'When you've got false ones you can just throw them
across to me!' I added.

'You know something,' she began to say. 'I'll still love
you even when I'm no longer able to run my fingers
through your hair.'

'Because of my baldness or your arthritis?' I joked.

She tickled me in revenge until I pleaded defeat and then
we held each other close on the settee.

'Hugging you is like taking a hot bath,' I told her.

'Relaxed, closed eyes, floating safe in the dark. By the way, did you remember to take the pill this morning?'

'Well I certainly took something, that or the aspirin,' she replied.

The first happy mating days on the pill, together in a room of our own. A new beginning for us both where the present was ours but we talked of growing old together.

It was good as long as the outside world didn't, as it inevitably must, interfere. In the mornings I sometimes warned her not to go out there and to stay in bed with me. The out there was her lectures, me signing on and doing the shopping. I know now that she wanted to get on while I had always wanted everything to remain the same. I wanted her as a fifteen-year-old school girl waiting for me dressed only in a T-shirt. I was jealous of what she could do, and would be without me.

She was in transition from playing at being a woman to a new life among her campus peers and her contraceptive pills. She was moving ground, from being radically Welsh to not wanting to offend anybody, from saying what she wanted to holding her tongue. And she needed to meet new people who were interesting while I thought I was the only one who had anything original to say and all I needed to be happy was for her to realise it too.

Siân would apologise to visiting student friends for the lack of space but reassure them that there was an actor upstairs. We met him for the first time at the foot of the stairs. He introduced himself as Peter. Older than us, about thirty, he was tall and very slim, with an underfed, tired look.

177

'Students?' Peter asked us.

'Siân is,' I replied. 'Maths.'

'How's your room?' he asked. 'In my pad there's no room to swing a dead cat.'

'Where we are there's no room for a cat flap to swing,' I added and stared at them as they laughed, arrogantly pleased with myself.

'That reminds me of a famous mathematician,' Siân began to tell us. 'He had two flaps put into his back door, one for the cat, the other, a little bigger, for the dog!'

'Ah, clumsy, like the rest of us mortals,' Peter said thoughtfully after we had stopped laughing. 'My play revolves around how we mortals can only ever walk backwards into the future.'

'*Gŵr dieithr yw yfory,*' Siân then said, quoting an old Welsh proverb. 'That means "Tomorrow is a stranger".'

'Oh, how lovely!' Peter exclaimed.

'Do you speak Welsh Gaelic too, like Siân?' he asked me.

'You mean Welsh, Brythonic, Cymraeg,' I corrected him. 'English is my mother tongue. Welsh is, so to speak, the tongue of my mother.'

'The old dialect has so many consonants,' Peter claimed. 'One placed after the next! It's as if someone was playing Scrabble and made words without ordering the letters,' he laughed.

Our small talk faltered. I looked to Siân to help me out but she didn't react. Just the fixed false smile on her face, as if the beginnings of a laugh had stuck on her lips.

'Well it might seem like that,' she finally said. 'But only from the outside.'

'I know taxi in Welsh is tacsi with an S and a C,' Peter said laughing. 'But what's mathematics in Welsh?'

'Well, it's mathemateg actually,' she explained sheepishly. 'We've never been good at numbers. Even now we use Welsh for making love and English for counting!' she added, referring to her own experience.

Siân could always talk her way out of a jam. And when she spoke I admired her, and remained silent.

18. *1981*

During the first month living with Siân I found out that Will was homosexual. I was in Gorseinon for the morning, at the library with Old Tommy when I saw Will pass by the window. I asked Old Tommy if he minded and went out and called to him. He looked as if he had been in the wars.

'Wow, now that's what I'd call a real black,' I began to say.

'I don't know why they call it that, it's more a light-blue and dark-green colour mix, isn't it?' he said, lightly touching the inflamed wound.

'Well, OK. Wow, now that's what I'd call a real light-blue and dark-green colour-mixed eye,' I began again.

'What time is it?' he interrupted.

'Twenty-five past opening time,' I said, looking at my watch.

'Now where would we be if the Celts hadn't invented beer?' he exclaimed as we moved off.

'But shouldn't you be at school?' I added as we walked in search of mild alcoholic intoxication.

He had stayed on an additional year to finish his A-Levels. He had English under his belt but they failed him on Economics and History. He had answered all the questions, he said, but maybe not given the required answers. But then I had warned him against quoting Herrs Marx and Engels.

'I only ever go to Flasher's Macro Econ classes these days,' he replied. 'He's the only one left that can put up with me.'

'Anyway, what happened to your eye?' I asked him.

'It was all a misunderstanding.'

'How many were there? Just a twelve-year-old schoolgirl, hey?'

'Something like that, but he wasn't twelve. I sort of met a new friend, things went OK, but then I did something stupid. Don't laugh, but I said I liked him,' Will explained.

'Now, there's nothing wrong with that, is there?'

'It's not easy, you know. Try telling a boy you like him.'

'What do you mean, mun?'

'Well, you know,' he said. I had never seen him so inexpressive before, except when the conversation was about girls.

'Look. I go in for people of the same sex,' he said very quickly as if the speed of the delivery made it easier.

I didn't say anything. It was a surprise at the time but not completely unexpected. I had always thought he was a later developer sexually, I put it down to shyness. But really I never noticed before because I only ever thought of myself.

'What do you think?' he asked me.

'And the eye?'

'Well I told the guy in a roundabout way.'

'Yes.'

'And he went berserk and gave me a hiding. He's called Al. You don't know him. It must be short for Alsatian because he's a vicious bastard,' he said. 'I didn't do anything. I just opened my mouth. But he fought me like a tiger.'

'You had it coming, you did. This is what you get when you mess with strangers, especially those that don't come with a book of instructions,' I said, and suggested we do him in, Will, Dai Panda and I.

'No! I'm not a sociopath you know.'

'How long have you been gay?' I asked.

'About as long as anybody is anything.'

'I'd never have thought. You didn't say anything.'

'It's not something you go shouting out about around here, is it?'

'You sleep with men then.'

'Not exactly. I haven't yet but I try.'

'And that's what you get,' I said, pointing to his eye.

We talked of Welsh society, puritan still in most ways. We concluded that people who wanted to express their sexual preferences were forced to go somewhere else.

'Perhaps many heterosexuals are just repressed homosexuals,' I said to cheer him up.

182

'Certainly there's more to it than common morality in those on the lookout for queers,' he said. 'You won't tell anyone, will you? They'll only start calling me names. Not even Panda. If I tell him it'll be in my own way. You know, I haven't exactly got posters of oily bodybuilders hanging on my bedroom wall. I'm only just trying to get to terms with my sexuality and God, I'm dying for a lover. I'm alright on my own, if you know what I mean, though I imagine sex has all the pleasure of masturbation but with someone who's beautiful. What am I supposed to do? Put an advert in the *Evening Post*? Or wait outside the rugby club at closing time?'

He was relieved to have told me. I tried saying to him that since we were friends he had nothing to fear from me. He explained that the wrong words went through his head each time he tried and the moment never seemed quite right.

'I have to admit I've been jealous of you and Siân, seeing the two of you together. I could never be so happy. What would you do? In my place, I mean,' he asked.

I mentioned the university community in Swansea. I felt sure that gay students come out more, and if they don't set the rhythm nobody would. Some student friends of Siân were having a party that night and I invited him to come along.

'At least it might cheer you up a bit, getting drunk and wrecking a flat and all.'

Later that evening we met at my bedsit and I tried to give him sexual hygiene advice.

'If you get it on with a nice boy, don't worry. Just pour

some vodka over everything when you've finished.' And I gave him a condom from an old packet I still kept.

He showed me his new system of rolling joints in public without anybody noticing.

'Look, with a rolling machine,' he explained taking the materials out of his duffle coat one by one. 'Here in this sachet of tobacco, the normal stuff fills more than half the packet while covering the marijuana below. To roll, take a bit of tobacco and a bit of marijuana, mix the two up still in the sachet and put it in the rolling machine and roll as normal. Nobody knows you're rolling a joint.'

'They only know when you're smoking it!' I replied.

Siân came in, laden down with books for the weekend, and was surprised to see Will.

'And don't say he's got a black eye,' I laughed.

She examined him close up and looked to me for an explanation.

'He got it fighting for equality,' I said.

Will occasionally would get up and go look at his face in the bathroom mirror, looking for signs of infection.

As Siân and I smoked the joint he had prepared, we counted the coins we could pull together to buy alcohol. On the way to the party we decided to buy a bottle of red each, hoping someone would have a corkscrew at the flat.

'If not we'll just have to push it down into the bottle,' I said.

As we walked, Siân told Will of her recent conversion to vegetarianism. He was critical.

'What's to be done with all those pigs and heifers if

184

everybody went veggie? I'm pro-animal, that's why we ought to eat them,' he joked.

'Rubbish,' she exclaimed. 'That's no argument. It's like saying what'll we do with the slaves if we abolish slavery. They'll obviously have a new life. Factory farming is immoral.'

'I'm more worried about the conditions of factory working,' Will countered.

'Being concerned about one doesn't exclude the other, does it?'

'But the reality is,' he began to explain.

'The reality is,' she interrupted, raising her voice.

The reality was that they argued the toss like two dogs over a slipper, neither yielding their point.

I tactfully forced a pause by asking Will to tell her about Taylor MA. The headmaster had been unimpressed by the fast of the leader of Plaid Cymru, Gwynfor Evans, in support of a Welsh-language TV channel. It wasn't a real hunger strike, Taylor MA had mocked, more of a diet.

'Luckily for Taylor MA it isn't a real hunger strike; if it were and Gwynfor Evans dies, Wales'll start looking like Northern Ireland!' Will argued.

Siân didn't express any passionate opinion on the matter; her radicalism diluting as she mixed with middle-class English students. I'd always thought that it was during their student years that the middle class were most radical.

As Will rolled another cigarette she said she thought he was trying to cut down on tobacco.

'Sometimes at night before going to bed I think to myself, tomorrow I'll cut down,' he replied. 'But when the

185

morning comes, like every morning, I light a fag so as not to feel alone. I guess I'll die a lonely old man, burnt to death in his armchair after falling asleep with a forgotten fag.'

'What do you do when you're not smoking?' she asked.

'Well I've still got my A-Levels to finish. By the time I'm ready to take them they'll have changed the syllabus.'

The party was overcrowded at first; everyone seeking free booze had heard of it. Siân and I, hand in hand, wove around people and shouted above the music. We saw a young blond man offer Will a cigarette.

'I don't smoke much. Only when I'm awake,' he said above the noise. He then went on to borrow the phrase I had used earlier.

'Other people should come accompanied by a book of instructions, don't you think?' he said taking off his glasses to look, if not more interesting then at least more modern.

Later, well into the night when I was wandering, defensively gripping a near empty bottle of wine, I came across Will again, blowing up the condom into a round, nipple pointed balloon.

Later still I found Siân looking for me and I went up to her pretending not to know her, re-enacting the first time we talked, reminding her of my words about buses and refugees and it made her smile. And then we danced, tightly on weak legs until the night closed in on Saturday's dawn and we were left with a reduced group that slept on the floor. We joined them, too lazy to make our way back home. I held Siân close to me, said a few sleepy words to her and thought of how I didn't want to be anywhere else with anyone else.

19. *1981*

Weddings and funerals are the rituals of a community laying its fears to rest. It was Year Thirty-Six of the Nuclear Age and a wedding and a funeral were to change everything for me.

Sometimes on Saturdays Will, Dai Panda and I went to demonstrations in London. We were part of those bussed in from the provinces at dawn, adding up the numbers at anti-nuclear and anti-apartheid protests. We usually hung around at the end in Hyde Park, hoping for a bit of fisticuffs with the police, at a time when the radical groupings and parties began to make a name for themselves.

Will was still at school, retaking his A-Levels. Dai Panda and I were chronically unemployable and I was back at home with Mam and Fan. At Elen's wedding in Gorseinon we were surprised to meet Karen. Will's sister was married in High Anglican white, all princess veil and metres of silk tailed behind, at a bleak, black Welsh Methodist chapel. She was a butterfly in a coal mine. Karen was the groom's neighbour.

Karen had given up drink. She was almost as I remembered her. She was more Saturday morning hangover than Friday night pissed. While I had grown a few inches taller she remained as a developed fifteen-year-old. She wore her hair a lot shorter than four years before and there was no longer any sign of make-up. She was dressed in black cords, Doc Martens and a duffle coat, wedding or not.

She had a job in a department store in Swansea. The one I used to steal from with Dai Panda. She had to keep an eye on the customers but it was better than working on the tills, she argued. Someone like her could have caught me when I was eleven, I thought.

At the reception we went out the back for some air and some marijuana and returned to the hall again half an hour later ready for the revolution. We talked about politics, Scargill and Benn, about a nuclear-free Wales, the planned demonstration in Swansea against steelwork job losses, and about political groups, old and new, their successes and their failings.

We met again at the demo. Us four would become inseparable for almost a year. Over the following weeks as the summer of nineteen eighty-one approached we found we had more in common beyond protesting at the forty thousand job losses in the Welsh steel industry. We discussed the visible effects of Thatcherism in Wales, the language problem, how we saw Wales as a colony with a colonial direct ruler over us and the increasing problem of rural cottages being bought up for holidays, threatening communities. We didn't have perfect answers and there were gaps in our knowledge, but we had Will, who could fake his way through anything.

We were stimulated by ideas; by debate; by the world opening up; by history, by imagination and by words. We would stay up all night and then carry on the same the next day.

The tightness of our group encouraged me to give up looking for work for good and become a full-time revolutionary.

Mam was off with the Women For Life On Earth march from Cardiff to the US Air Force base at Greenham Common when Karen, Will, Dai Panda and I formed Bore Coch. Our first act was to write on a wall next to the bank in High Street Gorseinon the slogan *Nid Yw Cymru Ar Werth*. Wales Is Not For Sale.

We'd only got as far as writing NID YW CYMRU before being interrupted and we ran off. The abbreviation stayed on the wall for the following months until the council finally cleaned it off. We would go out of our way to pass it everyday.

WALES IS NOT. It was all a new beginning for us. We called it Year One, like Old Tommy had said about May twenty-six. By Year Two we hoped to attract more through our reputation, becoming a group to be reckoned with. By Year Three we would be marching towards independence.

Karen was constantly worried by the threat of nuclear war. She had nightmares of war destroying Swansea again, this time forever, laying the whole area under a grim nuclear winter.

The four of us had become so close in our shared secret that Will suggested we should live together in a squat. But I had to look after Fan since Mam was often away with the women, while Karen wanted to avoid turning into our cookcleaner.

'I'm not cut out for being a Welsh mam,' she argued.

One night at the end of summer we plucked up enough courage to drive around writing Wales Is Not For Sale in both languages along the M4 between Swansea and Cardiff, in the very part of Wales nobody wanted to buy.

One sunny Sunday afternoon we drove up to my Mamgu's house in Karen's VW. Calon Ddu had been empty since her death a few years earlier.

'Pity we've ruled out living together,' Will said as we stood at the gate to the old whitewashed farmhouse.

'We could occupy the place as a centre of operations!' he added.

'But it's too far from a pub for you lot anyway,' Karen pointed out. 'And I'm not driving you all around everywhere.'

She wasn't made out to be a Welsh mam, nor a taxi driver.

'And what's going to happen to this place?' Karen asked.

'Well my uncle doesn't look like he's ever coming back. He didn't even turn up for the funeral. Perhaps he'll sell it or let it rot away,' I replied.

'So she lived alone, did she, your gran?' Karen asked.

'Yes. Funny really, thinking about it; I never associated the old woman with my mam,' I said.

'That's because of their different lives. Take your mam, she's independent now and doing what she wants, but I bet your gran was tied to this place and her family until her last days,' Karen said.

'Even alone?' I asked with a laugh.

I then thought that yes, it was true, Mamgu was tied to the place even alone, trapped to the past in her mind. I was remembering Mamgu letting her mind wander, becoming suddenly lifeless.

'Well, let's break in, or what?' Dai Panda asked.

At that time Old Tommy became ill. He was seventy-one and chronic bronchitis had put an end to most of our arguments. The morphine the doctor brought helped him go with a smile on his face, taking his cough and his life with it.

It shouldn't have been a surprise but he had a religious funeral. It was the thing to do despite the wishes of the deceased, for once dead they had no say.

'I never darken their doors,' he once said of chapels.

I didn't know whether to blame his wife or the Presbyterian minister who must have persuaded her into it.

I went along, asked to help carry the coffin. There were about ten of us in all at the service that started inside the chapel with organ-accompanied hymns and it brought back to me what he once said.

'When I hear a Welsh hymn on the radio I don't know whether to cry or throw up.'

191

The elderly lay preacher had deathly grey skin and bloodless thin lips with saliva congealing at the sides of his mouth.

'I would like, on behalf of us all, to say a few words of congratulation to the royal couple on this happy day of their wedding in London. But today, as we know, is also a sad day, a sad day indeed when in the name of God we have to condemn an atheist and communist to Hell,' he began to say slowly and loudly.

DUW CARU YW was written in big bold letters on the chapel wall behind him. God loves you.

I hummed the Internationale, just loudly enough to be heard.

The minister then talked at length about Lady Diana and Prince Charles before returning to Old Tommy, never mentioned by name but just called an unrepentant sinner.

After the sermon and a few more hymns we were given a signal to take the coffin outside to lower it six feet under. Chapels, Old Tommy never let their doors darken him.

'Not even out of curiosity, to hear the nonsense peddled on the inside?' I once asked him.

'Over my dead body,' he had said.

At the end of the ceremony his widowed wife invited me back to the house with the rest. I apologised, thinking that I couldn't take it if it were to be strict tt. A few days later I learnt that in fact the tea and sandwich wake grew into a monumental piss-up which came to an end only after the police had turned up.

Leaving the chapel cemetery I saw Jenkins standing across the road from the gate, as drunk and tattered as the first time I had seen him at the library. I thought he didn't come closer because it wasn't his Protestant sect and he just stood there, perhaps thinking that Old Tommy was finally with Arthur's ghost.

'I'm Jenkins, an old friend of...' he began to say as I approached.

'Yes, I know. We met at the library once.'

'Did we indeed?' he replied.

There was a silence between us, him stuck in the past, me thinking of the future.

'Ironic, isn't it?' I finally said after a minute standing next to each other watching the others leave.

'Yes!' Jenkins interrupted. 'Old Tommy was an egalitarian communist all his life and he was killed by the Tories!' he continued without looking at me. 'This winter Old Tommy and his wife had to make do with only two hours of electric fire a day in order to pay the bills. There are thousands felled each year by bronchitis and hypothermia. I wonder, how many pensioners is this Thatcher woman prepared to kill? You said something about irony,' he added turning to me, a stench of whisky floating from him.

I left Jenkins staring and I walked away, going nowhere. I walked for hours, all the time carrying the phantom of Old Tommy around with me. Then I saw another ghost. She ran for a bus to avoid me. I couldn't have exchanged niceties on passing. But in a small town one should be prepared for meeting one's past.

Siân had let her hair grow in the six months that had passed. I didn't like it, it was halfway to somewhere, falling

193

down behind her ears. I wanted to run. I didn't think that I wanted to be with her again. I wondered what she thought. We had caused each other too much harm.

I began to walk, my mind numbed until an off-licence opening for the evening caught my attention. Opening a can of lager I began walking again and noticed it had been raining and had got dark.

I came across a youth on a dark damp street unsuccessfully trying to strike a match. As I passed close by he took a cigarette out of his mouth and asked me for a light. I shook my head. I saw that he wasn't alone, that he had two friends sitting in a doorway. He shouted out insults at me as I continued walking and something snapped in me and I turned, threw the half empty can of lager to the ground and ran a few steps towards him, jumped and landed a kick at his abdomen. I fought with the other two youths until somehow I managed to escape, bruised and battered. They didn't chase me for long but I continued running, until I tripped over some black plastic bin liners full of kitchen rubbish. I crashed down onto the floor, spraining an ankle and limped away as best I could.

A few blocks away I slowed my pace, limping on to who knew where until a middle-aged man pulled at my arm to stop me as I passed.

'Got any spare change? Got a fag, have you?' he asked, beer on his breath.

Startled I just shook my head as before without thinking but he let me continue on my escape.

'You look in a hell of a state!' he called after me.

I rested a while, sitting in a shop doorway, head back,

looking up and seeing stars in the starless sky, little flames coming and going, jumping around, encircling in front of my eyes like molecular creatures under a laboratory microscope.

Later that evening I got drunk alone, stupid miserably drunk. I ended the day walking tipsy curvy turvy in the empty street with a can of lager in my hand.

'I don't want to think, I want to drink!' I shouted out and then dropped to my knees.

I slept a while on the pavement. I was woken by a girl insisting her boyfriend ask. He wasn't keen but eventually did so.

'Do you ever have nightmares about the police, or is it just me?' I remember replying. I'd just had Police Dream number seven.

20. *1981*

We read library books and were dangerous compared to the apolitical vandals we had little respect for. For them destruction was a result of blind frustration, for us it was guided. Our breaking of windows was an attack on the state. The state was the English Imperialist State. The E.I.S., pronounced eyes, we spat out, where others used Britain. The Eis are constantly watching you, the Eis control all, we said.

We were dangerous because we were aware of what was beginning to be called the politics of identity. It was identifying yourself, seeing yourself as belonging to a class, or to a gender, and acting as such. Women were becoming feminists, the working class growing conscious of itself. It meant seeing yourself in cultural and linguistic terms, it meant being someone, belonging to something out of yourself and your time. We were dangerous because we wanted to do something which would provoke a reaction, anything to turn the nightmare of reality into a dream. Something was happening in Wales in the early eighties, and we wanted to be part of it. We had decided to act.

'It's a pity Lad and Parry aren't with us,' Dai Panda lamented.

'Oh, shut him up, will you,' Will retorted.

'All I said was...' Dai Panda began, his feelings hurt.

'Enough!' Will shouted at him. 'We don't talk about them, right,' he threatened with a sharpened pencil from across the room.

We were in my bedroom, about to compare texts on our press announcement for later that night. The room fed Dai Panda's nostalgia, the walls covered in my brother Huw's posters of Bruce Lee and his bits of motorcycles in boxes or spread across the floor.

'Have you prepared the release?' Will asked Dai Panda when he had calmed down.

'What, me? I thought...' he began to say.

'He's only joking,' I told him.

'No, really,' Will replied. 'Hadn't we decided that Panda would be the one to express our ideology in fluent English? I mean if it's good enough for the Queen then why can't Dai...'

'Don't take any notice of him,' Karen said. 'He's only pulling your leg.'

She and I had been trying to translate Will's overlong thesis into Welsh and we reduced it to a few lines.

'Is that all?' Will exclaimed.

'We're going to read it over the phone immediately after,' Karen reminded him. 'That's the idea, isn't it? We've got to be brief.'

'What did he write then?' Dai Panda asked.

'A bloody linguistic monster with arms of obscure historical precedents. All very nice but impractical,' Karen complained.

'We could keep it for a better occasion, as part of a manifesto,' I suggested, to keep Will happy.

'Oh, thank you! What have you censored out then?'

'Reduced,' I corrected him.

'Here it is,' Karen began, looking through the notes she had. 'This is the translation back into the medium of English from the Welsh of Will's version of our demands originally in English.'

We, Bore Coch, Red Morning, claim responsibility for the attack at twelve forty-five a.m. on the Army Careers Office in Castle Street, Swansea.

Cynically the English Imperialist State, at a time when it is actively stripping Wales of its industrial base, presents the young Welsh working class with only one option: to enlist as a mercenary in an army defending the very capitalism that is destroying Wales.

Taking from the industrial reserve army of the unemployed and giving to an imperial army in reserve for the oppression of the industrial working class.

What that state is presently carrying out in occupied Northern Ireland is nothing more than a practice exercise for when that state finally intervenes in defence of the last vestiges of its crumbling stale Empire.

Bore Coch, Red Morning, calls on the Welsh working class to actively remove English recruitment centres from our land.

> *Prepare for the liberation of Wales!*
> *Down now with the Imperialist English Army!*
> *Down with enforced economic conscription!*
> *Troops out of Northern Ireland!*
> *Troops out of Wales!*

Mam interrupted her way into my room at that point offering tea. Dai Panda was about to gesture acceptance when Will refused on our behalf, so that she would not interrupt again.

'No thanks, we just had one before coming up,' he said to her with a big smile. 'Is that it?' Will asked when she had gone, returning to the press release. 'You certainly did simplify things, didn't you?'

'I think we should just call ourselves Bore Coch, even in the English version, the press can make their own translation,' I pointed out, ignoring Will's comment.

'Nothing about my analysis of the actual behaviour of the security forces in Ireland, as part of the sectarian problem, raping, torturing and killing in the name of queen and country, nor even how since the beginning of industrialisation in South Wales we have been surrounded by military bases, set and positioned to intervene at any moment?'

'Look, we reduced it down to this bit about an imperial army in reserve for the oppression of the industrial working class,' Karen read. 'What is strikingly missing from your English version and which we failed to add due to lack of space is any reference to working-class women,' she went on.

She was fearless then, a warring feminist. She was a bit like Boadicea, but smoked.

'And of course the presence of the army here is also a women's issue,' she added.

'Is it? Anyway there are two options open to the Welsh working class at present,' Will insisted. 'Not just one.'

'We decided since our action is against the Army Careers Office,' I began to explain.

'Well we can insert it here,' Will said, taking the sheet of paper from Karen's hands. 'Yes, easily, instead of one option, the young Welsh working class now can have two! Emigrate to be exploited elsewhere or enlist as a mercenary in an army defending the very capitalism that is destroying Wales. What do you think?' he asked.

'Fine by me,' I said. Karen nodded and Will looked for a reaction from Dai Panda who was looking down at the carpet wishing either to be somewhere else or that this was not going to turn into another bloody argument. He said nothing.

'Well that's it then, three for and one abstention because Panda's in bloody Noddyland,' Will exclaimed.

The text still in his hands, he began to look for spaces to add more.

'Let's cross out Red Morning and keep only Bore Coch,'

I suggested and Will, armed with the pencil, slashed at the paper twice.

'What if we add the part about South Wales being encircled?' Will asked.

'The action is against the fucking Careers Office not the effing boot camps,' Karen pointed out angrily. 'It's like talking to a breeze block,' she added.

Will threw the piece of paper at Dai Panda, still motionlessly staring down. 'Well you try and rewrite it,' Will said to him.

After a while, to our surprise, Panda interrupted our fight.

'I see where we can add women to the text, look Karen?' he said and got up.

And the fifth paragraph soon changed.

Bore Coch calls on the Welsh working class, man and woman, young and old, to actively remove English recruitment centres from our land.

And we left it at that, after reading it aloud and timing how long it would take on the phone. In our paranoia we feared that more than a minute would allow some sophisticated device to track us.

The original plan had been for me to read our communiqué in English to the *Evening Post* at one phone box, and at a second, Karen would read the Welsh version to the BBC. But that afternoon we decided not to risk making mistakes reading in Welsh to the BBC for the phone box probably would have no light. The last thing we wanted was to sound like an amateurish group that represented nobody and faked the Welsh, which was precisely what we were. What we most feared if caught was that they'd find out that we were young, incompetent and nobodies, despite our grand, all-embracing intentions.

We had also decided that, sober, we would drive into town at around twelve o'clock at night, park the car in a side street with Karen waiting at the wheel and when the street was quiet enough Dai Panda and I would smash with bricks the glass door and window of the converted shop while Will sprayed in red on the adjacent wall the words Troops Out Of Wales. Then we would escape calmly away down High Street to phone the BBC studio in Cardiff.

We met up outside Will's house at nine o'clock that night, Karen in her ancient black VW Beetle, to finalise plans. It was much too early, the three hours until midnight seemed an eternity, and being together made us nervous. As a result we were in a pub by ten o'clock, drunk by half eleven. All except Karen, who was on the wagon, and anyway was driving. We drank mostly in silence, just looking at each other in the overcrowded saloon bar, Karen getting up occasionally to check the time of her watch against the clock.

'Have you got a date?' I asked her.

She had changed greatly over the four years that had passed since our Friday night date at the disco, when she left with someone else. When I was first with her she had been basically a child longing to be an adult. Now she was an adult regretting how she used to behave. The same applied to me.

We were among the last to leave when we began to make our way into Swansea. I was nineteen, it was summer nineteen eighty-one and the town was abuzz with life.

Saturday night on the golden half-mile of Kingsway in the centre of town. There were disco dancers dressed to shame Caribbean maraca-wielding waiters in their flowered beach party shirts, and glue-sniffing post-punks spitting. There were thirteen-year-old girls wearing miniskirts and trying on bras and seductive smiles for the first time, whooping to the passing police dogs and bus drivers, to the bikers and ageing Hell's Angels. And brightly dressed mamgus sipping from a flask of whisky, lightly laced with tea for the bronchi cough. Duffle-coated electronics students trying to break endurance records by eating twice a week on a dwindling West Midlands educational grant already spent on a Mumbles bedsit sound system, cursing the Welsh and their A-level results. And grinning, tight-trousered Valleys boys and high-heeled new-tech village girls, all wandering in a stupor, all looking for a drink and thinking of a fuck, and all on show and in synchrony, weaving in and out of the police sirens and radio taxis, and the endless nightclub cues and bouncers, and all because the pubs had closed and because it was Saturday night all night.

But we were stone-cold and frightened of ourselves because that night would be ours, a night to be added to the ancient annals of Welsh history, despite the alcohol flowing in our veins and despite the drying liver Karen carried around and kept as a souvenir.

Karen kept the engine running and Will stood next to her VW, faking a conversation with Dai Panda while he occasionally shook a paint canister as if he were preparing an exotic cocktail while I walked up and down Castle Street. It wasn't going to be as easy as we had thought and I went back to the car to tell them.

'Castle's pretty quiet but people turn into it at any moment and there is always someone who could see us,' I informed them.

'Let's go for a spin and come back in half an hour,' Karen suggested through the side window.

'No,' I insisted in fake confidence, not wanting it to be me who insisted on what might have to be an inevitable retreat. 'We'll just have to be quick about it, that's all,' I argued. 'This is the closest side street, blow the horn if a copper comes into sight. We'll be outside the place and when we see it's OK we'll do it.'

'The paint job is the most tricky,' Will said.

I looked him in the eye but he turned away from me.

'Do it first,' Dai Panda suggested. 'I mean, it's silent, isn't it? And when you've finished we'll smash in the glass and run back here.'

There was a silence as we thought about whether to turn and run away back home or stay there all night discussing our possibilities. Although Will thought Dai Panda to be weak-minded and somehow for that reason unreliable, I was glad he was with us. He was loyal and kept his word, and he was not a thug like Parry or Zed had been. We had decided to attack the Army Careers Office and this was what we were to do. You can be as clever as they come and claim to know when it is best to be cautious; for Will it was always that time, but if you hadn't the nerve you might as well just have stayed in bed all day. At least Dai Panda was willing to take risks. If it wasn't for him we would be back in Karen's car excusing ourselves with slaps on the back because we had taken, intelligently, the best of options, to run and hide. Our ideals would remain just as an idea we once had.

'As long as a copper doesn't see us we'll be alright,' I said after a while to encourage Will. 'When we get back to this corner, walk normally to the car and if someone looks out of a window above they won't suspect.'

'Let's do it then!' Dai Panda said.

'Alright?' I asked down to Karen; she nodded rigidly.

'Off it is with us then,' Dai Panda demanded, and we went.

On the way back to Gorseinon Karen drove especially and suspiciously slowly; the short journey began to seem endless, the minutes torturously stretched. Either time had slowed down or the velocity of our thoughts had made it seem so. We were either on the road to safety or to being stopped by a police car on the prowl for drunk drivers.

'God, did anyone take down the numberplate?' Karen worried.

'We should have stolen a car,' Will said, lighting a cigarette with the dying glow of the previous one.

'Next time, you steal one,' I told him.

'No, you're right, it's better like this. At least we can be sure that if they stop us it's not for any apparent crime,' Will reasoned nervously.

'But someone could have seen us and memorised the number,' she continued.

'Don't worry,' Dai Panda reassured her, sitting at her side with a big smile on his face, the only one of us already content about what we had done.

I was still clutching the telephone number of the BBC.

'Throw it away,' Will groaned at me and I crumbled the paper into a tiny ball, lowered the side window and tossed it out.

'I need a drink,' Karen said, breathing deeply. 'You haven't still got the spray on you?' she asked Will angrily, her hair waving in the breeze from the opened window behind her head.

There was no response from Will.

'Well, have you?' she screamed.

'He wiped it clean and threw it in a bin next to the phone box,' I reassured her.

'Shut the window, can you?' she ordered. 'My neck is freezing. God I wouldn't mind something strong right now.'

'We'll be back home safe soon,' Dai Panda said.

'Back to your home!' she corrected him. 'I've got to drive on to Clydach, alone.'

'You can spend the night at my place, you know that, don't you?' I offered. 'On the floor with the dog.' We laughed, an abandoned, nervous laughter.

'That dog of yours won't be happy about that,' Will pointed out.

'It can go and sleep in the car, if it wants,' Dai Panda added.

'Cleaner than your room,' Karen said, turning her head back to look at me, swerving the car in doing so.

'You sleep in it then,' I replied.

'In your street it might get stolen, and me with it,' she said.

'Only a blind man would do that,' Will suggested.

Back home in my bedroom the four of us, sitting cross-legged on the floor, celebrated.

'I think it was a good idea, you making the phone call,' Will said to me as I rolled a joint and he played with a rusty old motorcycle chain as though with giant rosary beads. 'Your links with the world of journalism qualify you for press relations. You were a paperboy after all,' he added.

Will and I talked while Karen and Dai Panda looked through my record collection, playing the odd song. Talk drifted to politics. We had become more aware of the referendum fiasco but we four had formed Bore Coch for different reasons. Will was against nationalism. I was against capitalism. Dai Panda was against the police state. And Karen, against all forms of dominance, especially male dominance. Our common enemies were, in theory, the English ruling class-dominated, exploitative British state, the Eis, and Tory ideology as represented by Thatcher. Thatcher haunted us, we choked on her name, whose expression was like saying fuck and being sick at the same time.

'What was it that Mayakovsky had to say?' Will asked me.

'Ah, something Karen quoted me once.'

I called to her but she was busy joking with Dai Panda with records around them.

'Now this is a real oldie!' she said across to us.

'That if the stars shine it means that it is in someone's interest that they do so,' I quoted turning to Will.

'The Who!' Karen whooped.

'There's stuff there Eileen left me, dating from the sixties,' I replied. 'Early recordings of the Stones, Dylan and Hendrix. And Cream and Blind Faith,' I continued, casual about some of the music I still listened to in secret.

'Did your sister smoke pot then?' Dai Panda asked me.

'Well, I don't know. I'll have to ask her, won't I?' I replied, puzzled. 'I really don't know much about my eldest sister, or anyone in my family for that matter. Nor you lot either. I was running around in nappies when she was a teenager. But I remember when she dressed as a hippie and went to concerts.'

'She probably did smoke then,' Karen concluded.

'Haven't got any Bay City Rollers?' Dai Panda asked sarcastically.

'That seems more like your generation, doesn't it?' I replied.

'Ours,' Karen corrected me. 'From when we were still little more than tots.'

'Tot you might have been, my dear, but not me,' I threw at her. 'I...'

'Oh no, he's going to begin with that paper round he had for ten minutes,' Will groaned.

The three of them laughed at me as the first chords of *Stairway to Heaven* arose from the speakers and I told them to listen.

'Boy that takes me back, that does mun!' Will said in a false deep tone of voice.

It was well into the early hours of Sunday morning when Will, hardly able to walk and out of fags, got up from the floor and said that he was going home.

'Don't worry, I'll be alright,' he reassured us but we were too tired to care one way or another.

'Open the window on the way out, will you?' I asked him as he tottered his way to the door and left without responding.

'I'll do it,' Karen offered. 'If I can find it through this smog. He'll be alright, will he?'

'Oh, yeah. He can make his way home under any conditions, like a homing pigeon,' I reassured her. 'But he sometimes has problems with the front door key and ends up waking the whole street calling out for his mam.'

She opened the window which overlooked the street and stuck her head out, breathing deeply and looked down for signs of Will. Dai Panda stood up and joined her and soon they were giggling at what was happening down below.

'He walks like a duckling my gran had once,' she said to me turning back into the room. 'Or more like a blind man.'

'Watch he doesn't steal your VW,' Dai Panda warned her.

'Well, I'd better be off then too,' she said.

'You're not going to drive back at this time of night, are you?' I told her, having thought that she would spend the night, perhaps even both of us in my bed.

'You can stay here if you want. I've got a sleeping bag and be alright here on the floor,' I offered.

'No, it's alright,' she replied, not looking at me as she began to adjust her pullover around the waist of her jeans.

It wasn't so much a hope that we'd be together again,

because I was no longer with Siân, but rather since we both felt free to do as we pleased we could, as friends, make love without any complications. True I hadn't thought much about her, I didn't even desire her as such, but I did desire having another body close to me in bed again after so long.

'She's coming to spend the night at my house,' Dai Panda said out of the blue, clarifying the situation. 'We'll drive into town to see the wreckage we've done tomorrow morning, won't we Karen?' he continued.

They left together and I felt a pang of jealousy. Although she had left no scar on me like Siân, a real lover in a real relationship, there was a time when I'd thought that Karen chose my friends in the hope of being near me. It was clear that night that it wasn't the case. I was left wondering what she saw in Dai Panda, eighteen years old in his funny glasses, who still acted like a boy and who had never had a girlfriend. Perhaps that was it, he didn't chase women like the rest and if he wanted to be with her she would be sure that it was because of how she was and not because he wanted to be with a woman, any woman. Karen had changed so much. When she was fifteen she'd thought sex made men like her, but at the time she didn't know what it was in her that she wanted to be liked, and later still she didn't seem to care at all.

They told me the following evening that council workers had already scrubbed Will's words off the wall and that nobody had mentioned the attack. There was no official news about the Army Careers Office until Monday, and then only a mention in the local press about a vandal attack in the centre of Swansea. Nothing of our press release, but at least there was a photo two days later which accompanied an angry letter in the paper from a retired major, a classic, a piece about queen and country, he talked of the natives as if he were still in India, liberally interchanging concepts like respect and deference. I kept the cutting and showed it to Will who wrote a letter to the paper in the name of Bore Coch claiming responsibility. They didn't publish it.

Soon we were to adopt a phrase from Antonio Gramsci on the origins of communism in Italy.

Against the pessimism of events, we had the optimism of the will.

21. *1980*

'Wales has always been a prison. Now the difference is that there's a colour TV in every cell telling us, in two languages, that the prison is OK,' I declared.

'I only said I wouldn't mind having a TV, that's all,' Siân protested.

She had hoped that with time we would have a TV, a fridge, a car, a telephone, then a newer, bigger, colour TV, a washing machine, a dishwasher, a Walkman, two TVs, a video, a new car and a house of our very own.

And babies. She said she had come out of someone and wouldn't be complete until someone came out of her.

She wanted all and all in order. From the beginnings of consumerism to its impossible end. Our parents had hoped that our future would be better than theirs. Theirs was to hope in ours. Ours depended on whether we could afford to buy it. It was the end of nineteen eighty. Most of the people I knew in Swansea were worrying as to whether their dole payment was coming through on time. A better future was to be able to do some shopping for basics. My disinterest in consumerism only reflected a lack of confidence.

We argued. We argued about destinies and shopping lists.

Looking back on it now, Siân must have thought I hadn't yet grown up. I had no real plans, finding it easier to be critical of society than to try to take part in it. She must have believed I didn't want to learn anything new, nor do anything different, just vegetate at eighteen with a pint in my hand surrounded by the same old boyhood friends.

As usual arguments resolved themselves in bed, huffing and puffing under the squirming sheet. But the fights always returned.

Christmas was on its way and the same old carols in the distance mingled with the hum of traffic. She wallowed in memories of the synthetic fir tree flickering annoyingly in the front window, the coloured decorations dusted down again. She began to wonder where she'd go for Christmas dinner. With me and my Mam or without me with her parents and some distant relatives.

'What's your Mam doing this year?' she asked.

'Stuffed elephant, as usual,' I replied.

'Mine's ordered a goose,' she said of hers, with a vegetarian's shudder at the prospect in store.

'We should celebrate it in Cuba. Or failing that, in Cuban style as a normal working day,' I suggested.

213

'Now that would be a thing, to see you working, even just the one day,' she replied.

'I'll probably end up doing the washing-up.'

'Domestic work, hey?'

'If your Mam pays I just might consider washing up at your place as well! Does she still remember what I look like?'

'My place is here,' she corrected me.

'Maybe they'll give me a present as well,' I hinted, pointing to the book Siân had been given that afternoon.

She picked it up from the floor at her feet and handed it to me. *The History of Mathematical Formulas*. An illustrated coffee-table hardback, placed where she would have had a glass-top coffee table, probably imagining its presence there in front of where we sat, at arm's length, next to the espresso coffee cups and a cut-glass ashtray. I had thought it must have been a present from her librarian dad but opening the front cover I noticed the remains of a rubbed-out pencil inscription. I continued turning pages, unable to distinguish the words. It must have been a gift from a fellow student I thought as she got up to make some tea.

It was silly of her not to say anything. Sillier still to have rubbed out the inscription. She must have been embarrassed, thinking I would either have become jealous or else have mocked it. When she returned with mugs I looked at her, she made an effort not to make eye contact and then sat down next to me.

'What do you think?' she asked.

I didn't reply at first but thought about her question.

A problem of reference, she would have said, in her meta-mathematician's logic. What did I think? About her liberal use of rubber? The book? Presents in general?

'I suppose it's practical. One of your student texts, is it?' I replied with a dryness in my throat.

'No, not really. But it's interesting,' she said offhandedly, looking down into her tea.

Yes, it was interesting. I imagined I had never felt jealous before. It seemed a new, strange irritation.

'You've been lucky,' I eventually said, almost unable to speak. 'Most presents are useless rubbish.'

With one hand I pulled at the stuffing through a hole in the arm of the settee, like dry, wiry candyfloss under the finger. With the other I continued to flick through her expensive book, blindly turning the glossy pages but seeing only inside of myself. There we were, seated in silence in the room. She was a young fish eager for the seas outside while I preferred the fishbowl, the sleepy grey water unchanged.

Siân had become progressively disappointed in me over the four months we had spent together in the room. She wanted to live, I offered a kind of death. I offered the prison of selfish love, I slowly built it a little more every day and was its guard. She wanted the world. In Siân I had what I wanted but was angry with the rest of life and took it out on her. Worse, I made the mistake of thinking she liked me as I was. Sex wasn't enough. She faced a lazy, cynical nightmare every evening after college, until she eventually found something to keep her from coming home.

Two days before Christmas I was alone awaiting her

return, a loyal puppy, tail wagging. To pass the time I practised Welsh and created my first ever play on words and was eager to show her what I had come up with. '*Lle mae dŵr mae bywyd,*' was one of the Welsh Water Authority's slogans. Where there is water there is life. My variation had Tryweryn and its flooded village in mind. '*Yn lle bywyd mae dŵr.*' In place of life there is water.

Meanwhile above, Peter the actor paced up and down the squeaking floorboards of his room, repeating over and over again the same phrase. He tried it out in different tones and rhythms: hammy; Shakespearean; angrily and even gaily happy. Nothing seemed to work for him.

There but for the grace of God go I, he repeated at all hours as he stepped above my head, struggling with the purely linguistic, the grammatical as I waited for my Siân to come back home. She came back very late.

'You're still up then?' she asked as she entered timidly.

'Richard Burton's been keeping me awake,' I replied, pointing up beyond the ceiling.

She began rummaging carefully through a drawer of clothes and pulled out a nightie she had never worn. She usually went to bed naked and I had only ever seen her put on a T-shirt that didn't remain on for long, when cold.

She stood up and turned round to face me, gripping the nightie to her breast.

'Look, I've been thinking. I think we need more space,' she suddenly told me.

'More space? We could open the window and stick our heads out!'

'No, seriously! Recently it's been tense here in such a

small room. We're just not ready to live together. We need more space, we don't have to spend every evening together. I need to study and if I had my own bedsit you could spend the night with me now and then or I could come round here. It would be ideal until I finish university!'

So the three of us had been preparing speeches that evening.

She turned away from me in bed that night, curling into a protective ball. It said more to me than her speech. It was the end. We used to make love every day, all day at first, even through days of blood. I stayed awake at her side, inches apart from her, staring at the wall of the night, resigning myself to living alone, to being free to have Will and Panda round at all hours, to spending all afternoon in bed should I please. To losing Siân forever.

There was a vacant room on the second floor and we spent Christmas Eve moving her things upstairs, sandwiching the striving actor.

Two nights after she moved we planned to go out. The idea was that she'd come for me after returning from her parents'. I waited past midnight and she still hadn't come so I went up to her room, seeing light come from under the door. About to knock I heard muffled voices through the door.

'*Rwy'n Pedr,*' she said. 'It's easy, come on repeat!'

'Ruin Peder,' the other voiced replied.

'No, Pedr. Pe Dr,' she corrected Peter.

Hardly able to support the weight of my body, I turned to grip hold of the banister rail. I had thought her teaching me Welsh to be something sacred and there she was with the actor.

I walked back down to my bedsit and lay on my bed all night until sleep crept into me. I dreamt about Siân.

I was with her in a deserted supermarket. I filled a basket with tins and packets of meats. At the checkout, Siân began talking to a man she seemed interested in. I thought he must have worked there. I was jealous of him. The girl at the only till in use was busy adding up the bill. It finally came to forty pounds. I was expecting it to be much lower. I only had ten pounds on me. I asked the girl to show me the receipt before paying but she, curtly, said that only after she had typed in the amount of money handed over by the customer could she finish the operation and print the receipt out. I called to Siân for help. She was close to me but didn't listen, she only took notice of the man. I asked the till girl to start the process of checking out again because with only one small basket of food forty pounds seemed excessive. She said it was impossible. I called to Siân again but still there was no response. I went up to her and waved a hand in front of her face. She didn't care, she was only thinking of impressing the man. I returned to the till, angry and saw that the girl wasn't there. Alone with my shopping packed in a plastic bag I waited a while and then angrily said, fuck it, and walked out empty-handed, leaving Siân behind.

I awoke from the dream feeling shrivelled. I'd feel worse later when in the early afternoon Siân came to visit.

'I thought I'd just pop by to say hello before going out,' she said standing at the door.

'Won't you come in then?' I asked gesturing, half-relieved she had thought about me, half-disappointed she wouldn't stay.

'Well, just a min. I'm in a hurry,' she replied staring at my bloodshot eyes. I reminded her of our plans.

'Last night! I must have completely forgotten!' she replied. 'I stayed over at home after dinner, there was family there...'

'You're lying!'

'No, silly.'

'It's none of my business, we don't live together any longer after all but...'

'I'm late. I've got to go,' she interrupted me, looking at her watch and turning for the door.

'Just a minute, oh please Siân,' I begged. 'I feel abandoned here alone.'

'Look,' she said pausing at the door. 'I thought we'd agreed that we wouldn't spend every night together...'

'But we haven't spent any night together since you moved upstairs.'

'You've got to understand, I need more space!'

'I almost believe you but I can't get it into my head that you don't want me anymore.'

'Look, I just want to live. I'm almost eighteen and I haven't done anything! Living with you is like vegetating!' she said, raising her voice and left, slamming the door closed behind her.

I went to the sink and tried to vomit, helping myself with a finger poked violently into the back of my mouth but nothing came out. And then I cried. I cried for myself, that selfish bugger inside, the child wanting to be spoilt, cry and you get fed, mope and someone will come to comfort you. Nobody came. I wasn't to see Siân at the Sketty house again. Nor Peter. The days slowly passed and I began to give up on her. I had already given up on eating, on turning on the light, on drinking, on caring about myself. Finally a protective covering formed like a cement shell, covering the boy that didn't want to grow up.

I opened the curtains on New Year's Eve and the damp room reminded me constantly of her. I had surprised myself when I had passed an hour or two without thinking of her. My only optimistic thought was that with time I would think of her less. I was alone in a midday winter West Glamorgan street. The light laced through the window. What we had to put up with for affection, a little huffing and puffing under the blankets. We used to look at the door, together seated in silence, unable to leave. On the wall our Polaroids were yellowing in the rotten-apple smell of rising damp.

22. *1974*

I had said good night to Mam after rolling exactly twenty filterless cigarettes for Father. It was something I always did. Obliged through charm at first, it had become an expected nightly routine, like brushing my teeth but taking longer. After so many years I didn't even get a thank you from him the next morning, just the occasional comment if I had left a cigarette limp, when I had been mean with his tobacco. He told me he preferred my little fingers at first, better than his rolling machine, later he'd complain it was like smoking just the paper. He wasn't really ever content with anything those days.

At the top of the stairs music could be faintly heard coming from behind Fan's bedroom door. The radio always helped her sleep. Mam would usually go in to turn it off on her way to bed and Fan would get up the next morning and break the silence with Elvis singing *Love Me Tender* on her record player.

Huw was fast asleep in bed. Surprisingly he was at home. He got in at about five o'clock that afternoon, had scoffed down something to eat and went to bed exhausted to snore until noon the following day and quickly off again, oblivious to what was to happen that night. He lived as if he were on the run. He smelt of petrol and dog's hair in the bed next to mine and I had begun to prefer him not coming home at all.

I was all warm and cosy under the blankets when I heard Father return, earlier than usual. Soon the raised voices downstairs kept me from sleep. They were having a row like nothing since when they decided to send me up to Mamgu's out of the way. I couldn't pick out any words, it was like a loud throbbing muffled drone coming from a distant TV. There was a brief silence, then I could hear Mam crying a long time until it died out. Relieved the argument was over I expected them to come up to bed, unable to sleep until then.

I waited and worried until I finally went downstairs to find the living room empty and the kitchen back door open. Cold in my pyjamas from the draught I went to look out the back but was surprised at the door by Mam and the dog coming in. Wearing muddy Wellington boots she looked terrified.

'Where's Father?' I asked.

'He's gone.'

'Oh, Mam, what do you mean?'

'You'll catch your death like that. Back to bed with you now, go on!'

I went back up, thinking it had all been a mistake. She must have been angry with him and he'd gone out for another drink. Feeling a heavy weight in my stomach I lay on the bed and became dizzy. Panic engulfed me. And I vomited. Cupfulls of dirty water retched up through my throat and out onto the bed, soaking the pillow. On and on until exhausted I fell asleep.

I woke hearing Mam move things around in the box bedroom. I tried to wake Huw to ask him to find out what was happening but he was like a stone. I went to take a look myself. From the landing I saw her hurriedly put some clothes into a suitcase, the muddied boots still on as she bend down to pick up one of Father's jackets that had slipped off the coat hanger in her rush. Something in her felt I was there behind.

'Go back to bed,' she demanded angrily in Welsh, turning to face me.

I returned to my room without protest and stood leaning against the closed door until I heard her drag the case downstairs. I followed in secret and saw her take it out the back. Feeling a weight in my lungs and unable to wait for her to come back indoors I went back to bed, stricken.

In my dream I was seated at a table eating with my family when I began to notice a fine strand of sawdust falling from a point in the ceiling above my head. I looked up and the stuff got into my eyes. Father and I decided to go upstairs to investigate. We got up from the table and walked out of the room and into the playground of my High School, wondering about which of the buildings we should go into to solve the problem of the hole in the ceiling.

We then found ourselves back home. This time the sawdust fell onto me wherever I moved. I stood on a chair and saw that from the hole ants and wasps were throwing the stuff at me. Father prepared cement to tap the hole, but the insects pushed through each time, until we invented a new cement mixed with bleach instead of water which seemed to work. Mam wondered aloud about why they were after me. What had I done to deserve all this. Eileen said that once when I was little more than a baby I used to chop up worms in the garden to produce lots of wriggly ones. I denied it. He doesn't remember, she said. And then I seemed to remember. Mam said it was the insects' revenge and I felt guilty.

A few days later I went into Mam's room, a stale warm shoe box, carrying tea with fresh milk to surprise her. She slept, as I did, with head hidden, her body a ball rolled under infinite layers of heavy blankets. She opened a weary dead eye, tinted as grey as her skin. It was the time when Mam stopped being Mam and I wanted her to get up, but she was wishing herself hopelessly away. A headache, she called her days, hardly breathing.

One night when I was twelve I awoke to movements as she got up for the first time, moving her body down the stairs to the surprise of the dog at the foot of it. At first she only talked to the dog. She said some sweet words and his tail responded in lazy whiplashes. He had joined her in the protest against what remained of existence and Fan's attempts to make food.

All of us had aged as old as dry stone. For Mam everything coincided with menopause, Nerys said, when she came home hearing of her illness. Stopping for men or something. She would sit at the kitchen table in the dark with her tired face.

'Why is she tired? She spends all day in bed,' Fan would ask. 'She'll make herself ill.' Fan knew what she was talking about.

My sisters talked about her in her presence like they were her mother. I didn't say anything but made her tea, which she received with a long, indifferent sigh.

She managed to talk eventually. She said she'd read in the local paper that a boy had been killed crashing his motorbike into a wall, and she wished Huw didn't ride his, he was too young. That was all she could face. The rest of us were down to living on child benefit, tinned spaghetti bolognese and the spuds I dug up from next door's garden, carefully replacing the foliage into the ground. The coal came from Dai Panda who would steal from home, a stone at a time, hidden in his satchel. His mother got suspicious, for he hardly ever went to school and had started to go off keen in the morning with the school bag hanging from his shoulder. Panda's homework we called it.

Later she had doctor's pills which Huw used to take secretly too, one by one, and the doctor thought she was overdosing and cut the prescription down, which helped her get off them. She turned to a bottle of Guinness before bed every night but Huw was getting withdrawal symptoms which turned him to a mixture of model aeroplane glue, petrol, aspirin, cider and the dog's flea tablets.

Mam seemed smaller, as if she had shrunk in the wash. Oh, I've left the dishes again, became 'the dishes have been

225

left again.' She took herself out of forgetting the washing up. She took herself out of life, didn't refer to herself, talked more slowly, never smiling, never caring about the rest in the street. She almost ceased to exist as we had known her.

She was to finally stop being Mam, a mother. But she became a woman.

There were no women in Wales at the time. Only the extremes of girls and mothers. We think we have come to know the Welsh Mam, but we know nothing of the woman. Only the girl to mam metamorphosis: the Miss Kafka into Mrs Dungbeetle.

She had a life before becoming a mother, showing her cleavage in a pub on a sunny Saturday afternoon to a young miner with permanent coal-grit stains around the eyes and a permanent bulge in his best trousers.

I remember when she used to go out for the night with Father. Watching her transform herself, taking out the curlers, adjust her stocking straps, adding sweet powdery smells and bitter lipstick. In the bathroom she talked of Jack Frost, his climb up the winter window, while cleaning her vagina with a towel. I would lie awake wondering if they had finally escaped for good.

And how she would begin fingering my hair for fleas, which if caught were crushed between her thumbnails. And I remember asking her about the new decimalisation system. 'You'll get used to it,' she said. And I did. We got used to everything, Mam and I, eventually.

I wasn't completely surprised at Father going. If kids in our street could disappear, why not their fathers too?

After a few weeks Nerys came home in answer to a desperate letter from Fan. With Mam in bed the three of us talked around the kitchen table as we carefully tore up an old newspaper into square sheets for the bathroom, as Mam used to do when there was no money.

Sitting around the table it was Fan who first tried to explain the situation.

'He's left home, buggered off for good, Mam says never to return, well, there's been no word, she's in bed all day, I'm sick of cooking, there's only potatoes now, the rent man keeps calling, there's no one to pay him, we hide upstairs when there's someone at the door, all we needed is you leaving for Cardiff one week then the next Father running off, we'll become a Shelter family soon, what's left of us, or out on the street or in care, the school inspectors are after us again, we're frightened to answer the door, I can't leave here, Mam won't get up, the dog's got diarrhoea and he there's up to no good I bet.'

That was me. She was wrong about my *no good*, it was more *not all that bad at the time*. At least I went to school and got hold of the potatoes. She was right about the rest though. What was left of the tribe was falling apart, reduced to numbers of unsustainability, in the face of complete extinction.

'We'll write to Eileen. Perhaps she'll be able to send a bit of money,' Nerys suggested. 'In the meantime I'll ask Elen's Mrs Jones to try to cash Mam's child benefit to pay the rent man. Keep avoiding him for now! Suppose Mam will have to make Father's leaving official and claim social security in her name. She'll have to get up and out of the house. As

227

for the school inspectors, we'll need a doctor's letter for you Fan, saying you can't leave the house. If he won't give us one I'll write it. For Huw we can say he's gone off with Father and we don't know where they are. God knows how Mam managed to put them off for so long. There must be a new crackdown on truancy! Anyway we've got to get all this sorted soon, I can't stay long. I'm missing my lectures.'

Nerys would sort things out. She might have hated her body but she knew how to use her brain.

As for Mam, there was no solution except time and lots of tea. We didn't bother her with little problems, like asking her how to run the house. All Fan and I did was to fake our way through it, learning to cook together and throwing away strange bills from the electricity board.

When we'd been without lighting for about a month I accompanied Mam on her first day out of the house, for air and groceries. We passed a mother dragging along her crying young daughter.

'Frustration!' the woman said to the child. 'You'll know what frustration is when you marry.'

We stopped at the corner leading into High Street when we heard female voices out of sight around the corner.

'She couldn't have more children, you see.'

'Get away!'

'Was going loopy, upstairs. Mark my words!'

'Well, jew jew.'

'Not straight in the head. Her sack was missing a few potatoes.'

'I knew it, I did. I knew it.'

'Anyway they say she did her husband in, she did.'

'The witch! I heard he ran away from her.'

'Hacked the life out of the man, in his bed.'

'Go on with you, and in his sleep too!'

'And buried in butcher's portions out the back.'

'Hasn't been seen for weeks!'

'And the dog they never feed began digging him up.'

'Well I never!'

'Locked herself away.'

'In the dark too.'

'Still shouts at him even now he isn't there.'

'Thinks he can hear her from under the roses.'

'Now they all start screaming blue bedlam at night.'

'Funny family anyway. I always said it, I did.'

We stepped into the High Street and they stared at us.

'There she goes, as if butter wouldn't melt,' one said in an audible whisper.

We continued walking, past the mini supermarket, Mam at a normal pace, but without looking around, without saying anything. I told her we had walked by the market but she took no notice. We went on and away from the row of shops. The words tore in her brain. She was all used up, and worst of all she felt guilty. As though kids would taunt and throw stones at the crazy old man killer from Bryn Road.

How could a lie be important? The fact was that others believed it, and they believed it because it was said. They were only words, words germinated by her absence from the world of gossip.

'I feel that they are spying on me, see everything I think,' she said, almost ashamed to have to talk about it to her boy. She felt guilty, but there was no crime, she was defenceless against the ridiculous accusation.

'They are by there, behind the doors,' she said coming to a stop, looking around her.

'Let's go back and do the shopping,' I suggested, always looking for the comforting normal mother in my Mam.

'It's like being raped,' she said after a while standing still, clutching at her straw carrier bag with one hand and at my sleeve with the other.

23. *1975*

Even bright colours became part of that all-embracing grey, from the cloudy sky down to the buildings, the walking heads and the wet street. Greyness wasn't only a colour in those days but a transparent substance that wafted day and night around our streets, a Passover curse that came calling through the keyholes, wandered around the house looking for grey matter, and on entering the brain, turned thoughts and feelings grey.

Even food.

'Everything tastes grey,' I exclaimed to Mam as an excuse for my lack of appetite.

'Try a bit of salt on it then,' she recommended, but to no avail for salt was the very crystallised essence of greyness. 'Are you sure now that you're not taking sandwiches with you?'

'And where does he think he's off to?' Fan asked.

'Ask me, ask me?' I told her.

'He's only going,' Mam began to explain.

'Down the mines!' I exclaimed.

'Oh where's he going, Mam?' she moaned.

'On the gold rush,' I added, for a change.

'He does it on purpose, he does!'

'Now, now then. Leave him be,' Mam told her.

'Oh, Mam! And why doesn't he make his own sandwiches?' Fan replied.

'Because he doesn't want any, that's why,' Mam replied. 'So I'm making him some just in case. You'll be wanting plenty of butter on it, won't you now cariad?'

Mam always did think I was too skinny for the fat of life.

I got worse, after Father, they said. A year had gone by and at school things were going badly. A good education gives you choices about how you go on to work and how you consume. Unskilled workers have no such options, they do what they can and buy what they are told, Mr Morgan, Tech Drawing, warned us, and he should have known.

Mam was becoming different. Eventually she had got a job with Will's mam as a dinner lady at the Juniors'.

I was on my way up the Amman Valley to where Father once took me fishing. I had Huw's old rod with me which had never caught anything, but my only thought was of retracing the steps I had taken with Father once, on a relaxed, lost afternoon when we almost became friends.

I stopped at an opening between the trees and stepped down from the riverside path. There was nowhere to sit but after having walked a while through the unfamiliar surroundings I decided that here was a good a place as any to throw out a line and, if lucky, reel in a bit of weed. I had hoped to follow Father's route but it occurred to me that the picture I had of the area was of somewhere else. It must have been a haunt from his own childhood but where was it now?

After a while I began to feel hungry. I hitched the fishing hook onto the reel and secured it into place by tensioning the gut with a half turn. I stepped up onto the path back to the village and to the first of the buses home when I saw a man come quickly down the slope between the trees towards me. He wore a waxed blue farmer's jacket, the type they wear at Carmarthenshire cattle markets. He had quickened his pace, seeing that I was about to go. I turned on the path, pretending to take no notice of him when ahead in the distance another man with a walking stick came towards me and raised it in silence as he looked up to the man who continued down the slope. I began walking towards the stick when from behind I heard a voice cry out.

'Hey, you!'

I didn't stop, I hadn't done anything and was going home. I was getting close to the walking stick who had stopped. He was older with a long clean white face and I wouldn't have imagined that the two men were together, but rather that the man coming down the hill was going for him. I heard him closing on me behind and stopped, half turning and stepping aside, expecting him to pass by but he was looking at me, having slowed down to a walk and

233

stopped in front of me. He held out his arms either side of my body to stop me from escaping. I thought of giving him a quick push and running for it but my path was blocked by the older man.

'Have they been biting for you?' Walking Stick asked as he approached, stopping at a safe distance from me while Outstretched Arms remained at the ready.

I shrugged my shoulders.

'Not even a little nibble?' he asked sarcastically.

I shrugged again in silence.

'Show some respect, will you?' Arms grunted down to me in what was a more familiar local accent.

I didn't know what they wanted of me and I thought of escape again.

'The young man's lost his voice,' Walking Stick said to the other.

'No I haven't,' I replied.

'Oh! One of them,' he said as if disappointed by my accent. 'You haven't come far then for your day's poaching?' he added.

Poaching? The word sounded ridiculous, something medieval and criminal about stealing sheep at night from farms, something nobody had bothered to do in the last hundred years, or so I imagined.

'I haven't been poaching, I just came to see if I liked fishing, that's all,' I replied surprised.

'You've been seen poaching. On my river, with that,' Walking Stick said, pointing to my rod.

I didn't say anything. I didn't know anyone could actually own a river. I thought the water was for all, falling from the sky and flowing down through valleys, taking the shortest route to the sea.

'Have you got a licence for it?' Walking Stick asked.

'Yes, of course,' I replied. It was better not to run away, perhaps they would get the police after me and it was a long way home alone. 'It's at home.'

'Ah, yes so you've got a licence. And permission for fishing on this stretch of river. Is that at home too?'

'Oh. I didn't know I needed one. I haven't been poaching, I just came to see if I liked fishing, that's all.'

'It's a serious offence. You're a very lucky young man, to be caught empty-handed,' Walking Stick went on.

'Won't catch nothing with that,' Arms said. He was more relaxed and lowered his arms to his side. 'No bait or lead or nothing,' he continued, looking down at what I carried.

I held the fishing rod out to him and let him take it to examine it more closely.

'There's a lot of trout in this river and I have to protect my rights,' Walking Stick explained.

'But the footpath is public!' I exclaimed, remembering something about the right to walk along the route of rivers.

'That may or may not be the case. It's what's in the river that is mine and without buying permission from me, well, that is poaching.'

The term sounded feudal.

'Are you from around here?' he continued.

I wasn't sure if I lied or not when I said I was, for me it was Wales and I was from it.

'From the village?' he asked, while Arms looked at me in

disbelief but didn't say a word to contradict me when I nodded.

I was also asked about my father and what he did for a living.

'He's a policeman,' I said.

'Is he? In the village? Who would that be?' he asked, turning to Arms.

'He works for the South Wales Police in Swansea,' I said. I didn't know whether he believed me or not but I was less likely to be contradicted on saying Swansea than Ammanford.

'I see. Well this is what I'll do. My gamekeeper will confiscate your rod and if you come back with your policeman on Monday I'll return it to you once I have made it clear to him what exactly fishing rights are!'

I looked around and along the path for someone who could be a gamekeeper but there was no sign of any such storybook character.

Arms pointed across to the other side of the river to the route from the village to the big house.

I had to explain that Father was away until the following weekend, the soonest I could return and then thought never to do so anyway.

'Midday Sunday, shall we call it then?' he asked and I agreed.

'And the gamekeeper?' I asked perplexed. Arms waved the rod in my face and smiled as if to say, look it's me.

On the way home I thought what to say about having no rod and of whether to return for it. I could have asked Old Tommy, who would give them a history lesson and then we would be thrown out rodless. I would have to return, carrying an excuse for Father. As the week went by, doubts cramped my stomach.

I brought up Watts-pumped mine water six days running.

I didn't tell anyone about what happened, not even Will. I told Mam that I had made a friend and lent him the rod for a week. She warned me about being tricked by strangers.

It was during that week that a recurring dream began. I would be on the landing alone in the dark, then go downstairs in search of a noise coming from out the back. I found a monster digging in the garden which turned to me, telling me to go away.

'*Cer yn ôl i'r gwely!*' it would say as I trembled at the kitchen door. Go back to bed. And I would find myself in bed again, awake.

That following Sunday I dragged myself down the gravel path drive to the landlord's house. I hoped he wasn't there, leaving someone else to hand the fishing rod over to me and at the entrance I thought of giving up and returning home.

There were four cars parked where the path opened out. I knocked on the heavy wooden front door of a huge house that seemed dead and I imagined Walking Stick living alone with chasing spirits. At first there was no answer and I was about to go, but a shadow came up to the painted glass panel in the centre of the door.

'Yes?' Walking Stick seemed surprised, but I knew he recognised me. 'Ah, you. Late, and alone I gather,' he added casually as he looked down the lane.

'My father couldn't,' I began to explain, preparing my speech.

'You had better come in.'

I followed him in through the hall to a large living room from where laughter could be heard.

It was somehow familiar to me. An impossible memory of a place I had never been and yet as strong as my very first memories in Mam's arms. Chambers of air swirled across the hallway. I could hear their voices, waves of laughter, as when Mam took me through to the lion's den of home. I wanted to turn and run as we went into the light, where they all stopped to look at me before returning their attention to their guns and dogs and glasses of chest-tightening whisky.

There were hunters at his house. Five of them with their guns, two seated and the others standing, all with glasses against the light of the large verandah window and the lawn beyond creating shadows through cigar smoke. Three dogs lay at each of their master's feet.

'This is the boy I told you about. Came alone!'

I looked round for the gamekeeper but he wasn't among them. Busy cleaning riding boots out the back, perhaps. With his tongue.

'Came alone, hey? Fearlessly independent, isn't he, I'd say,' one said, slumped in an armchair. He was the eldest of the group, thin and tired, with a blotchy birthmark raised from his forehead over onto his bald head.

'My father's bad,' I murmured. Nobody heard.

'He's just a little Taffy toe rag. Bagged something somewhat bigger last week,' another announced, the youngest of the guests, a glass of whisky in one hand, a shotgun in the other. By his long face and cultured voice he could have been the landlord's son.

'So what are we going to do with him?' Armchair asked.

'Teach him a lesson, I should think!' Shotgun suggested.

'How old are you?' A third asked, facing down to me. He was tall and very handsome, and I dubbed him Cigar.

'Thirteen,' I said.

'Looks younger!' a voice from behind me said.

'Must be the native diet. Too much bread and potatoes. It stunts the growth,' Armchair declared.

'But then he's raised to be a miner,' Shotgun added, knowing that he had been raised to tell people like me what to do.

'You know, my grandfather was a miner once!' Cigar said, turning to the others who looked at him in bewilderment. 'No, seriously. Until he sold it!' he joked and they all laughed.

The landlord left the room, closing the door behind him. I didn't bother to look at where the questions came from and stared down at the floor.

'My father's bad and couldn't come,' I said sheepishly.

'Is he? Bad?' one asked copying my voice, laughing. 'Bad at what exactly?'

I began to curse them deep inside.

If the landlord had gone to get my fishing rod he would soon return and I would be free. Meanwhile his guests began to forget me.

'Dumb animals!' one of the hunters suddenly exclaimed. He was becoming worn down by drink and dressed in state-of-the-art Victorian hunting gear. 'It eventually chewed its foot off,' he added.

They all turned to him, in silence.

'Caught in a trap!' he exclaimed.

'Oh, the hare,' Cigar said to help the others.

'Botched his foot!' the Victorian splurted.

The hare chewed through to the bone in order to be free, I thought.

'Did I ever tell you about that fox I caught?' Shotgun asked.

'Yes,' two or three replied together, dreading repetition.

'Wounded in the hind, I kept it tied up in my garage for weeks,' he went on oblivious to them, perhaps for my sake. 'Became quite the focal point in the village. Eventually died. We had grown somewhat fond of the little beast, in a way,' he added neutrally.

'Shot my own dog once!' Armchair said. 'A red setter, the best I ever...'

'One of these days I'll bring my boy with me,' Cigar said to cut him off. 'Next time perhaps.'

'Jolly good idea.'

'Yes, next time maybe, so that he can practise on one of the local girls,' he said turning to me. 'To test his spurs.'

The rest laughed.

'To show his colours. See how sticky the wicket is, you know. A few test shots to clean the barrel. I would have brought him before, to shoot, but his mother just would not have it. She's turning him into a little fairy.'

'That's what the local girls are for!' Shotgun exclaimed.

'Here, here,' some agreed.

At that moment the gamekeeper entered the room with his cap held close to his chest, interrupting their conversation.

'Ah. Sir Henry's chap,' Armchair exclaimed.

'Please, if you gentlemen are ready,' the gamekeeper began.

'Any children?' Cigar asked him with a wicked smile.

'Yes, three,' he replied innocently.

'A daughter?' Cigar continued, hardly containing himself.

The gamekeeper stood at my side close to the door where I had remained.

'*Ble mae dy dad di?*' he said whispering down, asking where my father was. 'You should've come earlier,' he then added in English, as if a late warning.

I didn't reply to him.

'How old is she?' Cigar repeated.

He knew they were all laughing at him, but he kept his composure, knowing what his job was worth.

'If you are ready,' he addressed them again. 'Sir Henry is about to leave.'

'Oh, yes,' Armchair replied. 'Shall we take the toe rag with us?' he asked the others of me.

'No, no, he's to go home,' the gamekeeper interrupted, raising his voice.

He placed a hand on my shoulder and without another word turned me around and led me out into the hallway.

'But we have to teach him a lesson!' Shotgun said as we left.

From beyond the closed door we could hear them

murmuring and laughing. The gamekeeper led me to a coatstand and pulled out my fishing rod from under some overcoats.

'You can go now,' he said handing it to me. 'And don't come back,' he added coldly as I stared at him and he turned his head away. I just stared at him.

Cigar came out into the hallway and approached us. We stood aside as he took his jacket from the stand and sat on a chair to put on some Wellington boots.

'Sir Henry could teach you fly fishing,' he said, seeing my hopeless rod. 'It will give the old bugger something to do.'

He then put on a flak jacket and went off back into the living room and out through the French windows onto the lawn, behind the others.

As we went out through the front door the gamekeeper asked me if I was really from the village.

I shook my head.

'How will you get home, then?' he asked.

'By bus,' I replied.

'Have you got enough money for the fare?' he asked.

'Yes,' I said.

He searched in his trouser pocket.

'Here,' he said as he handed me some coins. 'I've a boy your age.'

I refused the money but he gave me it all the same.

'Can I go now?' I asked and he turned without a word to enter the house to follow the hunters on their afternoon sport. I watched him close the door and I turned to walk away.

Walking quickly back, almost running, on through to where the path met the river bank back to the village I swore to myself that one day I would have my revenge on them and their kind. I slowed down, breathing and perspiring heavily and kicked at the ground as I squeezed the fishing rod in my hand. I stopped walking and began to thrash the rod in fury against the trees and bushes at my side, repeating what they had said. Minnow, Taffy toe rag, very deep, ho ho ho, bread and potatoes, while snapping the rod and cutting my hand. I lashed out more at the burning heat of my hand until I stopped, raising the wound to my face and saw it bloody and thought of what Father once said to me.

We are a conquered people.

I threw first what was left of the broken rod into the river and then the gamekeeper's pennies followed, and I felt calmer, surprised I didn't need to throw up. I resumed my journey on to the village and the first of the buses home.

There were now more people to add to my list of enemies to be cut clinically with Bonkers Bevan's old Stirling sub-machine gun. Him, rat tat tat, her, rat tat, Mr Taylor MA, Miserable Arsehole, rat tat atat tat. I would return to the house, open the door and corner them in the lounge. And then the birthmarked old bastard, rat tat atat and dead, the handsome snob, rat tara tat, Sir Henry, rat tat atat tat, and all dead, dead.

24. *1981*

Occasionally I stirred the gravy into the peas and mashed potatoes and all into an abstract mess with slow strokes of my GCC fork. I was withdrawn, my head a concrete helmet.

'Let's go for a ride,' Huw suggested. This was his first time home since I'd split with Siân.

Three months after I left the Sketty bedsit for home I found myself wearing a conventional helmet and we rode on Huw's motorbike. My head turned to one side, with air gushing into the cave of my mouth. Huw popped pills, one at a time from a plastic packet in his leather jacket pocket. He gave me one, putting it in my mouth as we rode and told me not to drop off.

Huw's biker mantra was to get there, wherever, in two hours or never. The drugs he took made him feel as if he were travelling light. He had long dark greasy hair and almost never washed. Nobody could say if he ever had a real beard, it just grew naturally until someone would take pity and shave it off for him.

We eventually turned onto a mud track tunnelled by high branches and wound our way down through dense wood to a small stream and a footbridge which barely took the weight of the bike as we crossed. On the other side a rusted, battered caravan manned the entrance to a grass clearing in a field deep in the forest. Huddled together in the centre next to motorcycles and a few small cars were a mixture of camping tents. There were small plastic-sheet huts, their roofs weighed down under pools, and attempts at tepees, some with fires and a lot of coughing at their centre.

'This is Maesmadrynbach,' Huw informed me as we dismounted his bike. 'It's one of two tepee villages in Powys. The other is really a village, like, and only tepees, but we are trying our best. What you think?'

So this was Broth's tribe, I thought. Camp site of those amateur fungus experts that stayed beyond the autumn, those that had nowhere to move on to. Once a fortnight they would organise an expedition and all go down to sign-on in Brecon.

'Have you got a wigwam?' I asked him.

'Tepee!' he corrected me.

He pointed at his two-man, conventional tent.

He had taken me up to the village on my nineteenth birthday for the beginning of about a week, perhaps less for time is so imprecise when you are permanently stoned.

I took mostly pot and barbiturates and felt like I had permanent flu, it was all part of his treatment. Most of the village's inhabitants took drugs. Most called themselves ecologists, all were doing their own thing. With dogs that did their own thing. Some took no notice, all wanted to be noticed. Doing your own thing meant lying around, playing guitar, coughing and the like, and sharing all, even each other, taking what you wanted when you wanted. Relationships were formed, lovers for eternity or the following Friday, whichever came first.

One woman, the mother of the tribe, made marijuana tea in a big iron kettle on a fire outside her tepee, which she drank all day. Her tent was the nearest thing to a centre of reunions, with tea-drinking at five, six and around the clock.

I didn't want to be there at first but at least nobody seemed to take notice of me, nor mind if I went straight to bed to hide. Straight to Huw's small leaky tent, wrapped in a wiry blanket, using my pair of jeans rolled into a pillow and something he popped into my mouth to help me sleep.

I awoke at an early breeze brushing against my bare ankles. I turned round and looked out, staring at the wet grass ahead of me, the rest of the village just out of sight and quiet all but for the distant song of a woman's approaching voice.

The monosyllablic tune closed in and with pieces of crumbly emotional cement still stuck to me, I thought to close the tent flap down over the entrance, when a pair of bare feet planted themselves in front. I looked up at multicoloured baggy trousers and a tie-dyed shirt.

'Do you like it here too?'

'It's like watching green paint dry,' I answered.

'You what? Can I come in?' she asked.

I didn't reply but made room as best I could as she squeezed herself inside the tent, lying down between me and Huw's immobile body, her head next to his feet, the three of us staring out, two faces and a pair of holey socks.

She was young and had run away from home. She was slightly plump with almost shoulder-length fair hair, a ring in her nose, and nail-bitten hands that nervously played around her mouth as she spoke.

'I just dig dawn, and sunset,' she said after a while. 'It's something, you know, spiritual. Want to see my tattoo?' She brushed her hair away from the side of her head and pointed to a small red and black butterfly, inked into her neck. 'You're Huw's kid brother, aren't you?'

'Huw? Is that what's he's called? We met yesterday morning and had eloped by midday! We haven't had time for names, but I've learnt that his feet stink!' I answered.

'You what? You're a funny one! Huw didn't say you were like that.'

She began to talk about eastern religions. 'There's no school vicars promising afterlife,' Butterfly said. 'Buddhism isn't just a religion, it's a philosophy for real life, meditation brings us back to nature. I want to touch the stars, be at one with all. Take Tibet! It's hundreds and hundreds of years old, wow. I'd just love to go there. Can you do mantra chants in Welsh?'

'I think it's the only thing we can do these days,' I replied. 'Om is wm, I guess,' I added, drawing out the sounds.

247

'Wm,' she practised, seriously, in a deep tone.

'Wm, wmm,' she continued. 'Yer, it's music. The Welsh are an old people too, aren't they?' I paused. 'What music do you like?' she added

I was always reluctant to answer such questions, usually making up the answers as I went along.

'Loud,' I replied. 'Except in the mornings!'

'You know people by the music they like, don't you think?' she commented. 'I want my own tepee, one day. It's my dream, and I'm gonna ride across the States on a Harley Davy, and visit Jim Morrison's grave, and fly and...'

'Where are you from?' I interrupted her.

'From Man.'

'Isle of?'

'Manchester,' she corrected me.

I let her talk because I had to and didn't have the heart to tell her to go away; she was friendly and made an effort, though I was as bitter as a real ale brewery. Butterfly eventually tried to get me up and out of the tent to socialise. 'Come and meet folk,' she said.

'Oh, I don't think so. I don't really feel like it,' I said.

'Nobody's up yet anyway,' she reasoned.

I began to wish I wasn't there again.

'I shouldn't have come!'

'Where do you want to be?'

'Nowhere.'

'But you are nowhere, silly. In the middle of nowhere!'

We went over to Tribe Mother's exaggerated kettle. Butterfly lifted the lid off and looked down into it. 'Do you want some cold tea?' she asked. If anything I had hoped for a bit of breakfast, but was to get stoned instead.

She went into Mother's tepee, the biggest and best built of the attempts and returned with a handful of crumbly biscuits for me.

'Marijuana cookies!' she announced.

It began to pour down and we went to her plastic shack until it passed. Her home was like a very cheap, soft spacecraft that would readily be blown away in a strong breeze. She began her meditation with a slow drawn-out abdominal 'wm, wm' chant and the rain fell noisily, clapping down onto the plastic sheets above us.

The first heads of the other villagers began slowly to peak out of their shelters, most to return to sleep, or to think of doing nothing until the rain eased off in the early afternoon.

Once out of her shanty refuge I went to look for Huw, taking careful steps, my memory absently leaping and losing itself. Tepee Mother called at me as I walked. I turned to face a big, strong, middle aged woman with long grey hair let loose over half her back, speaking to me in a Yorkshire accent. I pointed to myself in question.

'Managed to escape, lovey?' she asked. 'You must be Huw's kid brother.'

Huw, I wondered, thinking that I might have been looking for him, saying to myself to take it easy, relax, the effect will pass eventually. I stood immobile at the woman staring at me. Mother suddenly waved at my direction and I pointed at myself again. She continued waving and I turned to look behind me at a woman walking across the field towards the village.

I felt like a solitary pawn in the middle of a chessboard being attacked from all sides by stronger pieces. It will pass, I told myself. It comes and goes in waves. Take deep breaths and don't worry.

The woman approached carrying a gift of flowers. She waved and gave me a daffodil as she passed.

'One for you,' she said, moving on to Tepee Mother as I stared at her. 'Two for you,' she said to Mother.

The visitor had a clear complexion, sunny blonde hair, and was well dressed in Laura Ashley's collection for slim ex-hippies. She obviously had money and was probably into ecology and ancient mysticism. Her humour, though, prevented her from seeming freaky to me. She brought a sense of life to the place, sun after the storm and flowers from her garden. Soon other villagers were out of their homes and talking to her around the kettle. Too clean to be trusted, I would have thought but she was treated as a present from the forest.

When she turned to face me momentarily I realised I was not dreaming under the influence of tea and cookies and wished I was invisible. I went to Huw's tent to hide away. Huw had got up and left, taking his bike with him. His treatment was to get me stoned and abandoned.

In the evening Butterfly came and asked if I wanted to come and have some soup with the rest. I said I just wanted to sleep. She must have seen I was hungry for she returned with a bowl for me. As Butterfly spoon-fed me in the darkness of the tent she told me of Mother, of how they were all her children. She helped people with their problems, she had helped some off heroin. Some stayed.

'Shame you didn't really meet Laura!' she suddenly added. 'She lives in a house off the main road nearby. You'd like her, you would. Maybe tomorrow.'

Soon there were loud wild calls from the night for Butterfly to leave. She retrieved the spoon from my lips and put down the bowl, stuck her head out of the tent and shouted out angrily. 'Shut your arse hole, I'll come when I'm ready, you fucked-up junkie biker.'

Bringing her face back into the tent she resumed speaking to me in a calm voice but with a hand to her mouth biting her nails. 'Laura's the only one who doesn't mind us being here,' she said as outside the calls continued.

'Fuckin' come out now, you slag. Fuck you,' the voice insulted her.

Butterfly waited a few tactful seconds and decided to leave. 'I've got to go and see the Führer.'

'Getting off on his dick, eh? And what about me, bitch?' we heard coming from outside.

'He's not going to come and stab me in the middle of the night, is he?' I asked after her.

It must have been good there once, one long dry weekend when, despite the flies and gnat bites, they felt alive, free and, at the end of their first ever piss-up, at one with nature. Then later it rained, day after day, and damp and coughing they felt reality hit them.

I got up the next afternoon after having fantasised about shaving, washing and sleeping in a real warm bed. I rubbed at my eyes and went out to urinate close to the tent, just out of sight of a group gathered around the kettle that included Butterfly, Mother and Laura. Huw had disappeared and I decided that I would throttle him with his throttle cable when I next saw him.

I went over to them and tried to sound cheerful.

'Sorry about last night, like,' a boy who came to my side apologised. It was the Welsh biker who had shouted at Butterfly. He was a lot younger than he sounded, no more than seventeen. He stood next to me in waxy torn jeans, smiling through unshaved baby fluff which he scratched at with long oily nails. He probably lived on a mixture of beer and insomnia and would move on if he could ever fill his petrol tank.

'Oh, that's alright,' I said.

'But you were trying to take her away from me!' he added. 'Mind you I can't blame you, goes with the place, like. This lot can't even pronounce the name,' he continued before I could object to his jealousy. 'I'm from Llanuwchllyn,' he laughed.

Butterfly moved a few paces towards us, bringing Laura along. 'Come meet Huw's brother,' Butterfly said to her.

Laura looked like someone who slept in a real bed, who shaved her legs, washed her face and took a bath in hot water. She had money that afforded her a milky look. She might crack the cement of a lost failed lover in a forgotten field.

Tribe Mother closed in. 'Tea, anyone?'

'I wouldn't mind some real tea,' I replied timidly.

'Oh, it's all very real, lovey,' Mother replied.

'Yes, but it's a bit early for me to be drinking very real tea. Haven't you got any boring old real tea?' I said to her.

'I have a kettle at home,' Laura said to me.

I asked her if that was an invitation and she asked if anyone else wanted to come along. I wished she hadn't. Butterfly hesitated and decided to stay and fight with the biker and have some very real tea. To my relief the two of us finally left alone, crossing the creaking rotting footbridge, one cautiously after the other. I asked her about the abandoned caravan.

'Oh, that. It was here before me. Mother had the ingenuity to recycle the seats into her tepee. They've been here for about two years now.'

'And how did they get those two cars into the field?'

'I've really no idea! I suppose we'll have to ask them.'

'A minor miracle they got them down the lane, let alone across the stream!'

'Yes. I don't really know anyone well here,' she said.

'A visitor to the area, are you? You know, holiday home or something?' I asked.

'No, I live here. Moved with my husband four years ago,' she replied.

'I can only imagine people coming to live here to admire the rain or do a bit of fighter jet spotting,' I said. She laughed. As we walked down the lane Huw passed us, speeding on his bike. He stopped and turned round, coming back to us slowly with a big grin on his face. 'I suppose you know this one, do you?' I asked her.

'Alright?' he said as he came to a stop at our side.

'Where the hell have you been?' I asked.

'Shopping!' he replied, pulling a prepared joint and a few blue pills from his pocket, which he gave me.

He then turned and rode off with no further word.

'We're the last of the primitive Celtic druids,' I said to Laura as we began walking again, looking at what he had given me.

'Do you summon up the dead with that?' she asked smiling, but I imagined she didn't approve.

'No, it summons us up when we feel dead,' I replied.

We walked the rest of the way to her house in silence. In silence all but for the occasional unintended grumble coming from my stomach. I popped one of the pills thinking that it was something more solid than nothing. And did you eat well bach, I imagined my Mam asking me if I were ever to get home. Small blue beans, I could have replied.

We heard the occasional car sweep by on the main road when she led me down a short grass path that led to the back garden of her house. An old golden retriever sleeping on a mat outside the kitchen door awoke to greet us, head bowed and tail swishing as it moved towards us. In her kitchen she began to make me tea and toast, explaining how they, in the plural, had converted the two-floor farm house. It was bright, spacious, centrally heated, and had wood everywhere. All time and money, I gathered.

'It took us two years. I'm a book indexer, and it doesn't matter where I work. Here it's ideal!' she said.

As I scoffed down the buttered toast I asked if I could take a bath. She led me upstairs; I followed apologetically as I thought of warming my tired weak bones in a tub of scolding water.

'Wow, carpeted floor and a radiator! It must be four times the size of the one we have at home,' I said.

'There's a spare razor here somewhere if you want to shave,' she pointed out.

There were no visible signs of a man having used the room, I noticed, as she searched in a mirror cupboard above the sink.

When I came downstairs an hour later I found her in the living room seated at a desk covered in papers.

'I've got to index a book on the Dutch economy in the seventeenth and eighteenth centuries. One really does learn a lot!' she said turning to me.

'I'd better leave you to get on with your work.'

'No, I'm just eyeing what I'll have to do. It came in the post this morning. I'm still finishing a text on Central American birds translated from the German. I can return to it this evening. Would you like another cup of tea?'

She seemed to really want me to stay and with her husband not there something dark inside me thought of what it would be like to hold and caress a woman again.

She offered me an armchair and a glass of wine. I popped another pill and offered her the joint I held out, hoping she would give me a light. She refused and went to find a box of matches. We talked as I drank and smoked alone. She didn't seem to mind my vices but then again she was probably making an effort to be liberal and open-minded.

'I have a friend in London translating Confucius into Welsh!' she said. 'It's rather amusing. She's interested in proverbs in general.'

'The Latin version of Confucius is Confusion, isn't it?' I joked, feeling relaxed for the first time in months.

She laughed and I found myself laughing with her. She noticed that I was stoned. I became suddenly paranoid. I felt she noticed I did everything wrong, coming with her, eating her toast, using her bathroom, saying stupid things. I became dizzy, the room spinning round and she continued talking. I vomited, bending my head down over the side of the armchair, retching over her clean, almost new carpet.

When I was finished she placed a hand on my back as I gulped in air exhaustedly. When it was all over she helped me up to the bathroom, cleaned me with a damp sponge and led me into a bedroom and closed the curtains.

'You'll be alright,' she said to reassure me. 'You can sleep it off here.'

I lay on the bed and daydreamed, seeing small human forms dance in the pattern of the curtains, a mocking performance. I closed my eyes to them but felt dizzy again, gripping at the blanket under me, resisting the spinning world until deep sleep overtook me.

Early the next morning under the sleepy eye of the golden retriever, I left the house and walked back to Broth's green-grey, damp-morning tribe.

To my surprise he was there. He hadn't gone to bed yet.

'Alright?' he asked sitting alone in the entrance to his tent.

'No,' I replied. 'I've caught something. Think I've got the flu.'

He was always coming and going but mostly gone without a word, always needing to be on the move. A wonder he could move at all with all he took. While Mother was the laid-back soul of the village, Huw made it run. He scavenged for wood, went to buy drugs and food. He was its heart, the pulse that didn't want it all to end. All the village lacked was a brain, and good weather.

I sat next to him and he gave me one of two tiny green-coloured paper squares he held. He put the other in his mouth and I looked at him puzzled.

'Write a note on the back of it, if you wants!'

'Tastes of paper,' I exclaimed, sucking on it.

'It is paper, mostly,' he replied. 'Liberty Bells are the best: mushrooms, they are. That's why we're here after all, like. Best time is autumn but damp springs can be OK. The thing with mushrooms are you don't know what effect they've got. You know, you picks a few and nothing, then you comes across a really weenie tiny one and you're out of your mind. These acid tabs are just the right dose for travelling without moving, dreaming without sleeping, seeing without opening your eyes.'

I swallowed the LSD-impregnated paper tablet.

'Passed a village dance last night,' he said. 'Popped in for a quick drink and watch the local kids turn up on their tractors, like. Should have seen them! Some with a girlfriend standing on the foot perch thing as they drove up to park outside. Neat! An old bloke asked me if I was the bouncer. Can you imagine, like?' he added smiling, nodding his head slowly. He was then silent for a while, almost always on the point of saying something, a timid child trying to articulate half-developed thoughts.

'I believes in the nothingness!' he declared eventually.

257

I asked him for a definition.

'The nothingness is when you don't know what you wants, who you is, like. When you are lost. It's like running out of petrol in the middle of nowhere.'

There were only three destinations in his life, nowhere, somewhere else or Mam's.

'It's like the tank being empty inside...'

'Hungry?' I asked.

'No, mun. Like dead, but you don't know it. Like having started but you don't know where the finish is. It has a sound, an ear-aching silence. You know, sometimes it's as if I almost don't exist.'

I said I didn't know what he was talking about. I asked if he was in love. 'No, mun. Come off it like!' he splurted mockingly.

He must have been affected by Father. And he didn't know who he was. Geographically he was lost inside and the drugs took his mind to some other destination. To my mind Huw had seemed a child running away to the circus and returning three days later with other plans. There in the village he had somewhere, he had a damp blanket and others who needed him to go and do the shopping.

He moved to lie down on his blanket inside the tent and I to lie face up on the grass outside. I began to daydream, ordinarily at first then I imagined it raining coloured musical notation, dissected songs of chattering magpies, mantras and butterfly wings in flight, the 'cha cha wm wosh' parts of a tepee opera falling from the sky until I felt real raindrops hit my eyelids. Crashes of mercury running off the sides of my nose, around my mouth before I began to lift off the ground, floating in the water, with city streets around me flooded halfway up the doorways. But I wasn't there, I said. I was in the countryside. Perhaps I had drifted down back home. My fear of water returned and I panicked and had to suffer the nightmare until the effects of the drug wore off or until it stopped raining. I tried to call out and then again cried, heavy air drowning my lungs, my chest full of tears.

A girl's voice told me to relax. I was safe, it was only a bad trip and I would survive, accept it, the voice said. Butterfly who liked me, Butterfly who I ignored.

'Come, sip some tea, it'll make you feel better,' she said.

I couldn't move, nor open my eyes but soon she was back and raised my head up from the grass to help me sip the infusion.

After the tea I began dreaming and floated on my back in the air over the field, a balloon held on a thin string by Butterfly and Huw below until it broke and I wandered high above the field, drifted over Laura's house and then slowly descended to land next to the main road where I sank into deep warm mud.

It took me a day and a half to recover. In that time, Broth and his bike had fallen into the stream, crossing the bridge that collapsed under them and he had to take the engine apart and became depressed at his failure to get it started again. He had to go and sign on with the rest by catching a bus on the main road that passed twice a week. He must have been indignant, thinking of his mantra, two hours or never, on the back seat, a little ticket in his hand.

The following days and nights the villagers went on with their lives. Playing dominoes on LSD, the pieces untouched after eight hours, rain adding to the self-regenerating soup, the dogs on permanent heat among the emptied beer cans, the fuckin' biker keeping us awake looking for butterflies as she looked for spiritual inspiration with others with long faces and diarrhoea after learning the hard way about toadstools.

Occasionally a fighter jet too close above passed overhead, frightening the sheep and transporting us all from the forgotten medieval field back to the end of the twentieth century. After one jet thundered past, Tepee Mother told me she was worried that space rubbish could fall over them. Bits of satellite, NASA rocket parts and all the cosmic bolts and wirings circling hundreds of miles above us.

Butterfly eventually told me more of Tepee Mother. She had been battered first by an alcoholic father and then by an alcoholic husband, had escaped to live working the streets in Sheffield before prison and then she found Wales and marijuana and had a role in life. Childless and reborn she mothered young hippies and planned to be buried there in her field.

I felt like a plastic bag blown about in a breeze. I still thought of Siân. I went to see Laura in the evening with the excuse of apologising for having frightened her dog with my retching. I knocked on the glass kitchen door and she welcomed me in with a smile. I made my apologies and she introduced me to a man who was sitting in the armchair I had vomited over.

'This is Ian, my ex,' she said to me.

He waved a hand up in salute but made no further effort in welcoming the dirty, drug-soaked teenager standing in the entrance to what used to be his living room. Guessing he wouldn't understand, I said how do you do in Welsh. He left after putting the finishing touches to a quarrel with his ex-wife.

I told Laura that I wanted to go home. She didn't seem to hear me.

'He's just left his girlfriend. She was not what he was looking for, he said. I know what he means! Poor girl! Men!' she went on. 'If you're not pretty they take no notice. Personality doesn't come into it. At any party the woman that's the centre of attention is always the beautiful one, without having to do anything. Her presence is enough to have them around her like flies. A normal woman in such circumstances has to work twice as hard just to get noticed and once you are over forty forget it altogether. It's a young woman's world!'

Laura herself was in the group of the beautifully blessed but probably felt borderline at her age.

'But is it only men's fault?' I asked. 'When was the last time you heard of a woman spending hours getting ready to go out on a Friday night by reading Sartre?' It made her smile. 'It works both ways. Women themselves are attracted to handsome men. They claim it's not as important for them but with women it's not just body, it's appearance they look at in men. If I were rich and dressed so, could afford a suntan and a fashionable haircut I'd probably have more success with older women than I do now.'

'Older women?' she asked, intrigued.

'Yes, I'm attracted to older women,' I replied, hoping I got across the hint. 'It's relative of course. When I was fourteen an older woman was eighteen or nineteen. Now I'm nineteen I...'

'Nineteen! So very young still.'

'Young! I feel past it!'

'And not having much success, you were saying,' she prompted with a smile.

'I'm seen as unemployable. Women of my class are more likely to like me, but a woman with style wouldn't even look at me twice.'

'I'm saying that with men it's being pretty that's important, and you're saying that with women it's all about class struggle!'

'Well for a man a woman is attractive regardless of her class. Not the case with many women, or am I wrong?'

'For a woman, usually, a man is attractive if he is interesting, intelligent, amusing, takes notice and a bit of care with the woman he is talking to. Even if he's fat and unemployed or an extremely thin aristocrat. But yes, first impressions are rather physical, aren't they? For us too. It's just that men take it to the extreme. A dumb blonde piece is his ideal.'

I felt relaxed talking to Laura, forgetting I had gone there because I wanted her. We continued into the night over a bottle of red wine until she suggested it was time for bed. She showed me to the spare room I had slept in before and we said our good nights.

I began to dream I was back in Sir Henry's house to pick up my fishing rod. The hunters dragged me out onto the lawn, the gaming dogs pushing past me on their eager run to be first down through the bottom of the garden into thick wood. My tears began though I tried not to sob. 'I'll tell my father!'

Once among the trees three men surrounded me when the others said they were going after hares. They pushed me from one to the next until I was dizzy and fell to my knees. The one with the flak jacket knelt down to face me and then knocked me over onto my back with a push to my chest.

I could picture their faces for the first time, faces staring down, holding me down. One a very old face, a birthmark on its forehead. A worn face smelling of whisky and smoke, wide-eyed and smiling.

'He's like a little girl,' Flak Jacket said.

He pulled at my clothes, my jersey up to my shoulder blades, my trousers down. His head moved out of view, his arm close to my eyes, as the other two helped turn me over. Then I saw only the ground, dirt and rotting leaves in my face, the taste of country damp in my mouth, the sound of a gun dog sniffing around me and a stabbing pain in my backside.

Flak Jacket lay on top of me a few moments, the full weight of him squeezing my tight chest before lifting himself off in silence. As the other two walked away he remained behind, sweating and puffing for air as he got up.

I shouted out in my sleep.

'Ssh. It's alright,' I heard and woke shaking and

263

sweating with Laura sitting at my side on the bed. 'It's just a dream.'

I couldn't speak and closed my eyes again, feeling embarrassed and useless. Laura began stroking my hair until I was calm and found sleep again.

The next morning I awoke to find her sleeping at my side. Her body inches away from me. She must have smelt nice before she smelt of me. With that thought I got up and went to take a bath. On returning I saw her on the landing, dressed and suggesting breakfast.

'I got up with the idea to wash and return to you in bed!' I eventually got the nerve to admit to her over coffee and strawberry jam toast in her kitchen.

'I got up to have breakfast,' she replied.

'I suppose I'm too young for you. You were at my side in bed to comfort a child, not a man, I suppose?'

'I felt dozy after a while and you were harmless. And yes, you're too young for me.'

'Oh, come on,' I objected. 'If you don't want me, all good and well. I have no illusions anyway, because of class!'

'There you go, class again! But really, I'd fear a younger man leaving me for a younger woman.'

'Unlike a man your age?' I asked. 'It's a question of confidence, not age.'

'I'd feel embarrassed if seen with such a youngster.'

'How old are you?' I asked.

'Forty,' she replied.

'I thought you were thirty!'

'Oh, thanks for the compliment but after a few weeks

with me you'll think I was fifty and begin to miss girls your age!'

'You're being unfair,' I repeated.

'What do you say if you change the conversation and I drive you home?'

An hour later we left the golden retriever in the garden and got into her car. She said she'd let my brother know my change of plans. I told her I had already changed them even more. I'd try to get a job or go to London and try my luck there, or something. Anything.

After passing through the Swansea Valley she pointed out a messy muck foam floating white over a low land sprawl below the road.

'What's that?' Laura asked.

'It's the River Tawe,' I replied.

Dropping me off at the Gorseinon turn-off on the M4 we parted with a kiss. An innocent kiss.

25. *1982*

It was closing time on Gorseinon and goodbye and thanks for all the overpriced ale, the long slippery glasses, the dizzy spells over a stained toilet bowl and the furry-tongued beasts of the morning after. But just when I was adrift there came along the soothing tone of an Australian woman's voice.

'It's on me,' she said as she served me a pint of bitter, refusing the money I was trying to hand over. 'You haven't been coming to see me lately,' she added and I discovered that she had thought about me after all that time.

'Well if it isn't going to cost me anything from now on,' I replied after my initial surprise. She hadn't been in my thoughts for about four or five years.

'Will used to keep me informed. Didn't he tell you? You two, you're a funny act. You talk like old men,' she said and moved along the polished bar to continue serving other customers.

I wondered what Susie was doing there, lost in Old South Wales in her late twenties or early thirties. I supposed it was important to her to be away from somewhere else. When she came back along the bar she commented on how we had never run into each other outside of her working hours, in the street, at parties. A shame, I said.

'Then again I work from morning to night,' she explained. 'But at least it helps me forget Australia.'

'But has it forgotten you?'

'What do you mean?' she asked.

'I remember you saying that you used to spend your wages on phoning your boyfriend back home.'

'Oh, that,' she said as she turned to look up at the telly where, eight thousand miles away, Harrier jump jets were being counted out and in again. 'Yer, it was just an excuse I used to come up with,' she said, turning towards me again but without looking at my face. 'To put myself out of bounds, I suppose. Now I use a cheap imitation wedding ring. Look!'

'You shouldn't tell me these things.'

'Oh? I always thought you were harmless,' she laughed as she went to ring the last orders bell.

She was flirting with me now. Before it had been the virgin schoolboy trying to impress his way into her underwear.

'It always seems to be closing time in here,' I said after her, and drinkers at my side murmured ay ay in grunted agreement.

'If things get worse in the effing Falklands that fucking Thatcher might close the pubs altogether,' one of them said to no one in particular.

All evening the drinkers had been looking up at the war in the corner above as Susie took orders, quickly serving pints and making a mental note of them, all at once. She counted them out and counted them in too.

'Well I'd better be going, I suppose,' I said to her and began to finish my drink.

'Where are you off to?' she asked as if I had midnight plans.

'Oh, I don't know,' I replied without thinking.

'Oh, I'm going there too, can I come along?'

'We could go for a walk,' I suggested. 'What do you fancy?' She shrugged her shoulders as she stared at me. 'Today on offer we've got headline-flavoured fish and chips eaten out of yesterday's newsprint under the acid drizzle.' I was performing. 'Bus-shelter snogging against slag-heap scenery, being chased by fox terriers with rabied dreams or we could get arrested for loitering and breathing after hours. Take your pick. If I had the money I'd take you to Paris, but it's not the time of year for it really, is it?'

'Do you fancy a cup of tea instead?' she asked, her smile gone.

We went to her bedsit above the pub. I followed her into a back room behind the bar, out into the hallway and up the darkly lit stairs, four steps behind her, her backside at eye level above me. I had only ever seen her from the waist up before.

When we entered she saw me shiver from nerves; after

all this time I was unprepared for being with her. She said she'd switch on the electric fire that sat in what had been the fireplace, spitting at the dust and wisps of hair it scalded, leaving a whiff of burnt pork fat.

'It's not cold really. It's psychological,' I exclaimed and moved forward to take her in my arms. She reacted by moving away, telling me to slow down.

The room had the sour smell of moulding wallpaper, yellowing around where she cooked. The windows were stained with watermarks and car exhaust from the road below and the worn carpet was pierced with cigarette burns. Her smile was the only thing of herself she had added to the room; without that it would have been a place to hang yourself.

'It's not much but they don't charge me rent,' she said as she crouched over her bedside table, her face almost touching it, her hands to an eye.

'You should charge them!' I replied.

'In a sense I do. They pay me to work here after all.'

We talked about her job, about books and dreams, as I sat on her bed, she opposite me on a stool in front of the fire, occasionally getting up to make tea. After the third mug she began talking of her boyfriends, concluding that most Welsh men were machines that converted drink into sperm. She told me how she had come down from London on a weekend visit with the idea of looking for her origins and had stayed ever since. Prior to his transportation she had an ancestor from Carmarthenshire, a Watkins. Perhaps he could have been a prison guard or an ordinary colonist.

I asked her about Australia. I could imagine people

leaving here for there but who wanted to leave the sun for the rain?

'I'm from a lost rural village,' she began to explain, looking alternately up at me and then away to the floor as she spoke. 'Where nothing ever happens. Well, a few girls can expect to get gang-rammed or battered. I lived in Sydney for a few years to get away from it all, serving drinks in a nightclub, working on commission. But it wasn't what you might think. It was a normal, dead-end place, all you had to do was smile, add and subtract. One of the girls there was going to Earls Court and I went along on the adventure, thinking first London and then New York, but if you haven't got money you have to work. Or marry. But I don't want to be trapped, possessed. I don't think I'll ever return, to Australia I mean; if I leave it'll be for the States. But to do what? Pull pints and listen to drunks there too?'

Anxiety settled as she trailed off into silence.

'You could do something else, couldn't you?' I suggested after a while.

'What? Another way to get money? Money for what, to work to spend and work again because you have nothing at the end of it all? Sometimes I wonder what's happening to my life. Oh, don't get me wrong. It's not all hangups and worries, you know. I like it here, there's no movement, it's constant. I know that tomorrow will be like today, if I want it to be. You know, that's important to me.'

I had never seen her depressed before, it must have been for my benefit in the intimacy of the damp that was curling down the ends of the wallpaper. Before, she had always been the blue-eyed Aussie blonde piece but behind the sun there was a tired life. I imagined she had run away from what might have happened to her, like the rest of the girls in some dusty village.

I said I thought that because she was beautiful, she had the freedom to do whatever she wanted.

'You have to learn to become a good whore to get what you want out of life. Me, I don't want anything, just time to think and a bit of affection,' she said.

'And love?' I asked.

'Love? Love lasts two weeks. It's pretending for a while that what we want, what we need, is that man in front of us. The rest is just nostalgia for those first few days.'

'Oh, I don't know. It was all very serious for me when I fell in love,' I argued. 'The end of it all nearly finished me off for good!'

'But breaking up is a bit like the flu, isn't it?' she said cynically. 'It seems bad at the time but you always get over it, eventually. And it doesn't even leave a nasty cough!'

'And desire?' I asked.

'We are frustrated beings that look for consolation in others.'

'Me, I've had a life marred by being pursued by attainable women,' I said hoping to cheer her up. 'I was almost handsome once!'

'Once! You mean all those years ago?' She reminded me of someone else and I felt a chill walk up my spine.

'Yes. Now I'm only just about alright in a bad light.'

'You know,' she said. 'Welsh and Australian drunks are the same. Red-nosed, rowdy and incomprehensible after a few.'

I said I thought drink made us more articulate.

'Or that's only what you think when you're drunk and confident. Social drinking is a macho thing. Women, housewives mostly, keep their alcoholism to themselves, they sip alone in the kitchen and slowly fall to pieces.'

She asked me if my mother drank.

'Only social sherry. Mind you she can get drunk on tea. Have you ever seen that?'

'They never come in and order tea.'

'You don't serve it by the pint then?'

'Perhaps we should if your mum can get drunk on it. Why don't you bring her round for a drink?'

'I will one day,' I replied, thinking of when I used to try to get her out of the house to do the shopping.

Humour, as ever, relaxed me. Then she asked about Parry.

'He loved her, I supposed. Falling out of love, that mild bout of flu he had, turned him into a psychopath.'

'Oh, you're not catching me out with that trick,' she said, annoyed. 'Being lovesick doesn't turn you into a maniac! There were deeper causes, surely!'

'Well he was a bit unstable before. At the time I just thought he was wild from all that testosterone. But breaking up finally made him go off his head. You know, he tried to commit suicide before the trial. The version I heard was that he hit himself repeatedly on the head with a metal bar.'

'I suppose he'll be in prison a long time?'

'At her Majesty's pleasure!'

'He was under age, wasn't he? I mean to be condemned like an adult. Britain must be the only civilised country where kids can get condemned for life.'

'Here we're capable of anything!' I replied. 'Once they used to put pigs on trial, for eating crops!'

'Yer? When?'

'Oh, in the late Middle Ages. And up to the seventeenth century, along with witches they burnt black cats and mischievous goats.'

As we talked on I thought she would ask me to go at any moment and I asked her what the time was to test the ground. She didn't reply directly but after a pause she eventually asked if I wanted to spend the night. I looked at her bedside alarm clock thinking I had spent most of it already. I got up from the bed and knelt on the floor at her side.

'Wait until dawn comes,' she said to me and went to make another tea.

I got up from my knees and returned to her bed, lying down to watch her walk across the room. I asked her if she would bunker up next to me until the war was over.

Together on the bed facing each other on our sides, talking in whispers, she asked what an orgasm was for me and I wondered for a few moments if she'd ever experienced one. She wanted to know if I thought it was the same for men as for women. I said it was physical and emotional, affecting the body and the brain.

'It's funny,' she said. 'The imagery we create in trying to explain what is just an animal experience. Crashing sea waves or buying a new pair of shoes...'

I stopped her with a kiss.

The waiting ended as the first rays of the spring dawn came in through the window, adding a new light to her bedsit.

She began to clumsily take off her blouse until I helped her and our four hands took off the rest of our clothes without moving from our sides. And we finally made love.

Running up a shaded hillside, you're panting heavily to reach the top and then you lose your footing; your stomach feels as if you're being driven over a humpbacked bridge, but you don't fall but reach the top of the hillside. The brightness of the sunlight hits you full in the face from over the other side and you feel like a child who's just been given the present he had been longing for and the joy takes your breath, leaving only a whisper and a pause in the pounding of your heart and your skin is raw flesh to the touch.

Just an animal experience. The animal inside of me licked its chops.

Outside, below, workers were closing their front doors, off for the day. As morning came, what remained of the passing night was pushing down onto me.

She had wanted to see first if I was interested in her, in who she was and how she thought while hoping I was patient enough to listen while she told me. That was my first-night litmus test. After she set the alarm clock we fell into half-conscious numbness out of time, our legs entwined, strands of her hair against the tip of my nose, her mouth against my throat, her breath first a wave of long warm calm air and then again nothing.

'Susie,' I said to myself. I like the sound of her name. A new beginning, I thought and then I slept.

When I left her flat in the morning, just before opening time, after sharing her breakfast, I walked the streets home, druggy from tiredness. I felt that I still missed Siân.

Sex and everything with her was so easy and straight-forward. Everything turned her on and she came whenever I entered her. With Susie, I felt I'd always have to be patient if we were to build a relationship together.

I went to bed and slept until late in the afternoon with the impression of Susie pressed against my skin.

That evening I met up with Will, Dai Panda and Karen at the park as planned. While the spring sunlight lasted it was pleasant enough for us to sit on the grass drinking a flagon of cider and talk of war and revolution. Will was cautious as usual, he never wanted us to go too far, while Dai Panda on the other hand was playing around with the fantasy of stealing a double-barrelled shotgun from Karen's grandfather. Will would have none of it and insisted we discuss the possibility of getting caught. Karen emphasised the discipline of never talk and Dai Panda and I agreed.

'Anyway it could only ever be for vandalism and we can expect a fine or a suspended sentence,' she said.

'The pigs still send people to prison for trivial stuff,' I protested. 'Better not to get picked up in the first place.'

'Better still, not do anything to provoke getting picked up,' Will added.

'So we're just going to paint a few slogans and that's that, is it?' Karen said angrily. 'And we're going to bring down the capitalist empire? I might as well go and hibernate. Wake me up when Thatcher's gone!' She motioned to Dai Panda for him to pass her the bottle he was warming in his hands and took a long gulp.

'What we've been doing is better than nothing, isn't it?

Can't you see it's impossible to try to take them on all by ourselves,' Will reasoned, pausing to light a cigarette he had just carefully rolled. 'For the time being we have to limit ourselves.'

'The usual excuse of waiting until better times. Maybe until another seven centuries of English domination has passed, hey?' Karen complained.

'No mun,' Will exclaimed. 'The arrests that have already taken place are directed at destroying republican thought, so that the Taffies know their place. We won't do anybody any good in prison.'

'So we do nothing, you say?' I asked.

'We have to wait, can't you see that?'

We had recently planned to burn a Union Jack to protest at the closing of the last mine in the area, but we chickened out at the last moment. Will argued that the police would pounce on us, and anyway we couldn't find a flag big enough.

'It's been about a year now and there's still only four of us,' I said. 'I've tried asking people what they think of the Bore Coch slogans left on walls and all they say is that they must be another bunch of Free Wales nutters ten years too late! I can't see much future in all this, honestly I can't.'

'What if in the summer we went up to Gwynedd and were loud-mouthed about things,' Will suggested. 'Maybe eventually somebody would take us aside and introduce us to people in the know. It's the best we could do in the meanwhile.'

'I can see us getting nowhere unless we make a name for

ourselves,' Karen said, offering the cider to Will. 'Then at least the next generation will have something to base themselves on, you know. Historically we aren't alone, though it seems like it, just like us and the example of the MAC and the Free Wales Army from the sixties.'

'Twelve-bore shot against the door of the DHSS, like!' Dai Panda exclaimed with a smile, taking the bottle from her since no one else wanted to drink.

'Something real that will get us on the telly; it's a propaganda battle after all,' Karen agreed.

'But forget about guns,' Will said.

'What then, bricks and paint?' Karen asked.

'Are you still collecting press cuttings on Meibion Glyndŵr's holiday-home bombing campaign?' Will asked me.

'Pinned to my bedroom wall,' I replied.

Will too had his collection. 'Better destroy them, just in case,' he warned.

'I can't see why,' I said.

'They might think you've got an interest in the firebomb attacks, especially if the cuttings are on your wall,' he argued. 'We've got to be careful.'

'Are we just going to talk again, like?' Dai Panda asked.

The rest of us shrugged and timidly shook our heads and he drank the last few drops, holding it over his open mouth.

'OK, let's go and paint something then,' he insisted.

For Bore Coch it was still Year One. There wasn't to be a Year Two.

We were not much of a group to base a revolution on.

Will, while on the dole, spent most of his time studying, except Thursdays when he manned a gay phone line in Swansea. He was eventually to become a council planning officer for Lambeth. Karen worked in a department store in the centre of Swansea where she was supposed to spy on potential shoplifters but always turned a blind eye. Dai Panda in those days waited until he could go and meet her after work, occasionally offering to repair neighbours' cars for a few bob, based on his experience with Karen's Beetle. After she lost her job because of a mixture of bad eyesight and low productivity the two moved to Harlech on the north Wales coast, where they formed a cooperative taxi service and had a daughter that only spoke Welsh. Karen with a K, who was to become Caren with a C, managed to pass on her genes after all.

I was wondering what I was going do with my life. I smoked pot, drank too much and fantasised about seeing Wales in flames. I had no special abilities, not even for learning my own language. Where I lived it wasn't exotic. No one ever went there to visit. A place that's just a tiny grey stain on the map of the world.

As night's dusk began to arc over us, bringing a darker hue and dampness to the brilliantly green grass, we left the park and walked the streets, deciding on a wall to paint that night. If nothing else, at least Gorseinon looked like a focus of radical activity according to its urban literature, as Will called our graffiti. We chose, for aesthetic reasons, the wall against the Anglican church. The others wanted to do it at the usual time, after the pubs closed, but I objected, thinking of Susie. What was to happen was all my fault, all because of my hormones. We agreed to do it relatively early when there were still people about.

We went back for Karen's VW, drove to where we kept hidden our supply of spray cans and surgical gloves and set up the security of the operation. Karen waited in her parked car as usual, me on lookout on the main road for Dai Panda and Will to do the job in red paint.

NO MORE WELSH BOYS FOR THATCHER'S IMPERIALIST WAR
          Bore Coch ★

Our slogans were getting longer. Before long we might begin with 'A spectre is haunting Europe' and fill the walls of fifteen long streets.

Dai Panda listened to Will's last minute design instructions on letter height and separation, for if nothing else our political graffiti looked professional. I stood at the corner of the church, looking up and down the main road, and then signalled for the two to begin. Dai Panda, looking at me, flipped off the top of the car paint spraycan with his front teeth, mock biting a pin out of a grenade, and then pretended to throw the canister overarm. When he finally started, concentrating with biting tongue, a car came slowly down the side road, passed the VW and the two artists, turned into the main road, thought better and stopped.

Its only occupant, a man, stuck his head out of the window. 'Bloody vandals. What do you think you're doing?' he shouted.

Will dropped his canister and began to run away. I walked with strained calm into the side road towards Dai Panda and signalled to Karen to start the engine with a thumb and forefinger twisted gesture thinking of our escape by car.

'Come on Dai, let's go,' I shouted.

'No, I'm going to finish!'

I doubted for a moment, and then ran with pounding heart to where Will left his paint can, picked it up and sprayed our group's signature. I tried my hand at the five-pointed star, which looked more like a farm cock's crest. The man continued shouting at us from a safe distance. Keeping an eye on him, I saw that he had got out of his car and I ran two or three paces towards him and threw the canister with all my strength. It was almost full but weighed very little and I missed him by inches, hitting his car instead. It bounced off the roof and flew across the road out of sight.

'Come on, will you,' Karen shouted at us as she revved the engine.

'I'm done,' Dai Panda said and I ran to Karen's VW.

'No, check what I wrote first!' he asked me.

I turned towards him and I thought he was crazy.

'Great mun,' I said without even looking at his spelling, and he then ran to the car too.

We drove off at speed, the man fixed in his steps watching us go.

'We were lucky he didn't come for us. He looked like a rugby-playing copper,' I said breathing heavily.

We drove round the block looking for Will, and then to

the street where he lived, but there was no sign of him.

'Where the hell is he?' I asked.

'Hiding from us I imagine,' Karen replied, bringing the car to a halt outside his house.

'Why did he run like that?' Dai Panda asked, his loyalty challenged by Will's behaviour.

'He got really frightened, that's all,' was all I could say.

'Bloody coward,' Karen exclaimed. 'He just can't be trusted. Just wait till I see him!'

'Why doesn't he come home?' I asked, unable to think clearly. 'We should have waited until midnight, as usual. I'm sorry.'

Dai Panda turned and smiled at me, I didn't know why. Perhaps he had never heard me apologise before.

'Well are we going to hang around here waiting for him?' Karen asked. 'I'm thinking about the car. That bloke could have taken down the reg!'

We talked about it and decided that they had better not stay in Gorseinon and instead leave for Karen's village. If traced she could always claim she hadn't gone out in her car that evening. We decided to meet up again the following evening and not to worry.

When alone I walked back up around to the Anglican church. When I got nearer I saw from the distance the flashing spiralling blue and yellow lights of a police car parked next to the wall we had painted. I turned and walked the other way. There was no apparent reason why the police shouldn't be there but it wasn't usually the thing they did, we had never known them to take an interest in our urban literature before. It must have been because I threw the paint canister at the motorist.

I thought of Will as I walked away, where he was and what he would have been thinking. He could be capable of turning things onto their heads and would probably have blamed me for our reckless decision to act so early in the night. He would probably quote and then interpret some historic military tactic that led to the fall of Troy and prove that I was the wooden horse. But nothing would make me forgive him, he was done for as my butty after all this time.

I already began to miss his friendship.

A tall, bony-thin middle-aged woman passed me on the street. It was the beginning of her midweek reckless night out on the tiles. I asked her for a light and she said that I was Huw's little boy, was I not. She wore an imitation tigerskin overcoat and thick mascara over the creases around her eyes. I wasn't surprised that she had known him once, but by the fact she recognised me. As I walked on puffing at the joint I turned and saw her staring at me, but in pub and bed memories of the man I reminded her of.

Soon the paranoid effect of the drug enveloped me. Alone, I felt nervous. I would never get used to cannabis, never control the effect. Other people became resistant to it, they could smoke and continue as normal, but then why smoke if it doesn't affect you? But I smoked alone then as one would drink alone, to move the mind or punish the body.

I thought of Father. I couldn't remember what he looked like, I had only then the bathroom mirror reflection of myself as a possible image.

After an hour of walking Gorseinon the effect of the cannabis waned and I began to feel better as I made my way to where Susie worked. It must have been nearly closing time when I stopped to run my fingers through my hair, guided by the reflection in a side window cornering the entrance. I saw Susie through the glass behind the bar. When someone entered through the creaking hinged door she looked up with her smile to see who it was. I stood watching her a while. I liked the sensation of spying on her unobserved and stayed a few minutes longer.

When I came in she craned her head around a customer to see and when I reached the bar she was already pouring me a pint of bitter. We exchanged knowing smiles and meaningful talk and I went to sit at one of the tables as the pub began to close. I waited until after she and a barman cleaned before she had time for me. We left for my place; she said she liked being out in the air after being trapped inside all day and I noticed there was a hint of optimism in her. She asked me what I had been doing and I mentioned the woman I took a light from. She said that some of my father's old friends often talked of him; when drunk he used to curse people in Welsh.

'Poetic though,' she mimicked.

'He must have hated it, not having anybody to talk to when he felt lubricated and inspired,' I suggested.

'If you don't mind me saying, he was a bit of a ladies' man.'

'Did you know him? No, of course not. He was before your time. He was a ladies' man in the womanless world of men's heavyweight drinking.'

'Do you think about him a lot? You remember him of course,' she asked.

'Just his aftershave and false-teeth smile,' I replied.

We walked side by side without making contact.

'Things have changed on the council estate since I was a kid,' I said as we turned at the foot of the hill into the housing estate of the Bryn roads.

'You're still a kid,' she said and nudged her shoulder against mine.

'There used to be only ever the postman's delivery van in my street. Now there are more cars and less life, most of the kids that were my age have gone away. Soon there will only be pensioners left, with their cars parked out in the deserted street. That's where Will lives,' I pointed, stopping on the corner of a street.

'I'll just go and knock to see if he's in. We fell out earlier. I won't be more than a min,' I explained and we walked to his house.

She waited on the pavement as I walked down the four steps to the front door. There was no one there, not even his mam, who usually watched TV in the front room at night. As I looked through the window where the curtains were open I thought I saw the shadow of someone move inside. I turned to go and I took Susie's hand into mine as we walked back to the corner into the street that led up to my house further up the hill.

'Perhaps they've gone out for the night,' she suggested to me as I turned to look back down the road.

'I don't know. It looks funny to me. What the heck, let's go.'

'Your mother won't mind, will she?' she asked.

'No. Anyway she's away protesting for the week. There's just my sis Fan at home. She'll probably mind but don't you worry. Look, the lights are off, she's in bed. Shall we go in? I want to see you as naked as the sea,' I said as we closed on my house.

At the gate a car came down the road and screeched to a halt at our side. As I turned to look, uniformed police officers were getting out of it and Susie gripped hold of my arm as they ran the few feet towards us. They pushed me backwards and I fell over the gate to the ground on the other side. The fall left my brain flashing and the last things I remembered were time freezing, a calm peace and the distant sound of Susie screaming.

26. *1982*

The slag heaps became overgrown with moss and gorse stalks, nature fighting back against history's disaster. The makeshift toys left behind at sunset by the children of my youth were replaced with syringes and empty cans of weak lager.

The streets of my childhood had been vibrant with mischief. Now they lay stone cold in shame. Walking them once again, I was surrounded by death. The moulding, rancid decay of forgetfulness and torpidity.

Where the children played, the next generation numbed the brain with pinpricks before the comedown of bus shelters covered in porn. There in the early morning you can stare down to see page three of the previous day's *Sun* staring up at you from a puddle. It must be easier to accept it all without complaint when you have breasts to think about.

And it always rains. Almost always, except when it snows. At the beginning of February it used to draw the kids whooping out into the street. The falling flakes were confetti at a winter wedding. And the kids churned it all up into a dirty mass in their wars with their ice-burnt fingers like thin sausages. Winter and night was falling early, indifferent. The sky was orange bright with street lighting. I preferred watching the snow fall on the coast, flakes at the water's edge, factory fumes above, black and white merging into grey.

And rain or snow we are always there. Father had said Wales was some North American Red Indian reserve, the last concentration camp for the original natives of the island. The Welsh were expelled from the towns and hid in the hills. Now in the industrial wreckage of the empire we find ourselves lost today, in this Atlantic windswept wilderness. It is difficult to know what we have now, looking out at the world from the South Wales goldfish bowl, waiting for the revolution on the telly.

With the earth's natural resources of water and coal stolen from us, a quarter part of the population living in poverty, the land under their feet belongs to either absentee landowners, the military or reforestation companies. What have we got? An Anglo-American culture of mind-dumbing entertainment.

And look at me. Always been a bit unsure of himself. Just wants to fuck and change the world. Poor dab. I wanted, once, to be known. Now I just want to be like a small insect to get on with surviving. But I am haunted by tangled-up images of reality. Drowning in the pit pool, shotgun hunters, Parry with a bloody hammer, Mam digging out the back. I was drowning again, unable to breathe, back to an old miner's breath when four. Go on, gulp it all in, let it swim around inside you bach. My face pushed into the leaves on the ground, Parry's blood dripping from a hammer, the earth shovelled over Father's suitcase for going nowhere.

Then in nineteen eighty-two as the Second Parachute Regiment made their way to Port Stanley eight thousand miles away, I awoke to find myself detained in a closed windowless room somewhere.

In the cell there came to me an early memory, a mirror reflecting disjointed fragments. Mam is drying her hair. It's a bright summer's day in the back garden. She leans over me, a drop of water rolling down over her brow, off the tip of her nose into my eye, momentarily blinding me, making me cry. I blink to focus and see a prison guard's face over me instead. The sky is nothing but the ceiling above, the sun a naked forty-watt light bulb, and the breeze the bracing chill of an empty cell.

PARTHIAN

diverse probing
profound urban
epic comic
rural savage
new writing

www.inpressbooks.co.uk

Llyfrau ar-lein
Books on-line

PARTHIAN   n e w   w r i t i n g

p a r t h i a n b o o k s . c o . u k